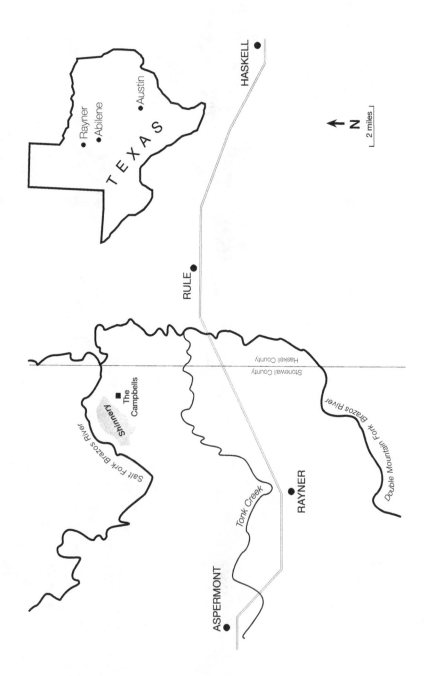

THE
SHINNERY

A Novel

KATE ANGER

UNIVERSITY OF NEBRASKA PRESS | LINCOLN

The University of Nebraska Press is part of
a land-grant institution with campuses and
programs on the past, present, and future
homelands of the Pawnee, Ponca, Otoe-
Missouria, Omaha, Dakota, Lakota, Kaw,
Cheyenne, and Arapaho Peoples, as well as
those of the relocated Ho-Chunk, Sac and Fox,
and Iowa Peoples.

∞

Library of Congress Cataloging-in-Publication Data
Names: Anger, Kate, author.
Title: The Shinnery: a novel / Kate Anger.
Description: Lincoln: University of Nebraska Press, [2022]
Identifiers: LCCN 2021059129
ISBN 9781496231383 (paperback)
ISBN 9781496233202 (epub)
ISBN 9781496233219 (pdf)
Subjects: LCSH: Honor killings—Texas—Stonewall
County—Fiction. | BISAC: FICTION / Westerns |
FICTION / Women | LCGFT: Novels.
Classification: LCC PS3601.N554427 S55 2022 |
DDC 813/.6—dc23
LC record available at https://lccn.loc.gov/2021059129

Set and designed in Adobe Caslon Pro by
Mikala R. Kolander.

For my aunt, Kathryn Barnes Hale, the story keeper,
and my mother, Kelly Barnes Noble, my heart's keeper.

Turn again, O my sweetest, —turn again, false
    and fleetest:
This beaten way thou beatest I fear is hell's own
    track.
Nay, too steep for hill-mounting; nay, too late for
    cost-counting:
This downhill path is easy, but there's no turning
    back.

—From "Amor Mundi" by Christina Rossetti

THE SHINNERY

Prologue

MARCH 1895

Jessa stood at the edge of the Shinnery. The grasses, which in spring would hide the shin oak, were dormant for winter. The thicket looked shaggy, its acorns long buried. She considered the animals burrowed for winter among the shrubs' roots, how they could suspend their lives until early spring. She wished to join them. Tunnel into the earth. Only she'd stay a bit longer, July by her calculation—if she wasn't sent away entirely. What else would they do with a girl like her? Her body had healed from the beating. No sign of the bruises she'd worn for over a month, yellow-brown splotches, the color of brackish water.

It was cold on the prairie, and she was glad for it. Her nose ran and her cheeks burned, and this mild suffering brought her comfort. She pulled her shawl off her shoulders and let it dangle on the ground. Red had followed her out here, but the dog had since waded into the acres of brush on his own, his head bobbing in and out of sight. Below her, in the distance, Jessa could see her father putting out salt for the cows. He would walk back to the barn soon, and she would join him there, speak the words she never could have imagined speaking. Maybe such things were better delivered in pieces, like swallowing mother's bitter teas. Only sufferable in sips. She couldn't worry about whether she would say it wrong. She knew she would.

Haskell Free Press, MARCH 16, 1895

KILLING IN RAYNER

Parties who came from Stonewall County Thursday evening for a coffin reported the killing of a young man . . . The killing was done with a shotgun and, while no particulars could be learned it was said to have been on account of some family trouble.

MAY 1894

Jessa sensed something was amiss as soon as her father pulled up in the wagon. He'd gone to Rayner for supplies. They'd run out of sugar and were low on coffee and cornmeal. Though he'd taken a batch of their usual trade goods, butter and eggs, the wagon was empty. Especially vexing to Jessa was the lack of melon seeds, the very thing he'd gone after. They'd been planning on the melons for months, had dug a channel off Sometimes Creek for water. They were already late, going for an early fall harvest, but they'd heard about a fellow over in Haskell who'd made a killing the year before. A proprietary seed and fertilizer. Mama thought it a scheme.

"Where's the seed?" Jessa asked.

Papa didn't answer as he climbed down from the buckboard. His face looked grim, and Jessa wondered if it was on account of pain. Everything he did, he did stiffly.

"Bring this in to your mama," he said, handing her a small sack of coffee.

"But where's the rest?" It irked her that he wouldn't explain. She wasn't a child, but a partner in this venture—or this almost venture.

Just then Agnes, nine years younger than Jessa, came rushing up. "Did you bring me anything?" From his pocket, Papa pulled three pieces of orange candy. Agnes plopped them in her mouth all at once. To Jessa, he handed a single butterscotch drop, for which she had no appetite. "The melon seeds?"

"Take the coffee. I'll be in in a minute with some news."

"News, shoes, clues," Agnes sing-songed in a candy-garbled voice.

Jessa didn't want any news. Not the way he'd said it, head down, talking to his shoes. Had he picked up a letter at the post? Was someone ill—or worse? Considering the number of very bad things he could be waiting to tell them, Jessa knew being upset over the seed was petty. Still, she had the urge to kick something. They were a few years into what the papers were saying was a nationwide drought. It'd wiped out corn across much of the Great Plains, causing droves of homesteaders to return east. Although Stonewall County had been spared the worst of the drought, the Campbells were always worried about getting enough rain for their cotton and sorghum crops. Money, and the family's need of it, was never openly discussed, but it was always there, staring back at them in their half-empty larder and worn-out shoes. Jessa looked out over the empty field they'd spent three days grooming. The Bradford was said to have a rind so soft you could cut it with a butter knife. For a second, she could taste one. What could be so important, or terrible, that he'd come home without the seed?

With the family all gathered in their small kitchen, Papa delivered his news. His hands were folded in front of him, resting on his belly, as if he were making a speech in church. "You'll be settled with the Martins," he said to Jessa. "The ones that got the mercantile."

"Settled?" She didn't understand.

"A mother's helper."

"What?" she said. No such thing had ever been discussed before. It was as wild to her as if he'd come home saying, "I've added a wife," or, "We're trading the horses for elephants." Papa explained she'd board with the Martins and come home to visit. Everything she knew about the world seemed to flip. Visit home? Home was the place you left to go visiting. What on earth had happened when Papa went to town?

She was Papa's right-hand man—he called her that, despite her sex—and had been since she'd stopped schooling four years earlier, when she'd turned thirteen. Her two younger sisters could not begin to take her place. It made no sense for her to leave. She objected in the way she could, in measured tones, as if panic weren't overtaking her. She wasn't quick with words like her sisters. Feelings and ideas would get stuck on the other side of her voice, no words to carry them across. Or she'd start talking and her words would fail, trail off, evaporate, everyone staring at her, waiting. Papa wasn't in a waiting mood. He seemed uncomfortable, brushing dust that wasn't there from his britches.

"It's an opportunity, Jessa."

She detected something false in her father's voice and wished the two of them could talk outside. She wanted so much to take his hand and pull him out the door, but the thought itself embarrassed her. She had to act like a woman grown if she was to secure a say in this. "I . . . I appreciate your . . . your, um, efforts, Papa—"

"Good to hear."

"But—I'm ill suited. Terribly. Mama still chides my housework." She looked over at her mother for a word of agreement, but Mama wouldn't meet her eyes. "I burn cobbler. Cobbler, Papa." She felt sick thinking about being cooped up all day in a stranger's house, about leaving the Shinnery.

"I wish I could go," Nellie chimed in.

Yes! thought Jessa, Nellie would save her. Nellie, her pretty sister, who loved towns and cities, and shoes and stores and children and cobbler. It would be—

"Perfect," Nellie said, "only I can't."

Jessa's head started to ache.

"I need another six months up at the schoolhouse if I'm to pass the teacher's exam."

Nellie was less than a year away from turning sixteen, old enough to qualify for a teaching certificate. Jessa felt like she was in the midday sun watching her sister take the last sip of water. She turned to her father, straining to keep her voice steady. "But what about the melons?"

This seemed to amuse him, relax him even. "That's my girl, head in the dirt."

How dare he make light. She wasn't only asking about the melons. What about me? she was saying. What about tomorrow, at first light, when we'd planned to be out in the field? What about the birds, sing-ing their truest songs at that hour? And the satisfaction at the end of the day, when we stand together, looking out over our planted earth?

"Is it about money?" she asked. Her mother had been sick the past winter, and their scarce cash had gone toward the doctor and medicines. "Because if it's—" Before she could finish her sentence, he broke in.

"You're barkin' at a knot. It's done," he said. Jessa and her father had only ever talked about money they hoped to make, never about money they didn't have.

"Papa," her little sister interrupted, "I was thinkin' . . ."

Papa turned away from Jessa, eager to talk with an eight-year-old, who wouldn't bring up subjects that made his jaw tight. "You were thinkin', huh?" He pulled Agnes close and gently rapped his knuckles on her frizzy blond head. "With this thing here?"

Jessa felt like pushing them over. Their easy affection in this moment galled her.

"I was thinkin' you might have more candy," said Agnes.

Papa patted his empty pockets. "Seems like I'm breaking all the ladies' hearts today."

How could he equate Jessa's plight to Agnes's lack of candy? Jes-sa's despair was met with a rising fury. "But why are you sending me off?" She'd never raised her voice to him this loudly. The room went church silent.

Papa cleared his throat. "You're of an age, Jessa."

"An age where I can work hard here. You need me."

"I can use you, but I don't *need* you."

Her cheeks went flush, tingled, as if she'd been slapped. It made her want to argue. He was half crippled, lead from Chickamauga still lodged in his thigh, half a dozen other war injuries, and now arthritis working to turn his hands useless. She'd caught glimpses of him in bed, Mama wrapping his hands in warm willow-bark poultices. He damn well did need her.

"See a bit more of the world," he said.

Nellie laughed but quickly clamped her hand to her mouth. Rayner, ten miles away as the crow flies, hardly qualified as "the world." Her sister gave her a look that said, What on God's green earth is he talking about?

It didn't make sense, until suddenly, it did. "Of an age" meant "marriageable." He must've wanted her to meet people. Now *he* was barkin' at a knot. Jessa didn't want a husband. Most took you away from everything you loved—sister Minta, thirty, a half day's ride away in Aspermont, and sister Jo, twenty-seven, in Albany, a distance of several days. They hadn't seen Jo in almost two years, and the last time they did, she'd cried in the kitchen after her husband snapped at her for an overdone roast. Jasper was as jolly a guy as you could meet, but his moods shifted like summer weather. When he was in a foul one, you felt that same prickly air as before a rainstorm, everyone trying to figure where the lightning would land. Only sister Maggie, twenty-three, had stayed close. She had found her husband, Solon Scott, when he came to the Shinnery to inquire about grazing rights. The marriage was a love match. As a man with six daughters and no son left to help, Papa was as excited as Maggie about the pairing. Still, no thank you. "I don't wish to marry if that's what you're thinking."

"You're getting ahead of yourself. I'm talking about work, looking after children. Seeing a little something. You don't want to confine yourself."

But she did. She had assumed every year would roll out similarly to the last, and it had given her a deeply peaceful feeling knowing that in spring, they'd calve and plant; in summer, harvest and preserve; plan and repair in the fall; and prune and make do in the winter. Many families had a daughter that stayed, looked after her parents. And though no one had ever said it, she was that daughter. The Shinnery was hers. She'd marry *it*. Dear shin oak and prairie chicken, ornery cow and morning sun, I take thee gladly.

"I do, Papa," she said.

"You do want to see something?" he said, one brow lifted.

"No, I want to confine myself."

He laughed. It did sound ridiculous the way she'd said it. Papa released her little sister.

7

"I'm gut-shrunk," said Agnes.

"Good thing supper's ready." He laid his hand on Mama's shoulder. "Smells good enough to eat." Mama granted him a slight smile, even though he said that same thing most every night.

"Mama?" Jessa said, her voice quaky. She wanted her mother to say something reassuring, maybe plead her case.

"The cabbage is ready" was all she said. Mama believed in getting on with whatever life handed you. "The cabbage is ready" meant "Move on, girl." Mama nodded toward the stove. Jessa grabbed the pot of cabbage and dumped it into a bowl, juice splattering. She made no move to wipe it before joining her sisters. When she entered the main room, where the larger table sat, she found Nellie laying out one of Mama's better tablecloths.

"Thought we'd make it special with the news and all," Nellie said.

Jessa wanted to pull off the tablecloth with the embroidered nosegays, maybe step on it. It seemed to mock her with all its starched cheeriness.

Nellie placed their nicest glasses at the table, three of them matching. "It'll be fun seein' new stuff."

Jessa didn't want to see new stuff, but she knew she'd sound childish if she said so.

"There was a gunfight in Rayner," said Agnes. "You better take a gun."

"She doesn't need a gun," said Nellie.

Her sisters argued over firearms and the relative need for them while Jessa slid her hand under the tablecloth to the bare wood. She found the place where her late brother Newt's awl had slipped while repairing her shoe, the marred surface precious to her now. She bet Papa wouldn't have sent Newt away. He'd been gone seven years now; a fever took him. She tried to picture her brother's face, but only his hands, working a piece of leather, came into focus.

"Jess!" said Nellie.

"Huh?" she said, lost in her thoughts.

"The knives."

She put a knife at each setting, trying to remember where the family all sat when Newt was alive and sister Maggie was still at home. Agnes followed with forks and spoons. Nellie fussed with each place setting, a chip on a plate turned to the bottom, knives facing in, and glasses just so. The point of it eluded Jessa. It would all be washed and back in the sideboard in an hour. For Sunday suppers, when sister Maggie and her husband Solon came, Nellie put a handful of whatever was blooming on the table. In early spring, she cut branches from the fruit trees coming awake in the orchard. All through those meals, Jessa stared at the blossoms and thought about the fruit that would never be.

"What do you think you'll eat at the Martins'?" Nellie asked.

The thought made Jessa's stomach lurch: eating with strangers.

"I bet you'll have candy every day," said Agnes.

"Do you think you'll eat with the family, or are you more like a maid?"

Jessa didn't know. Didn't know anything. Papa had said "mother's helper," as if she knew what that meant. Maybe if he'd asked her, it would've made a difference.

Nellie moved the salt bowl from the sideboard to the table. Everything was set.

"I will miss you fiercely." Nellie's blue eyes glistened.

They'd never spent more than a few nights apart. Jessa pictured herself alone in an unfamiliar bed.

"Sister," said Agnes. "I'll grow the melons for you."

The melons. A field of sweet, fat melons. It was all she'd thought about for months. Now that plan was dead. Or it seemed to be. Papa had not answered her. Jessa's eyes went misty too. Nellie put an arm around her. As her sister gave her a squeeze, Nellie was moving a drinking glass closer to the spoon. So much to know about a simple table. She was sure the Martins were getting the wrong sister.

•••

There wasn't much to pack. A couple of dresses, a nightdress, a shawl, and underclothes. Agnes's black stocking was stuck to the back of her folded apron, but rather than remove it, as she should, she left it and placed both items in the satchel. Tomorrow morning they'd leave for town. Jessa felt queasy thinking on it. Lying flat on the bed, she stared up at the rough-hewn planks of the ceiling, a dark stain in the corner where it had leaked. Maybe she was ill, she thought, too ill to go, though she'd been sick only a few times in her life. After a moment, Jessa made herself get up; it wouldn't do to waste her last day at home inside, chewing on everything she'd miss. She caught sight of her reflection in the hanging mirror Nellie had commandeered. The mirror was old and had gone misty around the edges, but the middle was clear enough. Jessa studied her face. Her eyes were deep set and brown, like Mama's. Too small for her face, she thought. She liked her lips best, the deep pink of the winecup poppy that bloomed every summer. Her dark locks hung limply, a brown tangle near her ear. She was not like Nellie, who brushed her hair a hundred strokes every night before bed. Jessa knew she'd have to improve her grooming habits; folks in town seemed to care about stuff like that.

She moved the satchel to the floor, surprised by how light her things were, her life away from home as insubstantial as lint. The satchel had been a gift to Mama on her eighteenth birthday, back in Tennessee. Jessa's grandfather, Elijah White, a some-part Cherokee, had crafted it. He'd burnished Mama's initials—MJW—into the leather just below the worn handle. It had traveled a thousand miles, across three states, from the Smoky Mountains, with their red clay earth and towering trees, to just below the Texas Panhandle, with its acres of prairie, rolling hillsides, and waist-high oaks. She tried to imagine the suitcase new and unblemished. They had only one photograph of her mother from this time, captured on a plate of tin that Jessa's father had carried with him all through the Civil War, and now sat on her parents' single dresser. Father said the photograph had kept him going. As he'd suffered seven bullet wounds and a stint as a POW, something surely had. In the photo Mama stared straight ahead, her dark hair parted down the middle and held in a bun, jewelry at her ears and neck—baubles long ago sacrificed to the cause of the Confederacy. She looked so unlike the gray-haired woman Jessa knew now. Eyes keen, lips full. Whenever she looked at the photo, Jessa sensed that this staring girl wanted to tell her something, something her mother had forgotten.

2

The next morning, when the sun was just warming up the day, Jessa started off to do the milking, but Mama said no, time for Agnes to take over the chore. Jessa hadn't even left yet, and she was already being replaced.

"Use two buckets with Sassy," Jessa called out to Agnes, who was headed to the barn.

"I won't let her kick," said Agnes.

"She doesn't need your permission. Pour off as you go; that way if she *does* kick—"

"She won't."

"So if she does, you won't lose all your milk."

"I know how to do it." Agnes ducked into the barn.

Jessa readied the buggy. Before she slipped the harness on Old Dan, she put her face to his and blew into his nostril like she always did. He responded in kind, a warm exhale that smelled like May itself: bluestem and switchgrass and horse. A lump grew in her throat. Then she silently chided herself for being sentimental.

Papa emerged from the house, carrying Jessa's satchel. She felt like she was watching someone else's life unfold.

"Sassafras!" Agnes hollered. "Hell fire!"

"You quit that cursing, Agnes Ida Campbell," Papa said.

Agnes emerged from the barn with an empty pail. "That cow waylaid me."

Papa placed the leather bag on the floor of the buggy. "Jessa sings her a song. Don't you, Jess?"

Jessa said nothing. When it was time to secure the horse to the buggy, she moved in unison with her father, sliding the shafts into the tugs and tying the breeching straps. No one else could match him the way she could.

Mama and the girls lined up to see them off. Although Jessa was not eager to be gone, she was eager to exit this in-between-ness. Settled in neither place. She climbed in next to her father at the reins. Mama reached up and squeezed Jessa's hand, and Nellie passed her a bouquet of wildflowers she'd kept hidden underneath her apron. Blackfoot daisies and firewheels. Jessa wasn't sure what to do with the bouquet. It seemed like something people in those novels Nellie liked to read would give as a parting gift. But as the cart pulled away, and Jessa had the sensation of falling, she was glad for something to hold. The hounds followed the buggy as far as the end of the family's property. Then stopped, as if they'd read a surveyor's map.

They had ten miles to travel, a distance that seemed a hundred times farther this morning. They'd go south and then west, crossing Tonk Creek midway. The rolling hills and mesquite prairie still held a touch of green. Miraculous, really, the way the view could change utterly with a spring rain. That color between yellow and green, as bright as the sky was blue, was all the more treasured for how briefly it lasted. Spring seemed like something she'd dreamed.

Papa didn't say much, comments about the neighbor's bull, the growing heat. Otherwise, they were silent. Jessa realized she didn't know anything about the Martins beyond the fact that they owned the store. They could have two children or ten. Mrs. Martin could be gentle as a lamb or mean as a badger. Jessa absentmindedly ran her thumbnail up and down the stalks of Nellie's bouquet. She noticed she was doing it only when the stalks were all but shredded. As they approached Rayner, Jessa was struck by how each time she came, there seemed to be something new. The town had been platted only six years earlier and already boasted a cotton gin, a grain mill, and a blacksmith, one school, two saloons, three churches, a half dozen shops, and a courthouse. The town's stout, columned bank had somehow managed to stay afloat during the Panic of 1893. Hundreds of banks and even big railroads had gone under, which had knocked the legs out from under thousands of businesses and farms. Jessa couldn't quite grasp all the workings behind such an event, nor fathom that many folks on the drift, but she suspected it might be related to her family's current money situation. Banks weren't lending like they had been.

When they turned onto Main Street, Papa pointed to a brand-new building. "A barbershop. What would your mama think if I came home slick shaved and smelling of lilacs?" He was trying to engage her. "Or maybe rosewater?"

How could he act like nothing had changed, like this was simply one of their supply trips and they'd both be back at Mama's table before the sun went down?

Papa pointed to a half-built structure across the road. "You'll have to tell me what's going in there."

The idea that Jessa might soon know more about Rayner than her father did made her feel strange, apart from him in a way she'd never considered before. They passed a saloon. There'd been a shoot-out in front of one of them, but she didn't know which. She'd heard her father and some men at church discuss shutting it down but saw nothing amiss on this Saturday morning.

The most impressive structure in town was, by far, the county courthouse. It stood three stories tall, its base made of red sandstone cut from the cliffs along the Salt Fork of the Brazos. Papa, who had talent as a carpenter, had been one of the men to work on it, along with Maggie's husband Solon. They were also part of the crew who quarried the stone. Jessa couldn't imagine the work of cutting and carrying all that rock from the river. Papa had taken such pride in the courthouse, explaining how the lintel was set, how someone almost lost his foot when the cornerstone was laid, how a country was not truly settled until it had a courthouse to mete out justice and enforce the law. Jessa had been inside only once, two years earlier, on the day of the ribbon cutting. Citizens from all corners of the county had gathered for a two-day celebration, including a brass band from Abilene. The family had been so proud to see Papa up on the dais, invited by Captain Rayner himself, the town's namesake. To hold a county seat was to ensure prosperity for a town. The folks in neighboring Aspermont thought the captain had hornswoggled it. Rayner had authored a petition in favor of separating Stonewall County from Jones County, which had garnered favor. But when the matter went to ballot, he snuck in a vague clause making his town the county seat. Aspermont was still fighting it; when their brand-new town hall burned to the ground, many suspected the captain's men had done it.

Outside the post office, a girl about her age, with copper-red hair the likes of which she'd never seen, was talking with Mrs. Posey, the postmistress. She didn't know anyone her age that lived in town. A quarter mile past Rayner proper, they came to what Jessa assumed was the Martin home. White wood siding dressed the exterior, and up at the top, where the roof joined into a point, white scalloped pieces of wood overlapped, like feathers on a bird's chest. The roof was pitched with one gable. A porch with ornate wooden railings and corbels ran along the front of the house on the left side. On the right, the house jutted out and featured a large window, flanked by two smaller ones. No flowers, no trees surrounded the house. Only dirt, as if spring had never visited here.

Papa pulled up on the reins, and Dan stopped just outside the front gate. "Most girls'd be happy to get out, see a little somethin'," said Papa. "Maybe you'll surprise yourself."

Jessa felt pulled like taffy. On one hand, she wanted to be the good and faithful daughter, say, Yes, Papa, of course, Papa. I'll try, Papa. On the other, she wanted to hurl those words back in his face: *Most girls. Surprise yourself.* Did he not know her at all?

"Hello!" someone called out. They looked up to see the Martins spilling out the front door. Four people, a pretty wife with hair as white as cotton, two fair-haired little boys, and a husband, a little taller than

Papa, his back as straight as a board. Like Papa, he had a thick mustache, but unlike Papa's bushy broom, the husband's mustache was neat and trimmed, his face as smooth as a woman's. Jessa reckoned he made use of the new barber.

"Miss Campbell," Mr. Martin said, by way of greeting. Then he immediately turned to her father and launched into a discussion about longhorns, someone running a herd for him.

"Welcome. Jessa, is it?" The missus offered her hand and Jessa took it. Papa had taught all his children a firm handshake was a sign of solid character, but when Jessa took the missus's hand, she realized her grip was too firm. She also noticed a half moon of green slime under her thumbnail from scraping flower stems and hoped the missus hadn't seen it.

The missus eyed the limp flowers. "For me?"

Jessa didn't know how to say no to the lady. If she should—or could—say no. She looked over at Papa, but his attention was on the mister. Time seemed to spread, the silence begging to be filled. She handed the bouquet over, the flowers all bent at the stems.

"Charming." The missus took the bouquet and immediately placed it on the porch railing, where Jessa figured it'd soon fall into the dirt. The missus was the whitest woman she'd ever seen. At first, she thought the missus was wearing tinted powder on her eyelids, but when she got closer, she realized her blue veins were visible through her transparent skin. Her hair was white-blond, the color of something just sprouted and yet to see the light of day. Jessa guessed she was maybe six or seven years older than herself. Mrs. Martin gestured for them to move inside. Walking over the threshold, Jessa worried about knocking the pretties off the tables—vases in deep blues and greens, cut-glass lamps, figurines of birds, and even ferns. Two of them, right in the house. It was as if the climate here, just ten miles from home, was different.

Mr. Martin was speaking to her. "Very pleased you've come. Mrs. Martin has her hands full . . ." Mr. Martin continued to say things, welcoming things. Jessa noted his close-set hazel eyes and his hair, parted to the side, with visible comb lines through the shiny oiled surface.

". . . don't you agree?" Jessa nodded though she wasn't sure what she was agreeing to.

He focused his attention back on Papa. "Nothing like raising your own meat," said Mr. Martin.

Jessa couldn't imagine this man, with his slick hair and polished shoes, anywhere near a steer.

"Grant Goodsite offered a fair price per head. He'll run my cattle 'til fall then get 'em to Fort Worth. He's got East Coast investors as well." At this, the man seemed to puff up a bit, reminding Jessa of a banty rooster. "He didn't want to name the families involved, but I heard—" He paused, then whispered, "Rockefeller."

Jessa knew the days of getting rich in cattle were over. Overstocking, drought, disease, and, most dramatically, barbed wire fencing had changed the Texas cattle story. As Papa had said, even their family was ten years too late by the time they'd arrived in 1885. In a good year, after feeding themselves, they shipped fifty or so. When they made a little profit, most went back into the operation.

"There may be shares still available if you're interested, Campbell," the mister continued. "Mr. Levi Keyes set it up with Mr. Goodsite."

"Keyes, the saloon fellow?" said Papa. "Some trouble up at his place, I heard."

Jessa's ears perked at this. Maybe if the town proved dangerous, Papa would have to call her home.

"Outsiders," said Martin. "They've been run out. Once these reprobates know we enforce the law, they absent themselves from Rayner."

Papa appeared skeptical. "Think I'll steer clear of anything connected to Keyes, but thanks for the offer just the same."

When the topic turned to the West Texas weather—hot to hotter—Jessa more fully took in the room. A piano topped with a fringed scarf, the color of almost-ripe peaches, held center stage. A settee covered in dark-green velvet and a chair with legs as thin as a fawn's sat across from it. She had never been in a house as furnished as this one. The whole place smelled like sawdust and lacquer. She pictured Nellie in the open alcove off the parlor, touching the many books—at least fifty. More than Jessa had ever seen in one place, including the schoolhouse.

"Jessa," said Papa. "Mrs. Martin asked if you are hungry."

"No, ma'am," she quickly replied, though she was. Hungry for her mother's cornbread and beans, her sisters' fingers in her hair, the scent of sage coming off the fields.

"I best be heading back," Papa said.

"Papa," she said, not finishing the thought. She was feeling wary, like a chicken in tall weeds. She wanted to feel her father's arms around her, but she knew he wouldn't embrace her in front of these people. Probably best, she thought, for she'd cry if she breathed him in. He left without another word exchanged.

"May I show you to your room?" the missus said.

Jessa had never had a "your room" before. She followed the missus down the hall to the back of the house, kitty-corner from the kitchen. The boys tromped after them. The room appeared freshly painted; the walls and the curtains were both a warm white. A single bed topped with a fat pillow and a white coverlet sat under the room's one window. Jessa looked through the dusty glass. The yard was as barren as the house was lush.

"Our bedrooms are all upstairs, so Mr. Martin rigged this bell in case you're needed at night." The missus closed the door to reveal a black bell attached to a piece of metal shaped like a shepherd's crook. A fat wire came off the black contraption, snaked up the wall, and disappeared into the ceiling. On tiptoe, the missus stretched to reach a black rod. *Da-ding, da-ding, da-ding-ta-ding-ta-ding*, the bell demanded. Not the somber weight of a church bell commencing worship or the confident clang of the triangle bell calling all hands to supper. This bell seemed to complain. The ugliest sound Jessa had ever heard.

"Can I do it?" the older boy said.

"I'm afraid you're too big for me to lift. Mama can hardly reach it herself."

"She can do it." The boy pointed to Jessa.

"Her name is Miss Jessa, Matthew."

"Missjessa," he said, running the words together, "I wanna pull it."

Jessa lifted him by his waist. A spindly thing. He pulled and pulled and pulled the lever—a terrible racket—then glowed with satisfaction. The sound made the younger boy cover his ears.

"That's enough. Gabriel doesn't like it at all," said the missus.

Jessa lowered the boy back down.

"You have to come when we ring," Matthew said to her.

"Mr. Martin loves his gadgets. Last week we acquired a double egg poacher and something called a rotary flour sifter. I'm supposed to test them, but I can't see either catching on."

The younger boy was now at the window, his hands making smeary prints on the glass. "Kitty," he said, looking out.

Jessa knelt to his level. She didn't see a cat. Gabriel put his damp hand to her face, and she turned to him. His eyes were wide and turquoise-blue, his hair white-blond, like his mama's, a headful of wispy curls. Under his tiny nose, a small patch of snot had crusted, and his cheeks were bright red.

"Yessa," he said.

She was hit with a pang of longing; he pronounced her name the way her sister Agnes had when she was little.

"Let me show you the water closet." The missus led her to a small room off the hall. Inside was a nickel-plated hopper with a wooden seat. Above it, and connected by a pipe, was a wooden tank with a pull chain. "First one in the county."

Matthew took hold of the chain. "This is how you flush."

Jessa had never seen such a thing. It didn't seem sanitary, relieving oneself inside. She worried she'd be so nervous trying to make water—or, heaven forbid, anything else—that she wouldn't be able to go. Her face must have given away her distress because the missus was quick to mention they had a privy outside as well.

"Thank you," Jessa said then felt embarrassed. Why was she thanking the missus for use of the outhouse?

"I'll have our boy bring in your trunk," said the missus.

For a moment Jessa thought she was referring to scrawny Matthew.

"One of our stock boys, helping out today."

It seemed that everyone who worked for the Martins was "theirs." This was the first time Jessa would belong to anyone other than her family.

"No trunk, just the satchel."

"Oh," said the missus, "don't fret about it."

Jessa hadn't thought to fret about her lack of a trunk until the missus told her not to; never had she felt so unprepared.

•••

That first week Jessa missed the animals. They had dictated her days: feeding, milking, cleaning, letting the chickens out, putting the chickens up, egg collecting, moving cows from barn to pasture and back again ten hours later. The Martins had no animals. Not even mice. Because they owned the store, they didn't need to make the things most people did—at least the people Jessa knew—like butter, soap, and socks. Those items, and all manner of foodstuffs, could be procured through the store or in trade with their customers. This freed an enormous amount of time for the missus. Jessa had never known a woman with less to do. Same with the boys. At home even young children were given chores. Jessa had collected eggs as soon as she was old enough to work the latch on the henhouse. She thought about starting a garden, giving them all a reason to get outside and smell the earth, but when she searched the small newly hewn shed, she found it empty as a beggar's pocket.

Jessa spent the early days getting acquainted with the house and its workings: the stove, where to pump the water, the daily chores and how they were to be done. The missus was most particular about clothing. Jessa had received an upbraiding for her lack of technique with the iron. She'd scorched a petticoat. She'd failed at pressing shirtwaist pleats. She also struggled with cooking times; the taters and peas would be turning to pap while the meat had another twenty minutes to go.

The mister was the hardest to please. When he came upon her dusting, he managed to scold her even about that. At home they cleaned with damp rags, but here she was to use a stick with feathers—a feather duster—which seemed to merely move the dust around.

"You must always begin with the topmost point in the room," he lectured. "In this case, the light fixture."

"Yes, sir," she said, as evenly as possible.

"Then you work your way down. Picture frames, mantel, piano, chair backs, tables. I run my household like my business. Efficiently. Pay attention and you will pass your probation."

"My what?" Jessa immediately regretted her impulse to speak. She usually took care to pose any questions to the missus.

"I invite you to look it up, Miss Campbell."

Her face went hot. She felt like she was back in school, trying to spell a word out loud, not able to keep track of what letters she'd already said. Even with simple words she knew how to spell, she'd get lost without a paper to look at. When the mister left the room, Jessa went to the massive dictionary, which rested on its very own stand in the alcove they called the library. She sounded out the word as best she could in order to find it. It took a while, and she worried the mister might scold her for dawdling. "Probation," she read, "the act of proving; proof." She would have to prove herself to the mister; that was clear. "Trial; any proceeding designed to ascertain truth; examination." She did not want to be examined by Mr. Martin. It was shameful to think on it.

At night she lay down in the empty bed, one pillow for her head, one to wrap her arms around. Loneliness pooled in the pit of her stomach. She thought about The Worst Things: What if she always had to live in town, passing from strange family to strange family? What if a fire broke out at their cabin and her family burned up and she never saw them again? What if a fire broke out in the Martins' house and the family burned up and the townspeople blamed her for it? She turned to her other side, taking the pillow with her, aiming to think new, better thoughts, but the flames still glowed in her imagination. She closed her eyes and tried to pretend she was back home, but nothing smelled right. The bed smelled like something from the mercantile, a cross between soap and ink. She recalled the scents of her real bed: the straw they'd harvested last fall in the ticking, the pillow down from Grandmother's geese, the summer blanket made from cotton they'd grown themselves, the winter blanket carded from a neighbor's sheep. The scent of the animals and the heat of the day lingering in her sisters' hair. The only thing that felt familiar was the sound of crickets coming in through the window. This was the passage to sleep; finally, she entered their song, *churp, churp, churp, churp, churp, churp*. Steady, and as constant as a heartbeat.

Mr. Martin had just finished his nooning and, as usual, had not been impressed with his midday meal: mutton soup and roasted squash. The soup, admittedly, was an unappealing silvery gray and the squash overcooked—mush really, like what Mama used to make for Agnes before she got her teeth and for Grandmother Campbell after she lost hers. "Have you *no* gifts?" he said, pushing back his chair. She began to wonder. Her father had let her go easily enough.

The iron gate creaked as the mister left and Will Keyes came through. The boys' piano teacher came twice a week. From the window Jessa could see him crossing the yard, loose-limbed, relaxed. Watching him she considered, for the first time, that a man could be pretty. He caught her spying and lifted his chin in greeting.

Mr. Keyes played little ditties between the boys' ministrations, so she aimed to keep within earshot of the piano for a bit of cheer. Today she was in sore need of a friendly face. For proximity's sake she headed to the library, the open half room off the parlor. She started dusting the bookcase and everything in it, working from top to bottom, as instructed. Out of the corner of her eye, she saw Gabriel clamber onto the piano bench. It baffled her that the family paid money to instruct a three-year-old. He could barely sit still, and his hands weren't large enough for proper fingering. Mr. Keyes mostly played duets with him, giving Gabe a simple pattern to repeat.

After fifteen minutes the little boy engaged in his favorite style of playing: making a fist and rolling it back and forth across the keys. "I done," he said.

Hearing this, Jessa stepped into the room. "A glass of water?"

"Yes!" said Gabriel. He slid off the bench and hugged her legs.

"I was asking Mr. Keyes, but I can also attend to Master Martin." She stroked the boy's damp head; the day would be a hot one.

Gabriel headed toward the kitchen. "Me first."

"That one's like a maggot on a hot rock," Mr. Keyes said, watching his pupil exit.

Jessa also stared after the boy and noticed how he touched every available surface on his way out, the way a dog marks its territory. She turned to the piano teacher. He was smiling. Dimples so deep they could probably hold cherry pits. His hair was light brown, wavy, and too long, her father would say. He didn't appear to be much taller than she was, and probably not a whole lot heavier. She knew she should probably turn away. Her sister Nellie had often scolded her for staring when they'd go to town or a dance. "You're giving folks the creep-eye," she'd warn. But how were you supposed to take in the world if you couldn't look? Mr. Keyes didn't look away either.

"Yessa!" Gabriel called from the kitchen.

When she came back with water, Matthew, the older boy, was at the piano. He started on what Mr. Keyes called his "scales." Jessa returned to the library and fixed her attention on the Devil Man— the name she'd given to the one-foot statue. He occupied a small table of his own, tucked into the corner of the library; he couldn't be seen from the doorway. The first time she had come upon him, he'd startled her with his bright red face and arms. Using the feather duster, Jessa made sure to wipe each fold of the green scarf topping the figure's head. Next, she dusted his face and arms, then his gold vest and purple bloomers. She wondered what Nellie would make of him. His long-fingered hands held a ball of glass, the only part of the statue that wasn't porcelain. Even though his head was bent down, toward the ball, his eyes looked right up at her, like he kept hell itself inside that ball and was inviting her in.

Jessa heard a familiar song. Matthew was haltingly playing "Skip to My Lou" as Mr. Keyes stood encouragingly behind him.

"Listen, Jessa," the boy said. "I can play it perfectly."

"Almost," said Mr. Keyes. He gave Jessa a wink.

His bold attention gave Jessa a little jolt.

Matthew called out, "Mama! Mama, come hear me!" and started the song again.

Jessa turned her attention back to the Devil Man. His glass ball was smeared. Gabriel must've been playing with it, she reckoned. With the feather duster tucked under her arm, she turned to grab her damp rag. But as she did, the duster handle caught on the arm of the statue and the devil came crashing to the ground. "AAHHH!" Jessa cried out. She looked down. The statue was shattered. Only the head intact. The rest of him in shards. The teacher must've come running when Jessa screeched, because he was at her side when the little glass ball, now free of the devil, rolled away from her and into the parlor . . . right to the feet of the missus. Mrs. Martin stood momentarily speechless. Then she fixed her clear blue eyes on Jessa.

"You stupid, stupid girl. You've no idea what that meant to me—"

"But Papa says it's a heathen atrocity," Matthew interrupted.

The missus turned to her son in an angry flash. "Well, it's not Papa's," she barked. "It's mine."

Oh, my goodness, thought Jessa, what have I done? She cursed the duster stick, the devil, and her own ungainly self. She did seem to be without "gifts" in this place.

The missus turned back to Jessa. "You ruin whatever you touch—cuts of meat, our linens, my favorite teacup, and now this! No debt of your father's is worth my home being destroyed. Get out!"

Jessa didn't know how to respond. Her father's debt? Was that why she was here? He did need her! She knew they owed a doctor for Mama's illness last winter, and money for a bull they'd leased that had gotten injured, but the mercantile too? She felt twenty different emotions at once. Shame that she was a mess of a girl. Relief that her father needed her—depended on her even. Fear that she was about to let him down. Before she could formulate words of apology—big words, contrition like she'd never voiced before—Mr. Keyes broke in.

"Mrs. Martin," he said. "I'm so miserably sorry." He bent down and picked up the statue's head, holding it like a precious gem. "I can't let Miss Campbell take the blame."

What? thought Jessa. Was he really owning fault? She halfway feared a trick.

"It was me. I broke it," he said.

"You?" the missus said, in surprise or disbelief, Jessa couldn't tell. She was similarly perplexed. *Why would he risk his job for me?*

"I was looking at it. I always look at it."

"You do?" the missus said, again with surprise in her voice.

"Nothing like it, am I right? It's such a fine piece, or was. I . . . I just feel sick about it." He crossed the room to the missus and took her hand. He placed the devil's head in it. "I'd offer to pay for it, but something like this . . . it sounds priceless to you, and I won't insult you with a paltry offer such as I could make."

He and the missus seemed to take each other in, and Jessa wondered that he did not let go of her hand. Mrs. Martin made a sad half smile, and he mirrored it, dimples subdued. It almost seemed like they were alone in the room, Jessa and Matthew invisible.

The missus sighed. "'Things without all remedy should be without regard': what's done is done."

"What's done is done, yes, ma'am."

"You know Shakespeare?" she said, brightening.

"No, ma'am."

She pulled her hand away, and a sorrowful look crossed her face again. "Miss Campbell, clean up this mess."

Jessa was still shaking, unable to believe she'd escaped dismissal.

"Aren't you gonna hear my song?" Matthew called to his mother.

"Not today," she said, heading upstairs.

"Then 'not today' am I going to play it." Matthew dashed outside, screen door slamming.

Jessa didn't know what to say. She spoke just above a whisper. "Thank you, Mr. Keyes, I—"

"Will," he said, equally low. "Time to dispense with formalities. We are partners now. Partners in crime. You a murderer, and me an accessory. The papers will call it 'The Assassination of the Genial Genie'—or was he a fortune teller?"

"I thought him a devil."

"Then you've done the Lord's work, partner."

Partner? He was teasing, of course, but suddenly, she didn't feel so alone in the house. He had done such a grand thing for her in taking the blame. She owed him. She thought of her father then, his debts to the Martins. She wondered how much money he owed and for how long he'd owed it. She wondered if her mother knew. Now she understood why the wagon was empty that day, and why there'd be no melons this year. If he had only told her. She recalled an oft-repeated proverb of Grandmother Campbell's: The rich ruleth over the poor, and the borrower is slave to the lender. Slave to the lender. Never had Jessa felt more deeply in debt.

•••

That night, as Jessa was clearing the table, the Martins squabbled over Mr. Keyes's employment. It had come up when the mister noticed the statue missing from the parlor and the missus explained the mishap.

"Even though he's done his Christian duty in breaking that monstrosity—"

"Would you please stop going on about it. It's art."

"An arguable point, but be that as it may, I'm not sure I want my children under the tutelage of a barroom entertainer."

Will played in a saloon? No wonder he knew such lively music. Jessa stacked the plates slowly so as to catch the conversation.

"Shady stuff going on there, Charlotte. Gambling and worse."

"For goodness' sake, he plays churches too. Besides, you've done business with the brother."

"Cattle business, but he's not the sort I'd summon to the parlor."

"But we have such a pretty piano," the missus countered, "and there's not another teacher within twenty miles. Besides, he's a boy."

Was the mister seriously considering letting Will go? Jessa got a dark feeling. She walked around the table and retrieved the butter dish, then went back and nested it in the serving ware. Jessa had worked to hide her lingering, but now she realized she had no need. She moved among them unseen, simply another of the house's features. Something you could purchase. A time-saving device like the mangle roller she used to squeeze the water from the Martins' freshly rinsed clothes.

"He's at least twenty if he's a day," said the mister.

"Without family, except for that brother."

"Exactly."

Jessa couldn't suss out why the missus would take up for Will this way. She wondered if she, too, was hungry for a friend. The Martins had only been in Texas six months. She knew they'd left family behind in St. Louis.

"So how is Will Keyes supposed to live out here, on the edge of nowhere, if he can't take work in a saloon?" the missus continued.

"A good name is more valuable than gold."

"Easy to say, Elias, when you have a little gold."

Jessa thought the missus made a good point. Will was doing what he had to do for his family, just like her.

"And I'm trying to hang on to it," he said. "Our name and our money. This is it. Need I remind you—" He seem suddenly to notice Jessa. "Will you excuse us, Miss Campbell?"

Jessa stepped out of the dining room but stopped at the other side of the door.

"This country's in a world of hurt, and we're into the last of my father's money. As outsiders here, we can't risk our reputations on anything or anyone."

"I assure you," the missus said, "that I supervise both the lessons and the musical selections."

That was a bald-faced lie. Mrs. Martin usually stayed upstairs reading novels while the boys took their lessons.

The sound of chair legs scraping across the floor alerted Jessa; they were done. She slipped the plates into the soapy water and then remembered the Martins wanted her to soap the glasses first, then the plates. So much to remember. The house and its demands pressed against her. She washed the plates quickly and slipped out the back door. The sky was a balm: the almost-full moon rising, the sun's last light glowing on the horizon, painting that section of sky orange and red with a line of purple. Sunset was her favorite time to be riding in the low hills at home. She'd hop on Dan with nothing but a hackamore and invent some last-minute chore—checking on a fence, a calf, a predator—then ride out to a little rise and face the setting sun. It was the closest thing to magic Jessa had ever experienced, the way the yellows and oranges, reds, purples, and gray-blues shifted in the sky. Something about feeling like she was the earth's lone witness in those moments filled her with gratitude.

After a few minutes, Jessa turned back toward the house. She could see the mister through the kitchen window. Was he looking for her, to gripe about something else? And what of his grumbling about Will Keyes? Surely, the boy with the dimples and green eyes was no threat to the Martin home.

4

It didn't feel like the Sabbath. No respite, no peace. It'd be another two weeks until Jessa would go home—a full two months of being away. Papa had initially said she'd go home once a month, but the Martins suggested she needed time to "settle in" before starting that part of the arrangement. Any more settled, she thought, and she'd be six feet under.

Now she was lingering in the privy. Instead of feeling fresh in the new day, she woke up tired. Exhausted from being on display and on call at all times, a never-ending test on a book she hadn't read: "Must you clonk, Miss Campbell? A light foot in the house." "Serve to the left, clear from the right." "Circular motion for silver, *with* the grain for wood." After learning precisely what her employment meant for her family, she'd vowed to do better, to meet the Martins' reproaches with a humble heart. Taxing, when a lot of the time she wanted to give them her own what for. She craved a few Martin-free hours. She considered begging off church. Her father wouldn't have let her skip worship— and she would not have asked.

At home on the Shinnery, a preacher came to the schoolhouse from Abilene once a month. On other Sundays, local men would take turns leading, or they'd worship at home. Mama quietly taught Jessa and her sisters to look up and meet God in creation. Easy to find God in the Shinnery. The sky so big and blue, kissing the wide-open land, and the red river, the Brazos, the arms of God. Río de los Brazos de Dios, as the Spanish had named it. Jessa always wondered what the Indians had called it before that, and if God Himself had names for things.

Mr. Martin, on the other hand, didn't seem as particular about keeping the Sabbath. He'd been fiddling with some sort of account books at his desk that very morning. Jessa sighed, dreading the pressed-down feeling she got being in the house. She finished her privy business. At least she could appreciate the rolled paper the Martins kept in the outhouse. Better than the corncobs back home.

Returning to the house, Jessa screwed up her courage and asked to be excused from church, but Mr. Martin wasn't listening, and she had to repeat the question.

"I'll allow it," he said. "But with this extra time, I expect today's pork roast to be a resounding success."

"Of course, Mr. Martin," she said, though she doubted the endeavor. Earlier he'd expressed a desire for a crispy top, while the missus had made clear she did not want a thick cap of fat. The fat was what made a brittle crust. When she began to trim the roast, she worked with the dispiriting knowledge that someone would be unhappy. She wondered what her mother was fixing at home, and who would be gathered around the table. The Martins were out of the house by nine-thirty, leaving Gabriel with her, which was fine. He was the easiest of the Martins to care for. With only him in the house, she felt free to take off her shoes, drink her coffee with too much sugar, and double butter her bread.

Tap, tap, tap. Jessa wiped her hands to open the door.

"Hey there, partner." The light behind Will framed him in a kind of glow, pieces of his hair floating and burnished by the sun. Mornings inside the house were dry things without dew and piercing sunrays, without critters and, seemingly, the world's wide turnings. Will brought the morning in.

"Do you think," he began, "I could . . ." He brought out a little tin cup from his pocket.

Was he going to ask for money? She did owe him.

"Coffee? You have any going?"

Jessa got the big enamel pot. She poured the coffee slowly, careful not to spill. He drank it down quickly, and she gave him a refill.

"A cure for what ails you," he said, toasting.

"Aren't you supposed to be playing the piano somewhere this morning?"

"That was the plan."

"Are you sick?" she asked.

"Yes and no." He picked up her half-eaten piece of bread and plopped it into his mouth. Then he wandered off from the kitchen as if he lived there. She found him at the piano, playing a song she'd never heard before.

"You play, Jessa?"

She shook her head.

"A shame," he said. "Music feeds the soul."

"My grandmother would say that it's the Good Book that feeds the soul," she said, and then she regretted it. Why'd she have to bring up her grandmother?

"The Good Book, huh? Then I shall feed you." He broke into song. "Blessed are they which do hunger and thirst after righteousness, for they shall be filled . . ."

Will sang the upbeat tune playfully, but all she could think about was what he'd said: "I'll feed you." She imagined the words from his lips flying into her mouth like barn swallows at dusk. She was tempted to open her mouth a little, to see if she could taste the music.

"From the Book of Matthew," he said. "Surely your grandmother would approve of that."

"Not with the piano."

"Come again?"

"She attends the Church of Christ now. No instruments but the ones God gave us."

"That'd put me out of business. I've played churches and revival meetings all through Indiana, Missouri, Kansas, Oklahoma, and Texas. So, Miss I-don't-need-a-piano, show me what pleases the Lord—or at least your grandmother."

For some reason, Jessa didn't feel nervous. She launched into a song she'd sung a hundred times, "Just as I am, without one plea, but that thy blood was shed for me, and that thou bidd'st me come to thee, O Lamb of God, I come, I come." Soon Will was playing the song note for note. She continued onto the second verse. He joined in the refrain, and this time his voice was quite different, no trace of tomfoolery. He had a rich baritone. If music were colors he was purple and red. She stared openly and he stared back. In the fullness of her gaze, she realized, he was the handsomest man she'd ever seen. Groomed, like a prize horse at a fair, hair shiny and just so.

"Because thy promise I believe, O Lamb of God, I come, I come," they sang together. He harmonized beautifully with her. She wished the song had a thousand verses.

"Where'd you learn to play?" she asked.

"My mama. 'Til the piano had to go."

"Hard times?" she asked. Every family had them.

"Something like that."

He got a far off look and Jessa felt it impolite to press him on the subject.

"Yessa," hollered Gabriel, breaking the spell. He tromped into the parlor. "We go outside."

She pulled herself away from the piano. "Sure. For a little bit."

"Imma get—" Without finishing his sentence, he hurried up the stairs.

"You sing like an angel, and you're pretty as one," Will said.

She blushed. His words were a poultice after weeks of stinging rebukes. She wasn't the "pretty one," lined up with her sisters, but there was no line here.

"Let's make it an outing," he said.

"Huh?"

"Going outside."

She wanted nothing more, but she had the roast to fix. She headed to the kitchen trying to calculate the minimum amount of time the pork would need to cook, and also calculating the risk she'd be taking spending unchaperoned time with the piano teacher. She felt fluttery inside thinking about it, like a fledgling perched on a twig. All shake and fluff.

"You need some fresh air," he said.

She couldn't disagree with that, but she didn't want to endanger her position. Still, he'd gone out on a limb for her. "I'm on probation. Mr. Martin seems half set on sending me home already. Don't want to give him more cause."

"Martin's a blowhard."

"What do you mean?" Jessa plopped the meat in the pan and placed onion slices around it.

"Doesn't know which way is up. That sign he's got on his store, 'E. Martin, Cattleman.' He doesn't even own any damn cattle."

"Yes, he does," said Jessa. "A Mr. Goodsite runs them."

"Goodsite runs 'em for any slicker dandy he can sell them to. Same herd, over and over."

Jessa put down the carrot she was slicing. "What do you mean?"

"Rumor has it, there's only one herd—and a measly one at that."

Jessa thought of her own family's cattle, how the drought, and lack of forage, had made them thin. "But the brand?"

"Alters it slightly."

"So you're saying the cattle Mr. Martin saw aren't his?" Jessa couldn't quite grasp how such a thing could be.

"I'm not saying anything."

"But—"

"But nothing. Everyone's got problems. I don't worry about Martin's, and he don't worry 'bout mine."

"What problems do you have?" she said. Will seemed so lackadaisical; Jessa couldn't imagine he carried worries.

"Same as every man: money, money, money, money."

"But the saloon," she said.

"Does all right. But we got a few debts from the Galveston operation. A misunderstanding. They got my brother's feet to the fire nonetheless."

"Who does?"

"Who does? You does," he cracked, clearly done with the conversation. "Let's get outta here." He cocked his head toward the door as if getting away together was something they did all the time. "Quick as a lick we'll be back."

"I've got Gabriel."

"You can chaperone him, and I can chaperone you."

It all sounded so reasonable the way he said it.

"We'll have a picnic," he said.

"A picnic?" She moved to the basin, put a few odd dishes in to soak.

"Yep, as long as we can round up some vittles." He lifted the cloth on the cold Johnny cakes and sniffed them. "These'll do."

"Will they?" She turned from the basin and marveled at his boldness, the way he marched in, asking not just for her company, but her food.

"That and a girl," he said, stepping closer, taking her hand. "Can't you see I'm sweet on you?"

"Oh," she said, ghost-tasting any number of sweet things—peaches, sugar, honey, molasses. Her mouth watered but she could not swallow. He was holding her hand, the very thing she'd wished for, his grip sure, and he was sweet on her. Suddenly, her other hand felt empty, her whole body unbalanced, and though some voice in her head warned her reaching out would be imprudent, she offered her other hand anyway. He took it and pulled her close. She bit her lip to keep from crying. She hadn't realized how much her body had missed her family. Gabriel had been her only source of touch, but he never lingered long on her hip or lap. Up close she could see the stubble on Will's cheeks, a bit of sleep crust in the corner of one eye. He kissed her cheek. Warm feelings rushed into a place in her body far removed from her face, and she marveled at it.

"Proper sweet. Serious sweet." He kissed her other cheek, slowly. It felt like a moth landing on her skin.

She felt dizzy. Was he going to kiss her on the lips? She stood dead still. He reached his arm around her, grabbed hold of her apron string, and untied it, the apron falling to her feet.

"Come on then, Partner."

"Gabriel," she called, "want to go on a picnic?"

They walked down the dusty road. The three of them, Gabe in between, little clouds rising at his shuffling, hopping, busy-boy feet, pausing to inspect yellow beetles and hidey holes and to pick up sticks that looked like swords and stones that looked like bones. Rayner, Texas, was so much larger when Jessa walked with Gabriel, seeing the vast distances through his eyes and experiencing the landscape through his small, distracted steps. Working against this vastness was a sense of the world shrinking as she walked next to Will. The sky and the earth seemed to press down, compressing the space—the width of the road, the length of their stride—into some sort of invisible box. The air between them was charged like before a summer storm, but instead of shuttering the windows, she wanted to throw them open and knock the lightning rod from the roof. He reached over the little boy and took her hand.

•••

An hour and a half later, the trio returned to the house. Will held Gabriel at the pump while Jessa washed his hands and feet. The act involved much splashing, and all three were laughing carelessly when they heard the back door swing open.

"Miss Campbell," said the missus.

They froze, even Gabriel who, like one of Jessa's dogs, immediately sensed the tension. The family had not been expected for at least another hour.

"What on earth is going on?"

Before Jessa could stammer out an explanation, Will handed Gabriel to her.

"Mrs. Martin," he said, "fortune has landed. I was comin' to speak with you when I ran into Miss Campbell here, arriving from a walk, was it?"

"Yes, a walk. A quick one." Jessa noticed Matthew, the older boy, next to his mother, the front of his shirt covered in blood. Poor kid was susceptible to bloody noses in the dry heat.

"So what was it you needed, Mr. Keyes?" Something in her tone told Jessa the missus was not buying the ruse.

"It's about Tuesday," he said. "I have another appointment. I was wondering if I could switch the boys' lessons to the morning, say ten?"

"Ten will be fine. And whatever you have bundled in my kitchen cloth, please return it to Miss Campbell. And Jessa, you can see what needs to be done with Matthew's clothing." With that, the missus went into the house.

Will handed the cloth picnic bundle to Jessa, a lone piece of cheese still inside. "She'll be fine." He was so sure of himself and his ability to move through the world.

Jessa wished she felt such confidence in the outcome. She could be walking into a firing, she thought as she headed for the back door.

"Jess?" Will said.

She stopped, turned around.

"I—I had a real nice time just, you know, walking."

Jessa thought she sensed a wistfulness in his voice, like walking was something he'd lost. She didn't know why that was; he walked all the time. "Ya, me too."

As she walked up the porch steps, Gabe felt heavy in her arms and ready for his afternoon nap. She laid him on her own bed to avoid going upstairs, where she could hear the missus creaking about. She assumed Matthew was resting as well. His bloody clothes littered the kitchen floor, but before she could work on the stains, the bell went off, *da-ding, da-ding.* All my eye! she thought. The boys will wake! If the missus had bad news for Jessa, she could at least deliver it quietly.

In the bedroom, jewelry was haphazardly spilled across the dressing table, the surface of which was cluttered with what Mrs. Martin called her "toilette." A powder puff in a blue-and-white china bowl, a wooden box for hair combs, and bottles of fragrance—one, Florida Water, with a label of an Oriental woman at the Fountain of Youth—comprised her collection. In the center a silver brush, comb, and mirror set, as ornate as the tea set downstairs. Jessa wished her sister Nellie could see the display.

"I couldn't find my pearl earrings," said the missus.

This was not what Jessa had expected. Did the missus think she'd stolen from her too, an added offense to the crime of an inappropriate visitor?

"Not the globes, the seed pearls," she went on.

Jessa pictured a plant sprouting from a pearl, its branches heavy with white orbs.

"But then I found them in the pocket of my gray gabardine."

Relief flooded Jessa. Better to be thought a sneak than a thief.

The missus moved toward the dressing table. "All these beautiful things and nowhere to wear them out here on the 'front porch of the frontier.'"

Jessa had heard that expression before and didn't like it. It made her home seem merely a place to pass through, a place to kill time until a door was opened.

"Go ahead," she said, "try something on."

Try something on? Why had Jessa been summoned by the bell unless to discuss the falsehood at the water pump? She was confused and didn't care to try on any of the jewelry, but the missus looked determined so she obliged. She chose a gold ring with a deep red, rectangular stone and filigree on each side—the pattern reminded her of leatherwork on a fancy saddle.

"From my parents on my eighteenth birthday," the missus said.

Jessa slid the ring on her finger. Her swollen, red cuticles competed with the red of the stone and made her embarrassed by her ragged hands, by her unfamiliarity with the things on the dressing table. Jessa took off the ring and placed it back on the table.

"I called you up to show you something, but you have to promise never to utter a word about it."

Jessa could not imagine what was coming next, but since it seemed like she was not in danger of being let go, she gratefully obliged. "No, ma'am, not a word."

The missus moved to the dresser and reached into the back of the drawer where she kept her underthings. She pulled out a handkerchief-wrapped parcel. After gingerly untying the delicate cloth, she lifted a gold chain. From it hung a locket the size of a small coin.

"My engagement present." She handed the locket to Jessa. "Open it."

Carefully, Jessa pried apart the two halves. Inside was a photograph of a handsome man who was not Mr. Martin. This man had dark, wavy hair and a broad nose, and there was something foreign about him.

"My fiancé," she whispered. The mirth was gone from her voice, the game of surprise over. She took the necklace back and stared at the photograph for another moment. "That's enough of that." She snapped the locket closed. "I know what's going on here with you and Mr. Keyes, and I'm here to tell you, it is folly. He is a pretty boy, but I'm not sure he's on the up and up. Either way, your family is not likely to accept him. Do you hear me? Don't mistake it for a game."

"But Will and I—" Jessa was trying to dissuade the missus, but Mrs. Martin was fixed and wouldn't let her finish.

"Even when the man is right and good, in the blink of an eye, your prospects can shrink, your family can . . ." Her words trailed off. She seemed to be talking to herself more than to Jessa. "And you'll find yourself crying over a broken statue, eight years after he won it for you at the Expo, eight years since you saw him last. It'll break you."

Jessa felt she had never known this woman. All their conversations and interactions had led her to conclude the missus was a little vain, in need of company, but above all, proper—a proper wife in a proper household. The locket with the image of another man was not proper. But why was the missus associating it with Jessa and Will? Mrs. Martin didn't know him at all, and if Jessa's family knew him—the real him—surely, they'd feel as she did.

Jessa stood up straight. Hands together. Proper. She wouldn't let the sweet feeling she held be taken away. "Mr. Keyes is just an acquaintance, ma'am."

"Well, you had better keep it that way."

5

Walking to town with the boys, Jessa tried to brush off Mrs. Martin's doom and gloom talk. The missus was not privy to how Will had taken the blame for Jessa with the statue. She couldn't see how he'd brought kindness to a home short on it. Still, the warning rattled her. She was "of an age," as Papa had said, so maybe it was right and natural to have let him kiss her. Maybe she'd been fooling herself to think she'd never fancy anyone the way her sisters did. She needed to talk to Nellie and would in another two weeks. She'd unload her heart then, when they were tucked up in bed, fingers intertwined, Agnes snoozing in the trundle.

The Martins lived a half mile from where the town's buildings began— the far end, when coming from the Shinnery. A line of soapberry trees had been planted on both sides of Main Street. "Pups," Papa had called them. They didn't offer much shade but held the promise of it. The boys made a game of touching each tree and then hurrying to the next, pretending the ground in between was on fire. It felt strange to be on her own going to town, the grown person in charge. She kept her eyes peeled for Will. She sensed seeing him would quell the unsettled feeling she carried.

The town was festooned in red, white, and blue, ready for the Fourth of July, two days away. Flags and bunting graced storefronts and lampposts—someone had even tied ribbons to the hitching post in front of the bank. There'd be a parade at ten and a picnic to follow;

the kids would compete in egg-and-spoon races, while adults would form tug-of-war teams and compete in blindfolded wheelbarrow races. Before the depression Rayner's celebration had been a two-day affair, with dances both nights, a series of foot races with cash prizes, and a parade with at least two marching bands. The Masonic Lodge would host one dance this year, but the missus had said it'd be a small party, only a fiddler and no midnight meal. Jessa was not keen on dancing, she had no grace for it, but liked to watch. Her family usually came into town for the celebration, but this year they'd be spending the holiday in Aspermont with sister Minta. It was just as well. The missus had made it clear to Jessa that she'd be duty bound to the children that day, holiday or no.

Mrs. Posey waved to Jessa and the boys through the open door of the post office. She had a letter for the missus. Jessa corralled the boys inside. As usual, the postmistress appeared to be holding court. The red-headed girl Jessa had seen that first day, coming into town with Papa, was there too. Mrs. Posey introduced her as Oneida Garrett. Jessa was intrigued by her complexion. Jessa thought someone fair with deep-copper hair should be covered in freckles, but Oneida's face was freckle-free. The girl looked trussed up for Easter Sunday in a wide-brimmed straw hat and pearl-buttoned gloves.

"Miss Garrett here's been down at Miss Brown's," said Mrs. Posey, by way of introduction.

Jessa nodded vaguely. She didn't know any Miss Brown.

Oneida seemed to pick up on Jessa's unfamiliarity. "Miss Brown's Young Ladies' Boarding School. In Houston?"

Though she said it kindly, Jessa hated having the world explained by someone her age. "Oh," she said awkwardly. "Is that so?"

"I'd bet you'd like to make tracks right back to the city," Mrs. Posey said to Oneida.

"That I would. My father won't consider it though. I've education enough, he says. Besides, it's 'dangerous' in the city, don't you know?" She smiled, her teeth as bright as a baby's. "I cannot wait to inform him that saloon patrons were set upon last night right here in Rayner."

Gamblers and thieves right in town. Jessa looked around the post office, wondering how she'd know who was who.

"Don't go crawling his hump, Miss Garrett. Only gamblin' money got stolen."

"Gamblers?" said Matthew.

"Little pitchers have big ears," said Mrs. Posey. She handed Jessa a letter for the missus.

As Jessa ushered the boys out, she heard a man behind her say, "I heard it's the proprietor himself sending thieves after flush customers." Jessa wondered which saloon and which proprietor the man was implicating, but she would not turn around to ask. It was no question for a young lady. She hoped the event would not reflect poorly on Will.

Between the post office and the *Texas Lasso* newspaper office, a new storefront was going up. While Matthew stopped to watch the workers put up the wood siding, Gabriel hunted on the ground for bent nails. One of the workers, a heavyset man with a rosy face, doffed his hat to Jessa.

"Afternoon," said the workman's black-bearded partner.

"Afternoon," she said, looking away.

This was new. Someone taking note of her. She'd thought maybe Will saying she was pretty was an aberration, but here was more of that kind of attention. Why had this never happened before? Had something changed? She'd have to add this to the list of things to discuss with Nellie.

Arriving in front of the courthouse, Jessa told the boys how her father had helped build it. Gabriel raced up the walk to the steps, but she caught him before he went through the wide oak doors. Matthew was more interested in the squat addition sitting at the rear of the courthouse, the jail.

"I could break out of that," the boy boasted.

Jessa had to agree that it didn't look very sturdy compared to the thick sandstone blocks of the courthouse.

Finally, they reached the store, the larger of the town's two mercantiles. Its sign read: Martin & Sons Dry Goods, E. Martin, Cattleman.

Jessa didn't know what cattle had to do with notions and hats, but Mr. Martin frequently referred to himself as a cattleman. The store, like the Martin home, was one of the newest and nicest buildings around, with its river rock base and pine siding. Mr. Martin had the only Dutch door on Main Street. Inside were two counters, each running the length of the building. There were bins of spices and sacks of grain—rice, oats, wheat, and rye. A large coffee roaster sat near the rear of the store. Jessa smelled the coffee straightaway, that and the new pine floor.

Jessa felt a bit shabby in all the newness. She was conscious of her shoes with their worn soles and her cotton dress, cuffs fraying, a long-ago hand-me-down from sister Minta.

"Good afternoon, Miss Campbell." Mr. Martin turned to his boys. "Are you after your sweets?"

"Yes, Papa," said Matthew.

"I have moneys." Gabriel opened his hand to reveal five bent nails.

Jessa feared the mister would dismiss the little boy's gesture, tell him to stop picking up rubbish, chastise her over his dirty hands. Instead, Mr. Martin bent down to his son's level.

"That is just the amount I was set to charge you, Master Gabriel, and frankly, I was worried about your creditworthiness. Are you employed?"

"I'm not 'ployed," said Gabriel.

"Good thing you can pay then." Mr. Martin opened his palm to receive his son's offering, which Gabriel dutifully deposited. "No hand in the jar, use the ladle."

Jessa crossed to the other side of the store. There were shovels and hoes and other implements she could not name, but what they had in common were their unspoiled surfaces. She had never seen a tool completely free of rust and dirt before. Never considered a tool's beginning point, unblemished, clean. The store was such an assembly of shiny and new—implements, bolts of fabric, harnesses, feeders, serving ware. Jessa wished she could take something home for Mama, something fanciful that couldn't be shared.

A man appeared in the doorway of the store. The sun was so bright outside that he appeared as a shadow-man on the threshold. Jess felt inexplicable dread, the same lurch in the chest she felt when a hawk flew over the chicken yard. Though she didn't think she'd ever seen him before, he looked familiar. Six feet if he was an inch, lean, long golden-brown hair like burnt sugar, and dimples like Will's but not as pronounced. Could this be the brother? she wondered. The maybe-brother sized her up and down, nose to tail, like she was a horse for sale.

"Afternoon, Miss," he said.

He was missing two teeth, his canine and the one next to it. It tarnished his looks, and for some reason Jessa was glad for it. On his hip, he wore a .45 six-shooter, and he walked as if ready for a gunfight in the mercantile. Papa would not approve. Guns were a fact of life on the frontier, and her father always carried one while traveling and ranging, but this was different. "Cock of the walk," her papa might have called this fellow. For young men to only have to travel from hand to hip to settle differences, real or imagined, was a danger.

Jessa had seen her father shoot out of anger only once. It had been a few months after her brother died. Newt had left behind a few goats. Angora crosses, for mohair. While some families might've treasured those stringy-haired goats as a link to their loved one, the Campbells did not. They were a reminder of what was lost. Papa had a vague plan to get rid of them, but grief sapped the energy even for that. The nannies were all right, but the billy was meaner than cuss, smelled worse than a skunk, and would not stay penned. He destroyed much of the kitchen garden. Got into the barn and tore up sacks of seed. One time he even broke a window, hopping onto the wood crib attached to the cabin, picking a fight with his own reflection. He'd butt anyone trying to put him away. Jessa and her sisters had been playing in front of the barn, in early evening, when the billy came after them, yellow eyes blazing. The girls hollered and climbed to safety in the wagon; Papa came as quickly as he could. The goat was waiting. He charged Papa, knocking him over, Papa's head hitting the ground. When Papa sat up, he had such a look of rage on his face—something Jessa had never seen before or since. While the goat made his way behind the barn, Papa flew in and out of the house. Winchester in hand, he followed in the direction of the billy, and out of sight. *Crack*, the rifle sounded, and they knew the goat was dead. In the blink of an eye. Papa got to work with the shovel. The girls got quiet and went inside. After skipping dinner that night, Papa sat outside in the dark for a long while. No one ever spoke of the billy goat again.

Although Jessa hadn't responded to his greeting, the man with the gun smiled and tipped his gray felt hat as if she had. Then he strode over to Mr. Martin.

"Afternoon, Martin."

Mr. Martin walked over to him straightaway. "Afternoon, Mr. Keyes." Jessa's ears pricked at this. This had to be Will's brother, Levi.

"Get that shipment in?"

"Straight from Kentucky," said the mister. He set a crate on the counter.

"Amen," said Mr. Keyes. "Need a sack of peanuts too."

The mister cleared his throat. "Uh . . . can I, um, expect a payment today on your, uh, credit?"

"I like to pay it all off at once, Martin."

"Yes, you said but—"

"Think I'm some kinda four-flusher?"

"Of course not—"

"If you're hurting, Martin, I can help you out, otherwise, we'll settle up next week."

"Right," said the mister, without conviction. He pulled his pocket watch out of his vest, glanced at the time. "Say, have you heard from Mr. Goodsite?"

He said this as if it were an afterthought, but Jessa knew better. Mr. Martin was obsessed with the cattle that were being run for him. The missus was tired of hearing him fret. "Elias, dear, must we keep going 'round about the cows?" she'd said to him last night at the dinner table. Jessa wondered if the mister asked everyone who came into the store about the missing Mr. Goodsite.

"Nope," said Mr. Keyes.

Mr. Martin took a handkerchief from his pocket and casually wiped the face of the watch. "I suppose he's busy with the stock."

"Nice watch," said Levi, eyeing the ornate gold timepiece.

"Thanks. A gift from my father upon my graduation."

"That so."

Mr. Martin tucked the watch back into his pocket. "Going back to Goodsite, I'm anxious to take a little trip out to see my beeves in their summer range. So if you see him—"

Mr. Keyes cut him off. "Haven't seen him."

"But if you do . . ."

Levi didn't respond.

"Anyway, much appreciated," said the mister, twisting the hanky. "Thanks again for the introduction."

Levi nodded. Mr. Martin exited to the storeroom in the back. Jessa was puzzled by their interaction. She had heard the mister rail against the unsuitability of having a piano teacher who also played in a saloon, a saloon of rather dubious reputation, and yet, here in the store, the mister appeared to be on downright friendly terms with the proprietor of said saloon. There seemed to be two sets of rules, one for home and one for business—or maybe three; at the Martins' there was a set of rules for the family and another for their "girl." As she watched Matthew approach the man with the gun, she realized she'd unconsciously taken a step toward the boy, as if she might pull him out of harm's way should it come to that.

"Are you a cowboy?" asked Matthew.

"Maybe. Or maybe I'm a gunslinger. You ever hear of Jesse James?"

"Jesse James is dead," said Matthew.

"Is that so?"

"My dad's a cowboy," said Matthew. "Fifty head of longhorn and fifty of roan Durham. When I am bigger, I'm going to drive 'em to Kansas."

Levi smiled. "You've got quite a plan."

"Sure you don't have any cows? Everybody does. Even Jessa."

"Jessa," repeated Levi. "This your sister?" he asked the boy.

"No, she's . . . what are you, Jessa?"

"Yes, what are you, Jessa?" the man echoed.

Though no one moved, she felt as if a shadow was crossing her. The same sensation she'd felt when he walked through the door. Jessa didn't answer the man. Wouldn't look at him. Instead, she removed Gabriel from the counter and put him on her hip.

"Jessa has mules too," Matthew said. "Beck and . . . what's their names—"

"A mule girl," said Mr. Keyes. "That right?"

Jessa didn't answer.

"You must know my brother then."

She held Gabriel more tightly.

"But somehow he's never mentioned you. Saving the pretty ones for himself."

Jessa was relieved Will hadn't seen fit to discuss her with this . . . this brother—another brother perhaps, an imagined kinder brother, but not this disturbing creature with a gun on his hip.

"Look, I'm just teasin'." Levi mussed Matthew's hair. "Aren't I, boy?"

Mr. Martin emerged from the back with a sack of peanuts. "Anything else, Keyes?"

This was her out. She grabbed Matthew by the hand and headed for the door.

"Bye, Papa," Matthew called, and Gabriel repeated it.

Jessa was relieved to be out of the store. She turned her face into the full sun. How could that man and Will be related, look so similar and be so different? She had felt for Will being separated from his kinfolk in Indiana, glad to know he had a brother here, but not anymore.

Haskell Free Press, APRIL 13, 1895

NO BAIL FOR DEFENDANT

Judge Hammer went over to Rayner Monday and heard the application for habeas corpus for bail for _____ charged with the murder . . . After hearing the evidence the judge remanded the defendant to jail without bond.

6

Jessa finished washing up the breakfast things, thinking about how next week at this time she'd be home. Four whole days. She couldn't wait to sit at Mama's table, walk the fence line with Papa, and hear the sing-song chatter of her sisters. The only downside was she wouldn't see Will. He'd been showing up every morning for his backdoor coffee. He came early, before the Martins were up, getting the first cup out of the pot. They'd stand on opposite sides of the threshold and whisper-talk—or just make eyes. He had started kissing her when he left, gently, on the lips. The first couple of times, she'd stood there, unsure. The last time she had kissed him back. What she felt was akin to hunger.

Yesterday, during the boys' piano lesson, he'd slipped her a note. She'd seen notes passed in the schoolhouse before but had never received one. Will asked her to meet him alone the next day. "If you feel as I do, you will overcome any and all obstackals to join me." She did and she would, offering the missus a convoluted story about how her older sister Maggie was expected in Rayner and how she desperately wished to see her. When the missus said she'd like to meet Maggie, Jessa readily agreed—even smiled—but then immediately followed up with an apology about how long they might have to wait in front of the court-house, as the meeting time wasn't precisely fixed. The missus, thankfully, declined. Jessa's actual itinerary did not involve town.

The afternoon was perfect. The sun was high overhead, a few clouds riding low, puffy and gray. Dry weather clouds, Papa called them. Jessa and Will walked the three miles or so to the Brazos, side by side, through fields and down paths, up hills, and across creeks. Jessa loved the way their footsteps seemed to shift the landscape as they moved through it, grasshoppers springing from bluestem, bobwhites spilling from under sumac, hummingbirds rising from sage, a horned lizard scurrying away; the scent of verbena, and the honey perfume of the Blackfoot daisy, all being released as they passed.

He was usually talkative at the Martin house. So sure of himself. Jessa enjoyed this quieter side. While she wanted to ask about his brother, she feared it might cast a pall on their walk. Instead, she asked about his mama.

"She has her qualities," he said.

"You miss her?"

"Of course."

It was a dumb question, and Jessa felt embarrassed by it. What she had meant by it was "tell me more."

After a moment, he said, "But I don't miss her husband."

"He's not your father?"

"Hell no, that man's a snake. A poisonous one." He paused, looked off into the distance. "He almost took the hide off Levi. Finally run him off when Levi was fifteen. Mama didn't do anything about it but cry. Course she'd had two more babies with him by then. I was only eight. He waited until I was twelve to start beating me. Always looking for somebody to blame."

Jessa couldn't imagine a family like that. Her father had never raised a hand to his children. "I'm sorry."

"Well, it's over," he said. "Over when Levi sent for me, train ticket and pocket money to boot. No one knew better than him what I was living through. Don't know how he managed it, but it was the single best day of my life."

Maybe Jessa had gotten it wrong about Levi. If he meant this much to Will, he couldn't be all bad.

When they reached the river, they waded in. Will hitched his britches to his knees. Jessa held her skirts in her fist, water up to her ankles. She could see dirty rivulets of water on her legs, where the flying drops met her dusty skin. She wanted to rinse the road off, but not with Will there, so she kept her skirt as low as she could without soaking the hem. A wet skirt might require explanation.

The only thing that hung between them—besides this warm, bee-buzzing feeling—was the shadow of his brother. She wasn't afraid of snakes, bobcats, scorpions, or bulls, but she was afeared of Levi Keyes. She was also worried that the stuff Will had said about Mr. Martin and his nonexistent cattle might result in Levi—and thus, Will—being run out of town. "So, tell me," Jessa said, "them cattle Mr. Martin saw, they aren't really his?"

"You hung up on that?" he said.

"How's it possible?"

"I don't know anything about it, right? But suppose Martin was a mark—"

"A mark?"

"An easy person. 'Spose this mark doesn't know what he's looking at, and suppose Goodsite, or someone like him, only shows him one or two steers up close. Misdirection."

"Misdirection?"

"Like a magician. You ever see a magician?" asked Will.

"No."

"Misdirection," he continued, "is where you focus someone's attention on one thing to distract from another. Like, look up there on that bluff." Will pointed to the layers of red sandstone that lined the walls of the river. "Over there. Do you see it? Creeping up?"

Jessa scanned the banks then—boom—he was behind her, inches behind her. His words dropped to a whisper.

"Misdirection," he said.

Just that moment, a cloud moved into the path of the sun. Jessa shivered. She felt immodest holding her skirt up, him so close behind, their bodies momentarily shadowed. Then Will stepped away from her. He found a big flat rock to lie across so he could put his face in the river to drink. He spit water at her playfully. Then the cloud passed, and all was in light.

"So, what happens when it's time for Mr. Martin's steers to go to market?" she said.

"Lightning strike, cattle plague. Let's just say, I wouldn't be surprised if something happened to his imaginary herd."

Jessa felt almost queasy. She'd heard tales of swindlers, distant stories about distant people, but she was learning now that deception lived close to home, that people set out to take from their neighbors. That was the thing about leaving home: the world shifted in ways that made it harder to walk through.

Will rose from the rock, a damp circle on his shirt. He picked up a couple of stones and tried to skip them across the moving water.

"Didn't your brother set the whole thing up though?" she asked.

"Why do you say that?"

"I heard the mister thank Levi for the introduction to Mr. Goodsite."

"An introduction, not a set up."

"You think Mr. Martin will see a difference?"

"Levi introduces a lot of people to business opportunities. Can't be responsible for how every one turns out, now can he?"

Jessa hoped that was true, a mere introduction, nothing to be gained or lost. "Should we tell Mr. Martin?"

"Tell him what?"

"About the cattle. The swindle."

"You need to forget all that. Whatever happens with old Pinch-face Martin, he's walked into it."

Pinch-face, thought Jessa, the perfect nickname for the mister. His face scrunched up and his nose flared whenever he had to deal with what he called Jessa's "limitations." The week before, she'd served him rice and beans mixed together—mixed together, like some kind of St. Louis crime. She'd tried to explain the dish called Hoppin' John, but Mr. Martin interrupted. "I don't want to eat your Indian food. It's fine for you at home, but not here." His criticisms stung less when

they were silly or, in this case, purely ignorant. Jessa knew Hoppin'
John was not a Cherokee dish. Mama said her people ate wild meats,
bean bread, and dried fruit, none of which Jessa was trying to put
on the Martin table.

"You have any part in, you know, your brother's business stuff?"

"Me? I'm just a piano player."

Will threw his last stone. It sank without skipping. "Them cows are
no concern of yours—or mine. Besides, you know what happens to the
messenger?" Will moved closer. "The bearer of bad news?"

Jessa shook her head.

"Why, they chop her head off."

Will hooked his arm around Jessa's neck and pulled her to his chest.
With his free hand, he rubbed his knuckles along the part in her hair.
Playful, like the roughhousing she'd done a thousand times with her
sisters, cousins, and school friends, and yet her reaction—her body's
reaction—was dead serious.

She pined for him even as he stood next to her. She thought of the
Bible verse they always said at weddings: "And they twain shall be one
flesh: so then they are no more twain, but one flesh." At those moments
the word "flesh" had always brought "meat" to mind, and she'd thought
how at odds the passage seemed with the pretty scene before her in
church. But not here, standing in the water, the sun sparkling on the
river and glistening in the fine hairs on Will's arm, which was now
draped around her shoulders. Flesh was as essential as water and sunlight. A body needed a body. Flesh.

Will released her and she leaned into him, her back to his front. She
looked off in the direction of the Double Mountains. Quanah Parker,
the last chief of the Comanches, and his band of Indians had made
their home there for a while. The Shinnery had been their hunting and
fighting grounds. Along the riverbeds, she liked to hunt for arrowheads
and tiny beads, evidence of these inhabitants who had disappeared
from the land.. She often thought about Quanah's mother, Cynthia
Ann, the white woman who had been kidnapped, as a nine-year old,

after her family was killed—revenge, no doubt, for how Indian families had been destroyed and driven away. The girl was taken from what was now Fort Parker, some two hundred and fifty miles away. Raised by the Comanches, Cynthia Ann forgot her former life and married a chief. The story went that, due to the chief's great affection for her, he never took another wife. When "rescued" years later, she mourned her return to civilization. Jessa thought about how Cynthia Ann might have leaned against her chief just like this, up on the mountain, how she would have looked down on the plains where Jessa now stood.

She worried Will would be as unwelcome a suitor to her family as Cynthia Ann's Indian chief had been to hers. Even though the saloon was Levi's, its reputation was dishonorable enough to taint Will. Father didn't have a blanket policy against liquor so much as a judgment of those who preyed on a man's weakness for drink. The stories of men being set upon on their way home from the saloon, with the insinuation that Levi was in on it, would not help Will's case. There was another story in circulation, one she'd overheard at the post office, about a washer girl who'd been living in the back room of Levi's saloon until her uncle arrived with a posse from Juarez and threatened to burn the town down. A misunderstanding, Will explained. The man was not a rescuing uncle, but an abusive husband; Levi was not a mistress-keeper, but a protector of the innocent. Jessa didn't know what to believe—the town seemed to thrive on gossip—so she put it out of her mind as best she could. Things had a way of sorting themselves out, her mother always said.

Will wrapped both his arms around her waist. She looked down at his hands on her belly, felt the heat of them through the worn calico.

"What's that in the willow?" he said.

She tried to focus on the scraggly tree on the opposite bank but could see nothing. The angle was such that she was looking into the sun. All she could think about were his hands. She closed her eyes and let the rays bathe her face in light. She thought of butter on hot bread, the way it melted when it met the surface, the way it glistened. And suddenly his mouth was on hers, soft and smooth. Jessa opened her mouth to his, a reflex, like a stick to the knee; the way the leg kicked, her mouth opened. *I am doing this*, she thought, *I am doing this*. He stroked her, his hands across her belly and her hips. For just a moment, his hand grazed her down-below. Even though she was wearing two skirts, she felt excited and alarmed enough to pull away.

"What's the matter, Miss Campbell?" he said.

"I best be getting back," she said.

"Best be."

He released her then and they started walking back, the river cling-ing to the damp hems of Jessa's skirts.

7

Jessa had been waiting on the front porch since early morning. She'd hardly slept. She hoped to meet her father before he dismounted and get underway before the missus knew he'd arrived. She worried the missus might mention her imaginary meeting with Maggie, or give a report on everything she'd done poorly or, worst of all, mention Will Keyes. The missus had caught them with their heads together at the piano just two days before. That was her news to deliver in her way. As soon as she saw her father, Jessa bolted from the porch and started down the road in his direction. He was riding Old Dan and ponying Beck, the mule, for her.

"How's my girl?" he asked, his blue eyes bright, a smile visible under his heavy mustache. His mustache looked grayer, his face older than when he'd dropped her off nine weeks earlier.

"Your girl's fine and well." She quickly started to unwrap Beck's lead from the horn of Papa's saddle. He put his rough hand on top of hers.

"I oughta speak to the Martins."

"Mr. Martin already left, and the missus has her hands full with the children. A real higgledy-piggledy in the kitchen this morning."

"Should you go on in and help her? I can set a spell," Papa offered.

"Oh, no, the missus said for me to get on my way. Said to say hello though . . . and wished us a safe ride home." For a girl who'd spent her first sixteen years tongue-tied, it nearly frightened her what a barefaced liar she'd become, the words flowing out practically of their own accord.

"All righty," he said.

Beck was tall at sixteen hands. Jessa had to take her skirts in one hand, grab the horn with the other, and jump a little to get her foot in the stirrup before she could throw her leg over. No ladylike way to mount the mule; she was glad the missus wasn't there to witness it. No one rode sidesaddle on the Shinnery. Then just as she threw her leg over . . .

"Mr. Campbell!"

The missus thwarted her escape.

"Good morning, Mr. Campbell." The missus walked directly to his horse.

"Good morn." Papa tipped his hat and started to dismount, but the missus stopped him.

"No need," she said. "Jessa, will you go in the house for a moment. Check on Gabe."

Jessa couldn't let this happen. "How about we all go in? Papa, I should have offered you coffee."

Papa looked embarrassed. "No, no."

If her bold invitation embarrassed him, she couldn't imagine what Mrs. Martin's news would do. She had to try to stop it. "I just feel I should say—" Tears erupted. Jessa was not a crier and yet they came. She couldn't bear to disappoint her father in this way. "I'm sorry, it's just, well . . . Mrs. Martin will probably tell you a few things about my work here, Papa, things I feel regretful about." She looked at Mrs. Martin on this last part. "I've not taken care like I should. Mrs. Martin's been a kind and understanding employer, and I am resolved, absolutely resolved, to please her." She turned to the missus, silently beseeching her. The missus exhaled, but Jessa couldn't tell what it might mean. Her father indicated with his chin that she should go inside, so she did.

After five minutes, Jessa came back out with the boys. Surely that was enough time for the missus to have decided her fate. Papa looked tight in the jaw. What had the missus said?

"Oh! And Mr. Martin paid her wages yesterday."

Did the missus mean her *final* wages?

"A third to her, and two-thirds to your remaining balance at the store."

Papa noticeably bristled at this. "That's it then," he said.

He said it in a way that felt like he was closing a book. End of subject. Papa picked up his reins and looked off in the direction they would head. It must be a sore spot, thought Jessa, to have a daughter pay one's debts. Debts never before discussed, now aired out, like laundry on a clothesline.

The missus addressed her sons. "Say goodbye to Mr. Campbell."

Jessa wondered if the goodbye was for three days or forever. Her father's face gave nothing away.

They rode in silence. Jessa was anxious to know what had been said, but she feared revealing her anxiousness would only draw attention to The Matter. The feel of Beck underneath her, his steady, rhythmic gait, and the scents of mule, and saddle, and still morning air calmed her. She pulled herself up straight, nothing like the crying girl she'd been minutes ago. She'd meant what she said: she was resolved to please the missus, resolved to stop sneaking off. Perhaps she could figure out a way to see Will above-board, and if there wasn't a way, she'd stop. Her father needed her.

Papa rode slightly ahead. When she was younger, she'd ride in front of him on one horse, his arms around her, holding the reins. She would lean against him, and sometimes fall asleep, rocked by the movement. Something had changed in the last year, a physical withdrawal between them. When she watched her father with Agnes, their rough play, the way her little sister would hang on him, Jessa felt most keenly aware of what was lost to her. She wondered when the last time was that Papa had grabbed her arms and swung her in a circle, or the last time she'd ridden on his back. She wished she had known it then: this is the last time. She could have made sure to remember.

They stopped to let their mounts drink at the creek.

"You sure you're all right, Jess?" Papa asked. "Takes a lot to bring you to tears. If you're ever in trouble, you know to come to me, right?"

"Yes, Papa." She considered his words: "*If* you're ever in trouble." Did that mean she was or wasn't in trouble now?

They rode on. When Jessa and her father turned left at the Krauss place, the old man waved. Mrs. Krauss was bent over a washtub, her large bosom threatening to tip her over. She often smelled like a pickling jar, gifting neighbors with cucumber, cabbage, beet, and green tomato preserves. The community valued her as one of its midwives. Folks jested that the babies she delivered all smelled like pickles. Jessa was glad her father was not stopping to chat today, as anxious as she was to get home.

From the road Jessa could see the far cliffs of the Brazos to one side and the edges of the Shinnery on the other. On the riverside the cottonwoods waved, their downy seeds dropping and floating like dust motes in rays of window light. When they passed the road up to the schoolhouse, Beck picked up the pace, eager for home. She let the mule go into a fast trot, and Papa's horse followed. At the soapberry tree, they turned up the lane to their place.

In the distance she saw the little cabin, the barn, the smokehouse, and the cold storage shed. In only two months' time, everything had gotten smaller, dustier, and more stooped. The cows in the pasture lifted their ears upon hearing the clomping hooves of the approaching animals. Sassy mooed. Dan gave a whinny and John, their other mule, answered all the way from the north pasture. That set off the hounds, who commenced to bark. Jessa watched the dogs rush-tumbling over each other, competing to be first to greet them. All the signs and sounds of home, but The Matter still cast its shadow.

Halfway down the lane Papa pulled beside Jessa and indicated she should stop. "Jess," he said.

Here it is, she thought. *Trouble.* Her mouth went dry.

"I hate to tell you this but . . ." he started.

She thought she might be sick. *What exactly did the missus tell him?*

"We lost a sow this week."

Relief flooded her momentarily, but then guilt reared its head when she realized how selfish she was being. "Which one?" she asked.

"The Tamworth."

Lilly Belle. She had been only two years old. Jessa had gotten her as a piglet from the Krausses. The sow had eight piglets her first farrowing, and a dozen her second. Nothing that pig loved more than a corncob and a scratch on the head. "What happened?"

"Fever. And I've got two barrows I'm watching."

Pigs, peaches, cotton, sorghum, and steers were their food and their money, and all so easily lost, and now she'd risked their store debt. "Papa, about the money . . . I'd be glad to give you all of—"

"Keep your portion of the wages."

"But—" Jessa wanted to free her father from his financial obligation to the Martins as quickly as she could, though she still didn't know exactly what was owed.

"It's enough of a mortification to send my daughter for my debts."

Jessa wondered if he'd feel the same if it was her brother Newt working, or if her brother-in-law Solon was giving Papa money. Was it worse because she was a girl?

"But what about the missus?" Jessa asked. "What else did she want to talk to you about?"

"That's a matter best discussed with your mother first."

Oh, Lord, she thought, he does know about Will. Otherwise why would Mama need to be brought into The Matter? She felt on pins and needles.

The dogs were at their heels as they reached the hitching rail in front of the barn. Agnes was the first to reach Jessa, with Mama and Nellie close behind. They all looked at her like she'd done something noteworthy when, in truth, she'd been a scrub maid, a lesser member of a lesser family, and had shamed them all with her duplicity.

"What'd ya bring me?" said Agnes. As soon as Jessa dismounted, Agnes threw her arms around her big sister's waist. "You've been gone forever!"

"I brought back your stowaway stocking."

"Is that all?"

"There might be a few gumdrops inside it," said Jessa.

"Yes!" said Agnes. "Thank you. I needed gumdrops."

Jessa patted her sister's back, hugged Nellie and Mama. Oh, how she'd missed everyone.

Papa said he'd see to Beck and Dan, while Mama took Jessa's arm and steered her toward the house.

"Tell us all about it," said Nellie. "Even the parts you think aren't worth telling." Nellie had set her hair special, braids going up both sides of her head with two Blackfoot daisies tucked in where the braids met at the top, as if it were an occasion.

They gathered at the little table in the kitchen drinking coffee and eating cold biscuits with blackstrap molasses and fresh peaches. Jessa had trouble swallowing and tried to quell her anxiety with stories of the boys, details about the house—very little about the missus. Mama reported on what had been harvested and put up: cucumbers, tomatoes, figs, and peaches; Nellie shared what she'd made and mended: two pairs of socks and Papa's cotton duck overcoat; Agnes shared what had died: a wren. From her apron Agnes pulled out a black-striped tail feather to prove it.

"You can have it," said Agnes, handing the feather to Jessa.

Jessa felt like her mother and sisters had saved up all these words for her, tucking a few aside each day she'd been gone. She'd never once considered the emptiness they would have felt in her absence, wrapped up as she was in her own loneliness—before Will anyway.

Sitting at Mama's table, Jessa thought the ceiling seemed lower and the kitchen darker. The spot where the stovepipe met the ceiling was black with soot, no one having seen fit to clean it. The sleeves of Nellie's dress rode high above her wrists, the cuffs soft with fray, and Agnes's ears needed cleaning, the wax visible from where Jessa sat. None of these things bothered Jessa. What bothered her was that she was noticing them at all, as if she had carried a piece of Mrs. Martin back to the Shinnery with her. There was a before-Jessa and an after, and neither self seemed to sit right on her bones.

"Oh, I almost forgot," said Nellie, "Solon's got a cousin coming to stay. What's his name, Mama?"

"Grover. Grover Scott. Solon's father's sister's boy. Twenty-two and a bachelor."

"Not if Katie Barnes has her way." Nellie flashed a wide grin. "Told Maggie she wanted to meet him the day he arrived."

"Poor boy," said Mama. She shook her head, teasing now. "Poor, poor, poor boy." Playful Mama was a rare thing. Jessa wanted to reach across the table and squeeze her, but she knew it'd break the spell.

"Mollie," called her father from outside, "you got a minute?"

Here it is, thought Jessa, my undoing. She watched her mother go outside. As soon as the screen door clapped, Agnes plunked herself down on Jessa's lap. She handed her *Peter Parley's Juvenile Tales*, one of the family's two well-loved children's books. Even though Agnes was probably the better reader and was three years past fitting comfortably in Jessa's lap, she wanted Jessa to read to her.

"You all right?" said Nellie.

"Fit as a fiddle," Jessa said, though her hands trembled as she opened the book. She took a deep breath and read, the weight of her sister grounding her.

After a spell, her parents came in. Papa needed no preamble. "Mrs. Martin isn't satisfied with one of my girls . . ."

Jessa buried her face in Agnes's back. The humiliation.

"Says she needs two. Some kind of swear-ay she's having."

What? That was The Matter they'd discussed? Not what to do with their conniving daughter? Praise the Lord!

"I'm invited?" said Nellie, practically breathless.

"Yes, invited to work. Cooking, cleaning, serving, like your sister."

Nellie's face burst into a smile, as if she'd been named the guest of honor. "Oh my goodness, when?" said Nellie.

"First part of September," said Papa. "Mama has agreed to make do without you for two weeks."

Nellie was overjoyed, and Jessa felt nothing but relief. She had been delivered and would make good on her vow: no more sneaking.

"That ain't right," said Agnes. "If Nell leaves, I'm gonna be busier than a cat with two asses."

"What did you just say, Agnes Mae?" Papa took a step toward her.

Agnes screwed up her face. She loved being the youngest when it suited her and hated it when it didn't. "Nuthin'." The fire drained out of her. "Can I be 'scused?"

"Excused," he said.

Agnes leaped off Jessa's lap and vamoosed. She usually tucked herself up in the Y of the apricot tree when she was out of sorts.

The remaining family members all looked at each other.

"Where on earth did she hear that?" said Mama.

Though his expression remained serious, Papa looked at Mama and meowed—meowed like a two-assed cat. For a moment, Mama held her lips in a firm line, but then even she gave in to the hilarity. All four laughed, mouths open, heads thrown back, bodies folding over.

"Guess I still got one wild daughter," Papa said.

Papa got up. A signal for the last work of the day to begin. Though Jessa had missed the bulk of the peach harvest, there was still a bushel or so to pick. Though it was probably a one-person job at this point in the harvest, she joined her father and they worked down the short rows together. They talked about the place, the hogs, how the cotton was looking. They laughed at Red going after a critter, digging at its hole like mad. The sun, starting its descent, shone hard in their eyes as they circled the trees. Jessa'd grabbed an old hat that kept slipping off. She felt her face starting to burn, but even that felt good. Sunshine was a tool for cleaning. Sheets, bedsteads, wounds. Blinded by the light, she felt as if the Martins were being scorched away.

That night in bed, lying next to her sister, Jessa didn't speak of Will. After her first outing with him and Gabriel, she couldn't wait to tell Nellie, eager for her sister to know how he'd sang with her at the piano, held her hand. She wanted to share the giddiness she'd felt. Now though, since their walk to the river, his mouth on hers in a way she hadn't imagined, it didn't quite feel safe to tell.

"What is the very best thing about Rayner?" whispered Nellie.

Jessa remembered Will's hands on her body, his front side pressed into her back. "Privy paper," she answered. "They make it on a roll."

Nellie poked her sister's side. "Disgusting! You're such a hayseed, Jess. I'll find something better than that in Rayner."

•••

August rolled by at the Martin home. Coffee at daybreak. Congressing behind the shed following the piano lessons. Will would press into her, Jessa's back flat against the wood, the weight of him as welcome as heat in winter. If the little boys came 'round, they'd call it hide and seek. It didn't feel wicked, but natural, a progression—like on the farm, from seed to sprout. It made her think of the way her father came behind her mother sometimes when Mama was working at the stove, his front touching her back. Just standing. And how Jessa would look away. It felt intimate, like watching someone pray. Though part of her very much looked forward to Nellie's arrival, she knew her trysts with Will would have to cease. That pained her.

The day before Nellie was set to show, Will showed up at the back door, a bit of straw in his hair and two days' stubble. He had either been up with the roosters or, more likely, had never gone to bed. Jessa could hear the creaking of the floorboards upstairs and knew the mister would be down soon for his eggs. She hastened pouring Will's coffee, splashing a little on the porch floor. He reached for her, but she pulled away, finger to her lips.

"I can't," she whispered.

"Can't what?" he said.

"Whatever you have in mind."

Her grandmother would call his smile wicked. "So, what's gonna happen if someone sees me? It's no secret I'm courting you."

Courting, thought Jessa, did he say "courting"? Courting as in courtship, as in marriage? She wanted so much to embrace him then. "It all has to be straight from the shoulder. Papa needs to meet you." She didn't say "approve" but implied it.

"I'll meet your papa; I look forward to the day."

"He's coming sometime this morning to deliver my sister."

"Shucks, I've got to help Levi this morn," Will said.

Something about his quick "no" made Jessa wonder if his morning duties were really that pressing. But taking into account his rode-hard-and-put-away-wet appearance, she decided maybe it was for the best.

"Next time." Will's hand went to her waist, traced her hip, started down her buttock—Jessa leaped back through the kitchen door and closed it.

8

The guests buzzed and fed like a guild of grasshoppers.

Nellie said, "Should I pass the almond cake?" Her hair was damp around her face, but instead of looking hot and sweaty, Nellie looked fresh and dewy, a morning flower turning toward the sun. Will, who'd been hired to play, seemed to notice too. Jessa caught him staring after her sister and the red-headed beauty Oneida Garrett as well.

Nellie repeated her question about the cake. "Do I pass then?"

The soiree, as the missus called it, was in full swing, hard to hear above the din. "No," said Jessa. "Wait 'til the coffee's brewed."

"This party's as fine as frogs' hair," Nellie said, using one of their late grandfather's expressions. "I hope it keeps going and going."

Jessa considered her tired feet and back. At 10:00 p.m. the party was still crackling. The mister looked drunk, his shirt damp. Jessa thought he might be airing the paunch by the end of the night. The missus also appeared a bit moppy, her neck flushed and her voice louder than usual, but she was wholly in charge of her faculties. She moved about the room like she was doing a contra dance, making patterns across the floor, left, right, across. Every guest had had the pleasure of her attention, hand to arm, an imitation of intimate conversation. Jessa knew for a fact that none of the thirty or so guests were her close friends; she could only reach her close friends by letter or daydream. The missus must have made peace with the fact that this group would have to do. The only woman not buzzing around Mrs. Martin, vying for attention, was Mrs. Posey, who set herself in the parlor's largest chair and let the town come to her. She got all the news first and was never stingy about exchanging it.

The women, including Mrs. Garrett and her daughter Oneida, seemed eager to hear about St. Louis from the missus. "The nation's fifth largest city," the missus had declared more than once that evening. When Edna Miller, the undertaker's very young wife, had made the unfortunate mistake of confusing St. Louis with Chicago and asked about the Columbian Exposition, the missus had launched into a spirited attack on Chicago's crowds, anarchists, and stench. Jessa wasn't sure what anarchists were, but she understood they were vile. "Of course, how silly of me. St. Louis is so much nicer," said Mrs. Miller, even though Jessa was pretty sure young Mrs. Miller had never been outside of Texas.

Nellie had taken to life at the Martins like a duck to water. Because she'd gotten the boys to sleep halfway through dinner, she'd been able to come downstairs to help. She was chatting with Miss Oneida Garrett as if they were bosom companions. The pale green dress the missus had given Nellie to wear had needed no alteration. She looked like a guest. Jessa was also wearing new clothes. A dark gray linsey-woolsey skirt, a percale waist, and a full apron, trimmed with a highly starched three-inch ruffle. No mistaking her for a guest. She stood against the wall, invisible, only there to fulfill someone's next request. In contrast, her sister forged ahead, refilling punch glasses and trying to look busy so she could remain downstairs. The missus didn't seem to mind. The plates had all been cleared and washed, and the Arbuckle's was brewing.

It felt close to ninety degrees inside. No one in Texas spent September entertaining indoors, but the missus would not be dissuaded. All the windows were open, but the curtains hung flat, no breeze to be had. Jessa could see Will, through the parlor window, smoking a quirley with Mr. Banks, one of Rayner's three attorneys at law, and Captain Rayner himself, who'd missed dinner and had spent most of the party outside. Will had played the piano quietly during the meal, but now the missus wanted him to sing as well. The missus approached Jessa, who was carrying a tray of meringues. She was just about to ask Jessa something when Nellie came up.

"Miss Campbell," she said to Nellie, "would you please summon the talent?"

Nellie froze, a look of utter confusion. Just as Jessa was about to hand her little sister the meringues and get Will herself, Nellie's puzzlement vanished.

"I would be delighted to procure Mr. Keyes," said Nellie, practically bowing.

Jessa wondered who this strange creature was that used words like "procure."

"Good girl," said the missus. "What would we do without you tonight?"

Nellie basked in the praise.

"And you too, Jessa." The missus spoke over her shoulder as she walked away.

Nellie bounded out the door. Through the window, Jessa watched her approach Will and the men. Her sister was no longer bouncing, but gliding, reminding Jessa of the missus—perhaps the length of the pale green skirt created the illusion. The lamps from the house cast a faint glow on the four of them, like yellow moonlight. Nellie shone, as pretty as the moon. Will stamped out his cigarette. He must have said something amusing because Nellie laughed. The men watched her in a way that raised Jessa's hackles. "Nellie!" Jessa barked from the window, as if her sister had done something wrong.

As Will arranged his sheet music at the piano, the missus summoned Jessa.

"Run up and get every last fan for these people. I don't understand not carrying one, but that's farmers for you."

Will started off with "Daisy Bell." Jessa could hear the opening lyrics as she climbed the stairs: "There is a flower within my heart, Daisy, Daisy, planted one day by a glancing dart." Jessa hurried to the bedroom. The fans were stashed in various drawers and boxes around the room. She went about collecting them but was in such a hurry that she knocked over the vanity stool. In the adjoining room, little Gabriel cried out at the noise. She stood as still as a broken clock, hoping he'd go back to sleep. One, two, she counted, and then he wailed. She rushed to the boys' room before he woke his brother. Poor lamb was a sweaty mess. She took a cloth from her pocket and wetted it with water from the glass beside his bed. She pressed it to the back of Gabriel's neck and squeezed a jot of water down his nightshirt. She made sure he was free of covers and lowered him onto the bed. She wiped the limp blond curls away from his face and, remembering the many fans in her pocket, unfolded one and gently fanned the boy. The *boom-de-boom* of the piano vibrated up through the floorboards to the bottoms of her feet, even through the prison of her shoes. She could hear Will beginning a new song but couldn't make out what it was. Her fanning got slower and slower. Again she was still. One, two, three . . . She tried to rise, but Gabe started to cry again. Whether he was awake or not she couldn't tell, but clearly he was miserable.

"*Shhhhhh*," she whispered, re-wetting the cloth. She was missing the best part of the evening. She felt resentment well up inside her, toward the child, toward Nellie, who was downstairs, toward Will, who kept on playing. The feeling rattled her from the inside, like bile. She could taste what it'd feel like to be mad at the world, and she didn't like it. No one had done anything to her. She settled her back against the headboard, flipped the cloth over to the cooler side, and waited.

When Jessa returned downstairs, the missus seemed irritated by the delay but wouldn't allow for an explanation.

"Our girl here has fans. Please take one," she said to the overheated room. "All right, Mr. Keyes, how about 'After the Ball' for our final number?"

Mr. Martin broke in. "Enough of that piddle. You must ride for the brand, young man."

"Yes, Mr. Martin, as you say. The boss calls it," said Will.

"Play us a cowboy song then. A clean one."

"Ah, there's the challenge," said Mrs. Posey. The guests laughed. Mrs.

Posey seemed to follow a different set of rules than Mrs. Martin or Mama, making bawdy comments, talking over the men.

The room went quiet, save for the sound of the guests fanning themselves, a delicate *whoosh, whoosh*, like the far off beating of insect wings. Will appeared to collect himself. He looked thirsty, and Jessa wished she had thought to bring him water.

When he began his last song, all showmanship seemed to vanish. Jessa had heard the song before but never so slowly.

> As I walked out on the streets of Laredo
> As I walked into old Laredo town,
> I seen a poor cowboy, wrapped in white linen
> All wrapped, for they had gunned him down.

The song was a lament, and as he sang it, she suddenly knew that he had things to atone for. Everyone did, of course. Romans 3:23 was as known to her as her own name: "For all have sinned and come short of the glory of God," but there was something else, a particular sin. He'd do anything for his brother he'd said. Somehow, the weight of what he carried made her feel more secure. They were both stumbling children of God. Flawed and in need of clear-eyed companionship. Everyone else fell away, and she was alone with him in the room.

> I see by your outfit, you are a cow puncher,
> This poor boy said from his lips of flame rouge.
> They done gunned me down, run off and left me,
> Here on this backstreet, just like I was dead.

Nellie must have been singing under her breath because suddenly the missus had her hand at Nellie's back and pushed her toward the piano. The spell was broken for Jessa when Nellie's sweet soprano joined Will's alto. Nellie seemed to match him in soulfulness, which surprised Jessa greatly. Nellie had always had a sweet voice, but a girl's voice; she sang because it amused her, not because it fed her soul. Or so Jessa had thought. It occurred to her that you can never really know anyone. Despite the heat a chill like loneliness settled around her shoulders.

Oh, beat the drum slowly and play the fife lowly,
And play the dead march as you bear me along.
Take me to the green valley, there lay sod o'er me,
'Cause I'm a poor cowboy, I know I've done wrong.

When they finished the song, Will took Nellie's hand, possibly congratulating her. They were both grinning and it made Jessa uneasy. Jessa heard a guest ask if Nellie was the Martins' niece, but she didn't wait to hear the answer.

"See to the guests, Nell," Jessa said curtly then poured a glass of water for her piano player. When she brought it to him, he slid his hand up the side of her leg and gave it a squeeze. She felt That Feeling again. His hand was so quick, so bold in the room full of people. A word came to her: misdirection. When she looked up, Nellie was staring directly at her. *Did she see anything?*

"Meet me later," he said.

"I can't."

Just then Oneida and the missus came up to the piano.

"That was lovely, Mr. Keyes, even if it was my husband's pick." The missus slurred a bit on "husband's." She fanned herself in an almost violent way then seemed to give up. "Please don't tell me it gets hotter than this."

"I won't tell you then." Will smiled, his dimples winking.

"I complained to Miss Garrett, but she doesn't seem to mind the heat. Do you, Oneida?"

"Oh, I mind, but you can't argue with summer, Mrs. Martin."

Will laughed like the red-headed girl had said the funniest thing. Jessa couldn't get over her coppery hair, pulled up in an elaborate twist, as sleek as silk, even in the damp, hot room.

"In St. Louis, we have the shadiest parks with enormous fountains," said the missus. "Perfect place to cool down."

"There's always the river," said Will. "Refreshment for the unrefined."

The river. Jessa remembered their legs intertwined, dangling into the cool waters.

"You call that piddly thing a river?" said the missus.

Jessa thought about how formidable the river could get when rain ran off the Double Mountain and fell faster than the prairie could absorb it, how it had almost kept her father from holding her brother Newt's hand on his deathbed during a great flood.

"When your measuring stick is the Mississippi, I'd imagine it does seem a paltry body of water," said Oneida.

"You prefer a wide and fast body, do you, Mrs. Martin?" said Will.

"And you don't, Mr. Keyes? You're satisfied with a skimpy little meandering body of water?" The missus practically tittered.

The three of them seemed to put unnecessary emphasis on the word "body," playing some kind of game. If Will was such a threat, a man to be avoided, why was the missus talking to him this way?

When the missus excused herself, Oneida reached out and touched Will's arm. Words were exchanged, but too low to hear. It would be so easy to lose him, Jessa thought. Perhaps she already had. Perhaps singing with Nellie had done it, or staring into Oneida's wide green eyes. Never had she felt this way about anyone. Just then Will looked up and locked eyes with Jessa. Oneida continued to talk, but he wasn't listening to her. He was waiting on Jessa. Jessa in the awful apron. Jessa with her jealous heart. She nodded.

After the guests left the Martins spent a little time discussing their triumph, and then Mr. Martin moved over to the table and lifted the damp cloth Jessa had placed over the roast.

"Seems to be quite a lot of meat left," he said.

"People don't like to eat a lot in the heat," said the missus. She moved to the sideboard and helped herself to another drop of sherry.

"Still. Seemed a little tough. Miss Campbell," he said, "you must be careful not to overcook the meat."

When Mr. Goodsite's man had delivered the meat that morning, supposedly from Mr. Martin's "yearling," Jessa could see by the dark color and large size that the roast was from an old cull cow, not a young, healthy steer. Still, she didn't want to contradict the mister. She said nothing.

"But look, it's pink," said Nellie. "I don't believe it's the cook time, Mr. Martin."

"You don't?" he said. "And what do you know about it, other-Miss-Campbell?"

"The meat was pretty dark to begin with."

"And this means?" he said.

"Maybe the animal's old. Isn't that right, Jess?" said Nellie.

"Could be." Jessa was afraid of upsetting the cattle baron.

Mr. Martin seemed to consider this. "I'll bet that's why Goodsite didn't deliver it himself. This is not one of my beeves. I knew it."

"You'll have to sort it out with him, Elias," said the missus. "I'm going to retire." The missus went upstairs with her sherry, but the mister carried on as if she remained.

"He's probably thinking of how much we can make on the hoof, doesn't want to part with the meat before then, but they're my animals, and I'll eat one if I damn well please."

Jessa and Nellie stood by. They wanted to collect the roast but didn't want to become part of the mister's growing agitation. Jessa's only concern was how to escape the house unnoticed.

"Bet he doesn't send jerky like this to Rockefeller. I've a right to a decent steer. If I get any runaround, I'm going straight to Keyes."

Will had assured Jessa his brother had nothing to do with Goodsite's cattle swindle; she hoped Mr. Martin would see it that way.

The mister went to the sideboard and bypassed the sherry in favor of the decanter of whisky behind it. He poured himself two fingers worth. "Those two better not turn out to be a pair of four-flushers 'cause I'll see 'em hanged." Glass in hand, he mounted the stairs.

9

On the other side of midnight, Jessa stood behind the saloon, scarf over her head and neck, a shawl covering her shoulders. As the moon was only a sliver, she stayed mostly hidden in the shadow of the building, behind a broken buggy. She wouldn't go inside. The plan was for Will to come to her on a break from playing. They'd go for a moonlight stroll, maybe discuss a time he could arrange to meet her father. Back at the Martins', she'd left a note on the dresser in case Nellie woke up: "Couldn't sleep. Out for a moon walk. Please don't worry." Her sister had been so tired from the party she'd gone to bed without washing her face or brushing her hair—two rituals she never missed. As Jessa had looked on her sister's sleeping form, she'd automatically said a prayer that Nellie wouldn't wake but immediately thought to take it back. *How could I ask God to aid me in what will probably go against His wishes?* This was of her will. At seventeen, she'd had little practice in exercising it. Instead of being afraid of God's wrath though, she pictured God sort of stepping aside for her, like a man on a walking path, tipping his hat in a sort of good-day-and-good-luck gesture. God may not be *for* her in this, she reasoned, but it didn't seem like He'd be against her either. If He had been, why would He have made it all so possible?

The saloon was like a little lantern, beckoning. She could hear Will's piano playing, fast and loose, jig music he'd called it. He'd only played a few riffs for her here and there, knowing that "low music," as the mister had called it, was not welcome in the house. This music was faster than anything she'd ever heard before. Exciting and wild, like a horse that's found its head. Her feet tapped on the dusty ground. Jessa imagined marching into the saloon and sitting next to Will on his bench. She could wade right into the music that way, bathe herself in those breathless, quick-shifting notes. Then Jessa heard the crunch of boots on gravel. It couldn't be Will because the music was still going. She crouched down, but the buggy didn't entirely hide her.

"Miss Campbell," a voice said.

She saw the gun at the hip before she saw his face. Levi Keyes, saloon proprietor and shady brother.

"A loitering lass."

Jessa said nothing; she stared at him and plotted the best direction to run had she need of escape.

"It's not safe out here. Come inside."

She shook her head.

"Not to the saloon. I know you're a church girl."

Just then Jessa saw another feller rounding the building. She felt acutely nervous, but the second man was stumbling and paid her no heed. He undid his britches and peed on a bush just a few feet away.

"Goddammit, Pete," said Levi. "Gotta shitter ten feet away, and you're trying to kill the one living thing I got out here."

"Good for it," the man called Pete said. "Nitrogen. My pappy always pissed his fields."

Levi stepped closer to the man, chin out. "He pissed you out and I'm gonna piss you back in if you don't knock it off."

The man was sober enough, or knew Levi well enough, to comply. "Yes, boss," he said, then he caught sight of Jessa. "Why don't you introduce me to your friend?"

"Light a shuck, Pete."

Pete stepped closer to Jessa. "Pretty as a red heifer."

Levi got between the man and Jessa. "You want I tromp your britches?"

"I ain't doin' nuthin 'cept makin' you rich with my drinking." He started to go but then stopped, turned back around. "Ain't you old man Campbell's gal?"

She turned toward Levi, panic in her gut. She'd been recognized.

Levi didn't miss a beat. "You're a lolly. This here's Henrietta of Galveston, and that's all you gotta know." Levi reached for Jessa and pulled her head into him, shielding her face. "C'mon, Henri."

Just then two more men rounded the rear of the saloon. Jessa had no choice but to follow. They entered the building through a side door; to her left, she caught a glimpse of men and tables, felt the thundering of the piano music echo off the walls. Her heart raced. They turned right and went down a short hall and through another door into a small room. A clear glass lamp illuminated the room's meager furnishings: a rickety bed, wooden stool, pitcher, and chest of drawers—minus the bottom drawer. What appeared to be a window was covered by an old piece of canvas nailed above the frame. Jessa wanted to run back to the Martins' as fast as she could.

"You're welcome," Levi said.

"Thank you." He had protected her identity, but he'd also brought her into the lion's den. Her scarf had slipped from her hair. She felt exposed, frozen in place. Then she heard it: the cessation of the piano. The silence was more beautiful than any notes she'd ever heard Will play.

Boom—the door flew open. Will bypassed Levi and swooped her into his arms like they were at a dance. Jessa felt dizzy.

"Ain't she the sweetest?" said Will. She could smell liquor on him, but everybody at the Martins' party had seemed in their cups.

"She's sweet all right," Levi said. He nodded to her and left.

"I love this girl," Will continued, as if someone other than "this girl" were in the room with him. She'd moved from peril to paradise so quickly that she felt outside of herself, like she was looking down on the scene. Will had said he loved her, or almost her, the "this girl" of her, this girl who had stepped into the night to meet him, this girl whom God had stepped aside for. Her mother had fretted on what would become of her, how she'd find anyone in their small community to marry. Mama had prayed on it, and in this moment, Jessa felt her mother's prayers answered. She saw now that the Lord had ordered her steps, even as she crossed the Martin threshold in secret. Knowing this, most of her fears fell away: the bad feeling about Levi and the man named Pete who'd recognized her, the worry that her sister or little Gabriel might wake. They all slid away as Will kissed her, like dirt down a bank, edges collapsing.

"Let's go outside," she said. That Feeling again, threatening to overtake her.

"I'm played out. Gotta rest a spell." He plopped down on the bed. "We'll go for that walk. Come sit with me, you must be plumb tired too."

She was. When she sat beside him, he took her hand. "Your sister was nice, not as pretty as you though."

That was a lie, but she kind of liked hearing it.

"Can't wait to meet the whole bunch. You live where? The shin-something?" He slurred on "shin."

"Shinnery, named for all the shin oak there. We've got quite a place—" She wanted to tell him about it, but it didn't seem like he was listening. "You ever see yourself farming, running some cattle?" she ventured.

"Sure, maybe. My daddy, rest his soul, was an Indiana hog and corn man."

"He was?" It cheered her to know his father had made a life off the land.

"Don't remember much about it though."

"You can learn," she said.

"I can? I can learn?" He slid his arm behind her, leaned over, and kissed her on the lips. "You gonna teach me?" His lips slid to her neck. "I think I could learn all kinds of things from you." His other hand moved to the top of her thigh. They kissed again. She felt greedy for him, but the pleasure moving through her body had the effect of jolting her awake. *I came to walk.* "No, I should—we should stop."

"We're going to be married, Jess."

Married; he'd said it.

"I never felt more at home with a girl before. So, it's hogs and corn, or cows and cotton—whatever people grow, I don't know. There's some kind of life for us, right? Say there is."

He slurred again, but he also got quiet on the last part. Maybe he was overcome with emotion. She had to work hard to think straight. "You've got to ask permission, Will. That's how it's done."

"I will. First thing. I'm gonna head on out to the . . . the Shinnery."

He had been paying attention.

"Think there's room for us to build a little place?"

Jessa said yes and went into great detail about precisely where they could build a little cabin. She could see his interest waning. He was tired, she figured, hadn't seen the place yet. What did he know of the landmarks she was mentioning? She was excited enough for both of them. To share what she loved best with the one she loved best—that was a life. She hadn't seen it that way before. Her vision had always been of *her* on the land. Now she saw how a partner, the right partner, could enrich her plan.

Will leaned in close. "Close your eyes," he said.

She did and listened to him rustling around in what sounded like the chest of drawers.

"Keep 'em closed." He took her hand.

She could feel him trying to put a ring on her finger, but it wouldn't go past her knuckle. She opened her eyes, even though he didn't say to, and watched him move a thin gold ring onto her pinky.

He looked up. "You caught me."

They both looked down at the ring. A delicate thing, a small stone in the middle that seemed to contain more than one color.

"An opal," he said, seemingly reading her mind.

The stone sat in a coiled circle of gold, one side damaged. Although the ring was too big for her littlest finger and too small for the next, it was pretty, and unlike anything she'd ever been given.

"My beautiful bride." He kissed her again. "I'm gonna meet your folks, and your cows, and your no-piano granny, but for right now . . ." He moved his lips back to her neck. "There's this. Are you mine, Jessa Campbell?"

She nodded, afraid of speaking.

He took her earlobe between his thumb and index finger and rubbed it ever so slightly. Shivers everywhere.

"You are something," he said.

The saloon sounds dissipated. The gruff voices a murmur, like summer cicadas, in the background. As Will pulled Jessa down on the bed, she thought again of that verse said at weddings, "they are no more twain, but one flesh." Though she'd never lain with a man before, it felt natural and right. One flesh. Their breathing went shallow, ragged. They could hear it, seemed to recognize it at the same time. And then an urgency. "I'm not cold," she said.

"You're not cold," he said.

"I'm . . ."

"Yes."

Will slid his hand up her skirt then kneeled down, his head between her legs, kissing her thighs. She'd never considered a person's face landing there—delicious. She undid her outer skirt, unbuttoned her shirtwaist. Will stripped them off and then her petticoat. She had removed her corset when the Martins went to bed so there was only a lightweight chemise. He took off his own shirt and pants as if they were on fire. Jessa had never seen a man's erect thing before, but her experience on the farm had prepared her. We are all animals, she thought, not for the first time. Naturally, the possibility of getting caught with child entered her head. But she reasoned that the likelihood was low this first time. When Will pulled back the coverlet, the fact that the bed was not entirely clean also registered with Jessa. But only for a moment.

"Want me to put out the light?" he said.

He looked so beautiful in the golden glow—they looked so beautiful. She shook her head and peeled off her chemise; she was as unencumbered as the day she was born. Will kissed her again and brought his fingers to his mouth to wet them. Jessa wondered why, and then she didn't. She had touched herself down there before, but this was different. Red, orange, purple—she saw colors on the insides of her eyelids. Dancing colors, like bobbing wildflowers on the plains. She wanted to tell him this but was overcome by such pleasure that she threw her head back and ceased to think of anything at all.

This night they made their vows, not in so many words—that would come later—but in their act of love. *I take thee, I take thee, I take thee.*

When Jessa stood to dress, she noticed a little blood on the sheets. She wished so much she could take care of it.

Will seemed to read her. "I'll wash 'em in the morning."

"Please, let me take it. I'll get the stain clean out."

"Don't worry yourself," he said. He went to the pitcher and poured water on a rag he'd pulled from the drawer.

"It's clean," he said, handing it to her.

She wiped between her legs and then commenced dressing. Will watched.

"My Indian maiden," he said.

This surprised her, that he thought of her as anything but white.

"Let's go live in a tepee together."

Jessa knew her mother's people had never lived in tepees, but in long-houses. The Indians of the plains—including the Comanches driven from this very spot—lived in tepees. But they were all dead now, or in reservations, which—according to her father—was a kind of death. Still, she would do exactly that, ride away with him on a pony as far west as they could go, if that's what he wanted.

Once she was dressed, Will gave her a chaste kiss on the forehead, as if all that had gone on before was between two other people. They heard a hard bang on the door. Jessa slid the ring off and went to stash it somewhere safe on her person.

Will said, "I'll take it."

Jessa was confused. Hadn't he just given it to her?

"Can't very well wear it yet. The missus will ask after it. How 'bout I keep it safe for now?"

Jessa didn't want to part with the ring, but he was right; it wasn't safe for her to have it.

"I'll see about making it a little bigger while I'm at it."

She wanted it to fit, so she reluctantly handed it over. She didn't like the way Will tossed it in the drawer, but she reckoned he was in a hurry. Immediately, Levi started banging on the door again.

"*Apúrate,*" Levi called from the other side of the door. "Get to playin'."

Jessa quickly tied the scarf on her head and wrapped her shawl around her shoulders.

"Let's get you back," he whispered.

"Will you go tomorrow?"

"Huh?"

"To meet Papa?" she said. "Ask for permission."

"Ya, darlin', real soon."

Earlier he'd indicated it'd be the next day. Again, he seemed to read her fear.

"Tomorrow if I can. Don't worry. I'm not gonna let you get away." At the window, he raised the canvas and the sash. The sill was so low they had only to step over it. As she swung her leg, she felt a twinge of rawness in her body from what they'd just done. She wished for a warm bath. Will reached for her hand.

"Boy," someone called sharply.

In the darkness Jessa recognized the voice, saw the tip of his glowing cigarette.

"Get yer skinny ass back in there," said Levi. "You can't be pirooting all night."

"Walking her home," said Will.

"My eye! You stop playing, they'll stop drinkin'."

Will took her hand. "I'll walk fast."

"Brother, we can't afford it. Go on. I'll see her home safe."

Jessa was thinking she'd rather walk home with wolves than Levi.

"Twenty minutes," said Will.

"You been out a good hour already. Patrons are going home." Levi grabbed Jessa's other hand. She was strung between them like laundry on the line. "C'mon, dolly, you don't wanna keep your boy here from doing his job, do you?"

She didn't wish to cause trouble. "I don't need anyone to walk me."

With a lift of his chin, Levi indicated they should get walking. "We Keyes men look out for ladies."

Will gave Jessa a sheepish smile and released her hand. "That's right." He turned to Levi. "You take care of her now."

The night got darker when Will went back inside. Jessa pulled her hand back from Levi. "I don't need an escort." She started walking at a good clip. Levi didn't reply but caught up to her. They walked together behind the town's buildings, hidden, only the sounds of their footsteps on the hard-packed earth. A few dogs barked, one followed for a while, but no people. Maybe Levi was looking out for her, she tried to tell herself. She was his brother's betrothed now; only natural he'd watch out. If that were true though, why was her body telling her to run?

When they got to the schoolhouse, he said, "This is as far as I go."

Jessa felt like she could finally exhale. The Martin home was just up the road.

"Soon as I get me that good night kiss." He smiled, his dimples more pronounced. The look was anything but charming.

Jessa couldn't scream or call out or she'd alert someone to her sneaking. "No," she said in her firmest voice.

"One little kiss?"

"I'll tell Will."

"Whatcha gonna tell him? I'll tell him you like my copper stick, can't keep your hands off of it." He chuckled at his own joke. "Just teasing ya," he said. "You're gonna get me that watch though."

"What watch?"

"That fat gold one Martin's always flashing."

Good Lord, she thought, he wants me to steal Mr. Martin's treasured watch? Not a chance. "I need to go." She started to walk away.

"Jessa." He grabbed her arm at the elbow. "You're in for Will, right? That watch'll fetch a pretty penny. And we need some pennies."

"I can't steal it. I won't—"

He stepped in closer. "Won't? You think you can do whatever you want without consequence? You ain't holding the cards."

What? What cards? What was he suggesting?

"Get the watch or I tell Martin 'bout you."

She was dumbstruck. How had she gotten herself into this position—and, more importantly, how could she get out of it? Pretend. "The watch, I heard you."

Levi released her. "I'm not trying to make things hard for hard's sake. We got problems to solve, and you walked through my door of your own accord."

You pulled me in, she wanted to say. By the time Levi disappeared back into the shadows, the goodness of the night had leached away. Had this all been a setup? Maybe on Levi's part, but not on Will's. He'd asked her there for his own true heart's reasons. Besides, she didn't have anything for them to take. Not a good mark, as Will had explained it. But then the fact that Will knew all about "marks" did concern her. She crept back into the Martin house undetected, a new weight on her shoulders.

"Jessa?" said Nellie from the dark.

"*Shhh* . . ." Jessa removed the earlier note from the dresser and slid under the covers with her clothes on, hoping her sister would fall back asleep so she could slip out of them.

"You all right?"

"Fine, go back to sleep."

"Where were you?" asked Nellie.

"I was thirsty."

Nellie went quiet, and Jessa thought she'd drifted off. At least one crisis averted. She felt queasy. What had she done? She wished she had the ring Will had given her, something solid to hold on to. Truly it had all felt good and right before Levi. Taking the mister's watch? She prayed he'd forget about it, or maybe accept something else. Or better, Will could talk him out of it altogether.

Nellie stirred. "I've been awake a while."

Jessa quickly recited her rehearsed story. "I couldn't sleep, all the excitement and everything. I went for a walk."

"By yourself?"

"Of course. Who would I walk with in the middle of the night?" Jessa regretted her words as soon as she'd said them.

"With Mr. Keyes," said Nellie.

"Of course not," she said, placing a firm period on the conversation.

Jessa turned away from her sister. The room got quiet again, and her racing heart slowed.

"You've always told it straight, Jess."

She turned again, this time spooning Nellie with the length of her body, her chin on Nellie's shoulder. "And so I'm tellin' it now."

Jessa thought of bitterly cold nights when it had felt like Nellie's body was the only thing between her and freezing to death; thought of the thousands of hours they had lain in a bed together, and how, before Will, her sister was the closest person to her in the world. Now he stood between them, not on purpose, just the way of things. She had an image of her sister in front of their home, standing still, while Jessa rode away; Nellie getting smaller and smaller with each cantering lope. She felt a catch in her throat.

"Who watches out for you?" Nellie said.

"What do you mean?"

"I mean, you watch out for Matthew and Gabe, who watches out for you? Mr. Martin?"

Jessa thought how ridiculous that was: Mr. Martin, who didn't know that his cattle were fake or that his wife pined for another, as her protector? If anyone was watching out for her, Will was. He checked on her practically every day, but she didn't want to mention that. Not yet. Jessa was worried about how the family might see Will, a twenty-year-old piano player who went to church when he was paid to—and sometimes not even then. But Will had farming in his blood. Working on the Shinnery, they could build a little cabin like Maggie and Solon had. They just needed to get a little money together, he'd said. Jessa had no idea how much, but her parents never seemed to have much, and they managed. "To him who labors, all fair things belong" was a favorite proverb of Papa's.

Nellie pulled away, sat up a bit on the pillow. "I saw what Mr. Keyes did."

Jessa rolled to her other side. Her sister was like a dog with a bone. "Go to sleep," she said.

"One hand was playing the piano, and the other—"

"Sister," Jessa hissed. "He did no such thing." She was glad for the dark. She felt her face go hot thinking of all the places he'd touched her that night, how his sliding hand at the piano was nothing. It'd felt so reasonable, so right, in the moment. But now the smallest doubt was creeping in.

"You didn't let me finish," Nellie said.

"Whatever you were thinking."

"I'm thinking you know what I was gonna say, which means—"

"Do you want to go home early?" Jessa spoke more harshly than she'd intended. This was dangerous talk. Moments passed. Jessa listened to the chirps of a lone cricket. Suddenly, she realized how very tired she was.

"Are you going to marry him?" asked Nellie.

It felt strange to hear the word "marry" in relation to her own self. Marry, wedding, bride. All those things she never gave a hoot about before. If she confided in Nellie, it would be real and true just as he'd said it—on the up and up, at least with her sister. Maybe this tiny almost-sick feeling would leave her. She needed that. "Yes," she whispered.

Instead of giving a little squeal of delight, like Jessa had thought she would, Nellie burst into tears.

"Oh, sister," she said. "He's so unsuitable."

El Paso International Daily Times, APRIL 7, 1896

IS HE A GUILTLESS FELON?

. . . if it was wrong for him to become the avenger of the wrong done to his home [then] custom and public sentiment should be changed.

Certainly there is something wrong when an honored, and honorable citizen, through the crime of another, is forced by the inexorable law of public sentiment to become a violator of the statute law.

10

The next day, when Nellie tried to broach the subject of Will, Jessa backtracked. "I like him and he likes me back, and that's all."

"But you said you're gonna marry him." Nellie pursed her lips like the schoolteacher she hoped to become.

"I said maybe I'd *like to, some* day."

"That's not what you said."

"It's what I meant. A storm in a teacup, Nellie. Not a thing to fuss over."

"But Papa—"

"Now I'm sorry I even told you." She turned her back on her sister. Nellie hadn't done anything wrong, but Jessa had to stop this line of inquiry. She'd apologize later, explain how she had to keep it secret until Will could make his way to the Shinnery, get permission from Papa. Surely Nellie'd understand then. Jessa wondered if he'd gone that very morning. Perhaps soon he'd come through the gate to celebrate, permission granted.

Only he didn't come that day, or the next, or the one after that. Each day the pit in Jessa's stomach grew larger. What if he never came back?

By the fourth day, she couldn't shake the thought that he'd gone to their place and Papa had refused him. But then she wondered, if that were the case, wouldn't Papa have come to fetch her by now? Then there was Levi. What he had asked was impossible. Maybe he'd been drunk when he said it. Drunk people were unreasonable; she'd seen that at a barn dance or two. Will probably didn't know anything about it. Still, Jessa had been watching. Mr. Martin carried the pocket watch on his person every day, and Jessa had no cause to be in his bedroom at night when he removed it—just the thought of seeing the mister in his nightshirt gave her the willies. Besides, that watch was from his father. His dead father. It'd be like stealing from a corpse, and she wasn't a thief. Will wouldn't want any trouble with the Martins either; they were his employers too. Anyone who wasn't family would be suspect and likely fired—and once word got 'round to the church folk about it, he'd likely be let go there too.

It'd been a full week since the party. Papa had come for Nellie but said nothing to indicate Will had ever been to the Shinnery. Will had also failed to show up for lessons or coffee. Every day, Jessa's worry grew. On Tuesday, a half hour before lesson time, she had installed herself on the back porch to wait. Sweeping imaginary grit, she saw Will in the distance. Something about his countenance troubled her. His eyes were downcast. Gone was the wide smile he usually wore, gone were the dimples. He trudged up the porch stairs. It seemed as if he aimed to walk right past her and into the parlor to begin the lesson.

"Mercy, what's wrong?" she said, her voice on the edge of breaking. *Mistake, mistake, mistake, mistake,* ran through her head.

"Nuthin'." His eyes were red-rimmed.

She got between him and the door. "My eye! Tell me."

As if in surrender, his face seemed to collapse a little. "It's bad, Jess."

"What's bad? Did my father—?"

"Your father?" His voice went low. "Is that what you're thinking about?"

Her cheeks flushed. "No," she said.

"Those men from Galveston, they want their money. Sent a couple of devils up here to beat the tar outta Levi. Broke his arm, cracked some ribs, and took every bit of cash he had. Now he can't pay the liquor men, or Pinch-face, or . . ." Will stopped and pulled out his handkerchief; he wiped his face then blew his nose. "And he still owes three times what they took."

Jessa didn't know what to say. She'd thought seeing Will would allay her fears, but now they were magnified. Was it really as bad as all that?

84

"At least tell me you have it," he said.

"Have what?" she asked but knew as soon as she said it. Will was after the watch. Not an ally, but a collector. "No, I can't. The mister'll know."

"Maybe it fell off its chain."

"It wouldn't."

"Sure it would," he said. "Just make sure to break the chain. Leave it where he'll find it."

"It was his daddy's."

"That's a shame," he said, sounding like he meant it. He took her hand. "I'm with you, I don't feel right about it either, but we're in what you call desperate straits. Levi—" His voice choked up on his brother's name. "I owe him my life, honey. He got me outta Indiana, saved me from getting the tar beat outta me every day. Then in Galveston, when I had that malaria, he nursed me better than our mama would've. Doc said I was a goner, but Levi, he never left my side."

She couldn't picture Levi looking after anyone, but it'd do no good to say so.

"We need that watch, and any cash you can get your hands on. They'll bust me up next. You don't want 'em breaking my arm or smashing my ribs, do you?"

Of course she didn't. Not a pinky, not a hair on his head.

"I can count on you, right, partner? You my girl?"

Girl. On Saturday she'd been his bride. He slid his hands under her skirt, one hand headed for her most private place. That feeling almost caught her, the one where she wanted him to stroke her in that spot, but she resisted, pulled her legs together tightly. "What about the ring?" she said.

"Ring?"

"The one you gave me. You can take that."

"Wouldn't fetch a tenth of the watch, Jess."

"Anything it'll fetch. I don't need a ring. We can go over to Haskell, to the clerk, and marry, or ask the Reverend Burchett, the Baptist minister. I bet he'd do it, real quiet."

"I tell you Levi and me got a price on our heads and all you can think about's getting married? I never pegged you for selfish."

Selfish? He'd never been anything but sweet to her before this day. Jessa was thrown into a daze, like when she was a kid playing in the river and would lose her footing on the slippery rocks. Everything water and bubbles, searching for the wavy rays of the sun to discern up from down. They'd gone too far, and she was trying to secure her footing. "I'm sorry," she said, although she didn't know what for.

"Look, I want to get out to your folks' place, make things right, but we're in a heap of trouble right now. This mess is a hindrance to any future plans. You can see that, right? We gotta get clear of it."

It did make some sense. At least the way he said it.

"That watch will buy us some time," he said. "Can you get it tonight?"

She shook her head.

"I'm sorry to tell you, but Levi might show up here and cause you trouble if he don't get it."

"Why would he do that?" she said. *How would that help Levi?*

"He owes the mister money. Trade a scandal for debt maybe. Like you said, Mr. Martin wouldn't like how you come out to the saloon."

"But . . . Levi pulled me inside."

"Still, Jess, you run off that night."

He said it in a way that made her feel ashamed, as if he weren't the one who'd asked her to come. She thought about the two of them naked in that room, how it hadn't bothered her then, how it'd felt familiar somehow, a matter of course, the twain, one flesh. Now though, it didn't even feel quite real. Had she really done that? Her throat went tight, and the heat of the day pressed around her.

"I'm not saying it'd be right for Levi to do it. I asked him to leave you out of it, I did, but he sees things I can't sometimes. Bottom line is we're not safe unless we've got something to offer those boys, so he's lifting every rock he can find."

"All right," she said. "I'll get the watch." The depth of what she'd done that night was dawning on her.

"Leave it behind the privy. Under a big rock or something. I'll find it."

• • •

Later that afternoon, the missus invited Jessa to walk to town with her and the children. The missus jabbered about some fanciful hairstyle called the Newport knot, and how feathers and flowers were now déclassé. Jessa only half listened, such a stew she was in over the mister's watch. She noticed that the purple groundcherry, growing flat along the road, had only a few scraggly blossoms left. The fair days of fall were spent.

Once they reached the mercantile, Jessa asked to be excused to go to the post office, saying she needed to collect the mail to take home to the Shinnery. Her hope was that Mrs. Posey might tell her more about what had happened at the saloon, if the situation was as dire as Will made out.

"In broad daylight, them fellers come in the saloon."

Jessa walked in on Mrs. Posey midstory. Didn't even have to ask.

"Charlie, that's the bar dog, he was polishin' some glasses, and Mr. Levi Keyes was settin' at a table."

Mrs. Posey had an audience of four, all men, none of whom Jessa recognized.

"He was eatin' his scrambleds, when these three fellers ambled in, like regular customers. One came to the bar and the other to a table. Charlie poured a couple a shots and went back to yawnin' on the glasses."

Ting, ting, went the little bell over the door. A lady Jessa recognized from the Martins' party came in. Jessa resented the interruption. She wanted to know the details of the beating.

"Nothin' today, Mrs. Meyer," said Mrs. Posey. The postmistress seemed eager to return to her gossip—gossip that apparently wasn't appropriate for the refined ears of Mrs. Meyer. She crossed her arms over her large bosom and put her chin to her chest as if to say move along.

"No letter from my folks in Georgia? You're sure?" Mrs. Meyer started to tear up.

"Bime by, it'll get here." Mrs. Posey came out from behind the counter, placed a hand on Mrs. Meyer's back as she walked her out the door.

"Texas women can't afford such tears. What do we save 'em for, Mrs. Meyer?"

"Snake bites and widowhood," she said, dabbing her eyes.

"That's right; you're learnin'."

Mrs. Posey picked the saloon story back up without taking a breath. "So Keyes does some evalu-tatin', decides these fellers is fine, only one sneaks up and grabs him from behind. The other feller pulls a pistol on my friend Charlie. They ask about the money Keyes owes, sumthin' 'bout gamblin' and bets he didn't cover. Keyes says he ain't got no money 'cept what's in the till, so they beat him: smash his nose, kick his ribs, and break his arm."

Jessa felt her bowels seize like she'd eaten a bushel of green peaches. So Will had been telling the truth. He was next in line if these roughs didn't get their money. She couldn't imagine someone hurting Will like that, though she didn't feel too bad on Levi's behalf, probably got what was coming.

"They took the till money and some more hidden in the icebox. Keyes gave up the location when he had his own Colt pointed at his head. To add insult to injury, them Galveston fellers stole that pistol as well. Charlie subsequently terminated his employment there."

"Those the only two that were there?" asked Jessa. "Nobody else?" She wanted to know if Will was implicated in any way but didn't want to ask outright.

"Nope. And a good thing too. Could've been a right nasty gunfight. Folks are already grumbling 'bout shuttin' down the place. Any more trouble and they will. The captain won't abide it."

Jessa left the post office only to realize, when she got back to the store, that she'd never asked about the mail. What would happen if Levi were driven out of Rayner? she wondered. Would Will go with him?

That night after supper, Jessa could hear through the walls of the kitchen that the Martins—minus the children—were discussing events at the saloon. Unfortunately, she couldn't hear well enough to glean any information about whether Mr. Martin was on the side of closing the establishment. When she hurried in with coffee, the missus was speaking.

"Matthew is progressing so well on the piano. Don't tell me you would interrupt his studies on the hint of a rumor?"

"It's no rumor." The mister turned to Jessa. "I feel for some cream."

Jessa practically leaped to the kitchen to grab the cream and get back.

"—a leader in this town," the missus said. "Your employment of him speaks volumes."

"Exactly. You, *of all people*, Charlotte, should know how one becomes tainted through an ill-advised *acquaintanceship*."

The temperature in the room seemed to drop ten degrees. No matter how much Jessa concentrated, she could not stop her hands from shaking. *Was he alluding to the missus's secret fiancé, Mr. Broussard?*

The mister stood, bumping the table with his thigh, the coffee sloshing onto the saucer. "I'd like to cease this discussion. There are things you do not know, things I recently learned. Things of *such a nature* that I cannot discuss them with you."

"Oh!" the missus said, as if suddenly understanding something significant. The problem was, Jessa had no idea what that thing was.

"So the boy—as you call him—will no longer be under my employ."

Jessa felt like the roof was caving in. No chance now for Will to get the watch himself.

•••

That night Jessa crept into the Martins' bedroom. Two dark mounds in the dim light. One lightly snoring. As she neared the bed, she saw the missus with her mouth open, a white halo of hair. Jessa went to the tallest chest of drawers. An inlaid rosewood box rested on top; from Switzerland the missus had said. She lifted the lid. The watch gleamed in the dim light. She picked it up. "EJM" was etched across the top in elaborate script. She imagined her own father having such a thing to pass down. The war had stripped the Campbells of all their valuable possessions—the few they'd had. This was a treasure. She couldn't do it. She put the watch back in the box. She had nineteen dollars of her own earnings, which she'd leave behind the shed. That'd have to do.

11

After a couple of missed throws, Papa roped a bull calf. Jessa rushed to flank it. Coming in low to the head, she got her knees under the calf, lifted his body, and brought him onto his side. It had to be done quickly, the momentum providing the strength. While working, she started to feel restored to herself, restored to her father. She wondered whether she would've had the chance to be as indispensable to her father if Newt had lived.

She'd finagled this trip home when Solon and Maggie had come to town to have their picture taken for Maggie's birthday. Solon had mentioned Papa needing to castrate a batch of summer calves, and Jessa had jumped on it. After failing to procure the watch for Levi, Jessa was in a state of all-overs thinking Levi might show up at the Martins'. She also had the added stress of waiting on her monthly. She thought she might be a day or two late, but she wasn't sure. Fleeing seemed the best option. A couple of days to sort things out before she went back. A couple of days for Will to ponder the unreasonableness of Levi's demand.

Once the calf was down, Agnes held the front legs and Jessa the rear. The hounds stood just outside the pen, as if waiting to be called upon to help. Agnes attempted to soothe the trapped calves with a tuneless song, lyrics changing with whatever was in Agnes's view. "There's a fly on your nose, but that's how it goes. Dirt is dirty, dirt is purdy," she sang. Papa made a quick incision and popped the testicles out. It took two cuts to remove them from their ropey cord. The first cut was partial, allowing him to make a quick scrape of the cord before the final cut, higher up where the blood supply was thinner. The whole operation took about half a minute.

"Blood, blood, redder than mud—ow!" Agnes lost hold of the foreleg and was grazed in the head by the calf's flailing hoof. Instead of crying, she flung herself over the calf's head and front legs, stilling its body with her own. "Can't kick me now." A bright red mark flared across her eyebrow.

"You are something," said Jessa.

"Something else," Agnes and Papa chimed in at the same time. Jessa had missed the joy of working together. Not like the Martins', where everyone was so separate. She hoped to work with Will someday—though, in truth, she couldn't picture him doing this particular chore.

After Papa castrated ten or so calves, Jessa took the knife. She worked swiftly and with precision.

"That's about as fast and clean as you can get," Papa said of her work.

"Just like you taught me."

"I guess the credit goes to me then," he said. He reached over and ruffled her hair like he used to when she was Agnes's age. She missed this other father, missed the girl she'd been.

After they'd cut thirty head, Jessa gathered the tender meat and went back inside. Everyone but Nellie liked prairie oysters. "Eeew," Nellie said when she saw the bucket. Mother had fixed a mess of greens to go with their regular pot of beans. Jessa dipped the balls of meat in flour and set them in the skillet with butter. Her cooking skills had improved, and she was half hoping her mother would notice.

Mama lifted the cornbread from the cast-iron skillet. "Solon's cousin got here. Grover Scott, a nice young man," Mama said.

"That so," said Jessa. Mama had never before played matchmaker, never even suggested Jessa should be thinking about a husband. Yet here she was, trying to introduce Jessa to Maggie's husband's cousin for just such purpose.

"Jessa already has a—"

"Nellie!" said Jessa, too sharply. She looked at her sister directly. "Can you *please* hand me that rag?"

Nellie knew what Jessa was asking and handed over the rag.

"That's interesting, Mama," said Jessa. She would not raise suspicion.

Maggie burst into the room, holding a pecan pie. She set the pie down and gave Jessa a hug.

"Those oysters look good." Maggie plopped one of the cooled ones into her mouth. "Jessa cookin' supper. That's a new one."

"Every day," said Jessa.

"Good for you, honey."

"I was just telling Jess about Solon's cousin," said Mama.

"Is he handsome, Maggie?" asked Nellie.

"It's a man's character you should be concerned with, not a pretty face," said Maggie.

Maggie had a pretty face, and Solon was handsome, so she didn't speak from a place of experience.

"If I have to look at a fella's face for fifty years, I'd prefer it be a pleasant one," said Nellie.

Jessa thought of her father's weathered face and his broken body, the scars and lines and wrinkles that told stories of love and war, of work and death. Did her mother still find him handsome? She knew she'd never tire of Will's face.

"Anyway," said Maggie, "ya'll are gonna meet Mr. Scott tomorrow. He's coming for supper. The picnic."

"Picnic?" said Jessa.

"Didn't Mama say? Minta's coming too. Dee's buying a horse off Slim Brown, so Minta decided they'd make a day of it. Haven't seen them since Fourth of July."

•••

Agnes said, "He's so skinny he could take a bath in a shotgun barrel."

The Campbell sisters all looked across the yard at Grover Scott, who stood in the doorway of the barn. It was perfect picnic weather. Jessa and Nellie had set up sawhorse tables in the barn to keep the food out of the sun and their oldest neighbors off the ground.

"Mr. Scott just needs some good home cookin'," said Maggie.

After eating and wiping down most of the plates, the sisters gathered near Mama's rose hedge, which was nearly six feet tall and full of pink flowers, clear into fall. Red followed Agnes over, in the hopes someone had a scrap in their pocket.

Jessa was fearful Nellie would spill her secret, here in the circle of sisters. Their easy camaraderie highlighted her own distress. She longed to be the girl her family thought she was, the girl before town, and she longed for Will Keyes to be the eligible man her sisters were discussing—someone recommended, accepted, ordained. She needed to broach the subject with Papa but didn't know where to start. A wrong word could cut her off from Will, and she couldn't very well ask for her own hand. At least her monthly had started that morning. Never had she been so relieved to see blood.

"Some lucky girl's gonna scoop Mr. Scott right up," Maggie said.

Jessa studied Maggie and wondered if she might be with child again. Maggie was only an inch or two taller than Mama but outweighed her by twenty pounds. She hadn't always been heavy, but with each miscarriage or stillbirth, she seemed to keep a little bit of the weight. Perhaps the bulk was a comfort to her, made her feel ready to carry the healthy child she believed God would deliver.

Minta chimed in. "Look, he's going back for seconds. Won't be a beanpole for long."

Minta was the oldest sister; her oldest child was nine, the same age as Agnes. Dark-haired Minta was on the taller side, like Jessa. She was a skilled horsewoman. Before she married she had broken and trained horses, but her husband Dee thought it too dangerous. Jessa hoped Will would never hold her back like that; Will had said he admired her pluck.

"I find Mr. Scott to be very polite," said Nellie, "though not exactly a Belvedere."

"His mustache looks like a caterpillar," added Agnes.

"My," said Minta, "what a harsh jury you are. What about you, Jessa? You find Mr. Scott worth considering?"

Jessa didn't answer, hoping the question was a jest. She busied herself rubbing Red's ears and kissing the top of his head.

"She should," said Nellie.

"Why's that?" Minta cocked her head to one side.

"Because she's over the moon for a man Mama would give the broom."

"What?" said Minta and Maggie at the exact same time. Their soft eyes turned sharp, a kettle of hawks, Jessa in their sights.

Jessa felt fire in her fists. "Shut up, Nellie! Why are you trying to poison things?"

"I'm . . . I'm not," Nellie stammered.

"What *things*?" said Minta.

"Nothing." Jessa regretted her outburst.

Maggie said, "You're awfully hot over nothing."

Jessa took a breath. "She's at the Martins' for two weeks and thinks she knows something."

"His name's Will Keyes," said Nellie.

This got Agnes going. "Keys, keys, if you please," she sang, sprinkling petals on the ground in circles.

"Agnes, sweetie" said Maggie, "looks like Mama's cutting pies. You best get yourself a piece before your nephews gobble 'em all up."

"Them boys are locusts!" Agnes tossed the remaining petals and headed off toward the barn.

Once Agnes was out of earshot, Minta turned to Jessa. "Who is this Will Keyes?"

Before Jessa could answer, Nellie spoke. "The piano teacher. He comes for the boys, and Jessa too, in the morning before the house wakes."

Nellie knew more than she'd let on at the time. Jessa wondered why Nellie hadn't confronted her with it then. "You don't know what you're sayin'."

"I'm sorry, Jess. I'm worried is all. When I saw him touch you—"

"What? What did he touch?" said Maggie.

"My *hand* as I served him coffee," said Jessa. She would put a stop to this. "True, it was forward. I should have corrected him." She stared straight at Nellie, daring her to contradict the account. Her sisters wouldn't understand about Will, about how they were practically married already. All would be forgiven when they were, when the family knew him as she did, but now was not the time.

"Wait," Maggie said. "Keyes . . . ? He's not related to the owner of that doggery?"

"One and the same," Nellie said quietly.

With the turn in conversation, home suddenly felt as dangerous as the Martins'.

"Mr. *Will* Keyes has nothing to do with the saloon," said Jessa. The fact that he played there would be a battle for another day. "Is Abel to be held accountable for the sins of Cain?" she said, grasping at anything that sounded biblical and righteous. "I feel sorry for him caught up in his brother's dealings."

Minta said, "Why, Jessamine, you are soft on this fella."

"No. It's not like that."

"That saloon brought road agents into Rayner," said Maggie. "A shoot-out on the street."

"Mercy!" said Minta.

"Solon says they're trying to get it shuttered."

"Well, Will has nothing to do with that." Jessa could hear her voice going up an octave.

"'Will,' huh?" said Minta.

"Mr. Keyes," Jessa corrected.

"We will have to tell Papa," said Maggie, getting her back up like a school marm.

"Tell him what?" Jessa could feel the muscles in her neck go taut, a hiss to her words.

"Well, that you—"

"I, what?" she interrupted. "I *nothing*. I'm 'soft' on someone who flirts and pays me no serious mind. How many boys in school did you go moon-eyed over, Maggie? And you, Nellie, who took nosegays from half the class. I never even looked at a boy, and so now I talk to one a couple times a week in the company of the children, and it's so terrible it must be reported?" She looked directly at Nellie now, daring her to bring up the night after the party. "Papa needs the money I bring home. You gonna worry him over something that don't warrant it? If you do, you are the most selfish sister God ever put upon this brown earth."

Nellie looked like she'd been punched. Jessa could see it on her face, the conflict, wanting to report everything she knew but not wanting to lose her sister and best friend. Jessa had put her in a mean position, but it had to be for now. And any hope of talking to Papa was now off the table; she couldn't risk him going to Nellie to get her take.

Jessa turned away from the group and marched straight to where Grover Scott was standing, Red at her heels. She would not draw further attention to herself by avoiding the visitor. She would play along, though not in too friendly a manner, lest he get the wrong idea.

"Mr. Scott," she said, "may I interest you in some pie?"

Mr. Scott was tall, over six feet. Long in the trunk, his legs appeared short in proportion. His hands and face were long too, but not unpleasantly so. He seemed startled by Jessa, taking half a step back. She had made a beeline to him. Now she feared he might get the wrong idea about her offer. Flustered, she scooped up a slice of pie and plopped it on his half-full plate, realizing—too late—that he hadn't actually said he wanted any.

"Uh, thank you," he said. "You make this, Miss Campbell?"

"No, and you're glad for it."

"Not a baker?" He reached down to give Red a pat.

"I'd rather do just about anything than be stuck in a kitchen."

Mr. Scott laughed at this; he had kindly eyes, large and dark, with long lashes that curled like a woman's. He motioned to where her sisters were standing. "Haven't seen too many roses in these parts."

"Papa's gift to Mama." He'd planted sixteen in remembrance of Newt, but it felt too private to say. "Bathwater roses, he calls them."

"Aren't they supposed to be yellow though?" he said.

"Yellow doesn't get on well here, not a good rooter from cuttings . . ."

Jessa realized he was referencing the song "The Yellow Rose of Texas," making small talk, and was not looking for a horticulture lesson.

"I'd guess Old Blush," he said.

"You guessed right." Jessa was surprised the beanpole knew his roses. Impractical knowledge out here. She wondered if he had the stuff to make it. She thought of Will. He'd spoken of being willing to farm, but he hadn't demonstrated any actual propensity for it. He was smart though, and with her guidance, he was sure to pick up the work quickly.

"Flowers: the proud assertion that a ray of beauty outvalues the utilities of the world," said Grover. "Emerson."

Jessa stared at him. Beauty outvaluing utility? If that's what Grover Scott believed, he definitely wasn't going to make it in West Texas. At least he'd gotten her away from the wobblin' jaws of her sisters, and the possibility of all her secrets being spilled.

12

The missus spoke to Will from the back porch. "I'm afraid, Mr. Keyes, with school starting, and Matthew needing to concentrate on his lessons, Mr. Martin has decided to discontinue his musical instruction."

Jessa listened through the half-open window in her room but couldn't see them. She hadn't spoken to Will since she'd returned from the Shinnery the day before.

"I see," he said, playing along with the fiction.

Matthew was an excellent student, far ahead of his classmates, and they all knew it. Jessa didn't know what Will's banishment would mean for her. She felt a little short of air contemplating it.

Will said, "I apologize for my frankness, Mrs. Martin, but I am in need of funds. If you can think of anyone who can use my services, please direct them my way."

He sounded so businesslike, so respectable. She wished her father could meet this Will.

After the missus shut the door, she marched straight to Jessa's room. "Mr. Keyes is a persona non grata."

Jessa did not know what a "non grata" was, but she didn't reckon it was good.

"He is connected to unsavory events."

"Like what?" Jessa said. She felt like she was missing some key information.

"Nothing the likes of you or I need to know about, so I'd better not catch sight of him again." The missus spoke low. "You are the company you keep."

After ten minutes or so, Jessa made her way to behind the shed. She had a feeling he'd be there waiting, and he was, only he didn't look like himself. His clothes were in disarray, one button on his suspenders missing, the brace dangling. He looked almost childlike, lost.

She embraced him. It felt like forever since they'd held each other this way. That hunger returned. "I love you," he whispered in her ear. They kissed, deep and long, his knee pressing into just that spot. She felt herself spreading her legs open even as her head told her "bad idea, bad idea." Somehow, they had switched places because her back was now against the shed. They were still kissing, and he must have undone his pants. She felt her skirts being lifted, and quick as a wink, he was inside her. She didn't know people could do such things standing up— or that this was where they'd been headed. She hadn't said yes, but she hadn't thought to say no either. Perhaps standing was a way to avoid pregnancy, she thought, as she felt Will's matter running down her leg.

Will fixed his britches and handed her a handkerchief. It made her think he'd done this before, the way he knew what a woman needed.

"You hear the missus?"

Jessa nodded.

"Honey, I need you to bring me the watch, and anything else you can get your hands on."

"I left you money last week," she said.

"You did. Thank you. I know you worked hard for it, and it helps, it does, but it's not enough."

Not enough. Everything she had. She didn't know what to say.

"Levi was fixed on coming over here, telling the mister 'bout you and getting some hush money."

"Did you tell him we're betrothed?"

"He's desperate. So it don't matter if I fancy you."

"Fancied" her? That was a far step from marriage.

Will said, "I told him to give you another chance at the watch."

She rued the night she'd gone to the saloon. Rued her decision, minutes ago, to give in to temptation. She pictured the mister's fat gold watch, thinking how she might wind the hands back and back and back to the time before she'd done any of it, a time when she'd stay in bed next to her sister all night long.

"I feel like I'm looking up a rope," he said.

She felt the same. The hangman's noose dangling just above her head.

•••

A couple of hours after everyone went to bed, Jessa snuck back into the Martins' bedroom. The watch was not in the rosewood box. She felt as sick as she did the first time, only now because she *couldn't* steal it. She found folded paper money; she couldn't tell how much it was, but she took it. She had to find the watch. The mister's vest wasn't in sight. She crept to the wardrobe, her bare feet moving quietly, but when she pulled open the cupboard door, a hinge creaked. As the mister turned over in bed, toward the sound, Jessa dropped to the floor and lay as still as stone. The wardrobe was slightly ajar, and she worried he'd get up to investigate. Nothing to do but wait. She counted to two minutes and then stood again. She slid her arm into the wardrobe and tried to feel her way to the vest. As she pressed her way farther in, shoulder into the gap, the cupboard door squeaked again. The mister's eyes flew open and looked right at her. Trapped, she moved toward him, as if she'd meant to wake him.

"Apologies," she whispered.

He sat up. "What is it?"

"I heard noises outside, horses maybe? Spurs? I got scared."

"Good Lord," said the mister. "Clear out now. I'll take care of it."

"Yes. Thank you, Mr. Martin."

Jessa waited in the kitchen for Mr. Martin to tell her what she already knew: no one was lurking outside. She felt sick about failing to get the watch. She looked around but couldn't see anything else that could be easily pilfered that'd match the value of the watch. She felt the folded money in her pocket but didn't dare pull it out to count.

"You can't be too careful," Mr. Martin said, heading back up the stairs.

When she was sure everyone was asleep, Jessa slipped out, money in hand, grateful for the sliver of moon and her new black shawl—a castoff from the missus. "Black is for widows and old maids," the missus had said. But the black wrap allowed Jessa to walk behind Main Street unnoticed, and it gave her something to hold on to when Will asked her the ugliest question a man can ask.

13

They stood in the dirty room at the back of the saloon.

"You want me to do what?" said Jessa.

"You heard me." Will rubbed the back of his neck, a gesture of weariness.

"Lay with another man?" She was falling, tumbling into a well. She thought of all her earnings already sacrificed, hidden under the rock, and the twenty-five dollars she'd just stolen. "I gave you everything."

"I know," he said, "but they need more. *We* need more."

"I can't," she said.

"You can, for us."

"No." Jessa stared at the cobwebs that stretched from bedpost to washstand, imagined the room abandoned. Cobwebs everywhere, a broken window, a foot of sand. That's what happened out on the prairie when folks gave up, moved back east, or farther west, or just plain died. She felt empty, abandoned. Dust in her throat, snakes at the door.

"I'll get the watch," she said. "I'll go back now, tear the house apart."

"They're here. I need to give them some more money tonight. More than this." He indicated the stolen bills in his hand. "You think I like this? My girl and . . ." He broke off. "It kills me to ask. What kind of man . . ."

Will sat on the edge of the bed, head in hands, shoulders shaking. Was he crying? She again felt the impulse to comfort him. That isn't right, she thought, her feelings so jumbled.

A bottle of what looked like whisky sat on the bureau. He poured some into a smeared glass and drank half of it. He held the remaining liquid out to her. She shook her head.

"Take the drink, please," he said. "You're making everything harder than it has to be."

She wasn't sure what he meant by that. She was here, wasn't she, giving him everything she had?

He held out the glass, and she took a sip. "No, sweetheart. Toss it back." He motioned for her to drink the whole glass, and she did.

Fire in her throat and then embers in her chest. She grimaced but did not cough.

Bam, bam, bam, a hand on the other side of the door, loud. "*Vamos, apúrate.*" She recognized the voice as Levi's.

"This is what we have to do. Otherwise, he's gonna pillory you in pursuit of some recompense." He poured another glass, more than half full this time.

She drank most of it.

"He's only trying to save his skin. They'll kill him," he said. "Do you get that?"

Levi at risk, always Levi. Levi, the savior, Levi, the protector. Couldn't Will see Levi was the weight, the giant rock tied to their ankles? "Cut him loose," she wanted to say, but downed the rest of the liquor. Then, "Cut him loose," she whispered.

"It wouldn't matter. I'm next 'lessen they get their money."

Could she really be the only thing between Will's life and his death?

"I'm headed for a pine box."

"No," she said. No to death, no to his request. No, no, no.

"Listen: Higgins was my brother's partner on the bit house down in Galveston, ran the tables, conned everybody, including Levi. These men kilt him. Shot him twice in the face. They're comin' for us. The only reason they haven't done it yet is they still got hope for more money. Just like I do. Hope, Jess." He poured another shot and placed it on the bureau in front of her.

She stared at his beautiful face, imagined it shot up. She picked up the small glass and drank it down, as if someone else were in possession of her body. Will stepped closer, brought his hand to her neck, and stroked her jawline with his thumb.

"One night," he whispered into her ear. "One night. I'm begging you."

"Please, no."

"These customers, they're not from 'round here. You'll never see 'em again."

"I can't."

"That's a lie. You have and you can. Please, honey. You just gotta lay there."

She felt the liquor starting to do its work. *You have and you can. You have and you can.*

He pulled her to him, his warm breath in her ear. "I need savin'. And right about now, you need savin' too."

Was it true?

"Jess," he whispered. He smoothed her hair in soft strokes like Mama sometimes did. "I'm sorry."

"No, please, no," she said.

"His horse is saddled."

"Whose?"

"Levi's. Blackmail, Jess. That's where he's headed."

"He'll go to Mr. Martin?"

"No, honey. He'll go to your pa."

Jessa's knees buckled. She slid to the floor. He would ruin her. The shame her father would feel. And it wouldn't stop there. Her family's name and the reputation of her sisters would be besmirched. "But Papa doesn't have any money."

"You'd be surprised what a man's capable of doing when it comes to a daughter. He'd get some."

Tears spilled down Jessa's face. She was out of words.

"Look, if'n this works though, he won't go. He promised."

The room tilted. She closed her eyes and prayed: *Please, God, deliver me from this.* She waited. Ten, nine, eight, seven . . . But no one burst through the door. She was not felled by illness nor lifted in death.

Will did not shout: "No! Never mind, I cannot ask you this!" Nothing happened. She opened her eyes. The dirty room was unchanged and unchanging. The course appeared to be set. She couldn't think straight anymore. Didn't know how to counter his pleas, so she sat there, defeated. The cost of love too steep.

"Thank you, oh, my sweet girl, thank you, thank you," he said, though she'd not uttered a word. He pulled her to her feet. "It'll go quick, I promise." Another whisky in her hand. "And we'll never speak of it again."

•••

The first one's name was Jim. He was as plain as pine. She only knew his name because Will had said it. No introductions. No need for niceties. Nothing nice about it. The room was dark. She stared at the wall and then the ceiling. Jim's hand traveled up her chemise. He pulled at her knickers without untying the drawstring waist. *Tugging, tugging*, his breath ragged. She thought about untying her drawers for him, but the thought made her gag a little, like when she had to swallow liver pills or lima beans. Jim found his way to the string. He yanked too hard and it knotted. The liquor helped her go away from herself. Another girl in the room.

The next was dark-headed and fat. He smelled like he hadn't bathed in a month of Sundays, and perhaps he hadn't. She gagged when he took off his trousers. Bitter liquid flooded her mouth and she spat it right on the bed. It went unremarked upon. This time she kept her eyes closed. He was done almost before he started. He tried to embrace her after he finished, but she pushed him away. He didn't seem surprised.

Will ushered in a third man, and a third glass of whisky. Jessa didn't look at the man's face. Not once. But she caught glimpses of his unruly red hair just the same. He talked a lot, but Jessa was drunk by then and couldn't follow. The fourth, the fifth. Like branding or cutting time, an efficiency to the way the animals were moved through the process. It took no time at all. It took forever.

14

The sun rose, as it always did. The floor was just as cool on her bare feet as it had been the day before. She built up the fire in the stove, the same as she had done every morning since her arrival. And yet she experienced none of it in the same way, not the warming sun through the window, not the bite of the morning on her ankles. She took no notice, let alone comfort, from the second batch of kindling sticks. She used two basins of water to wash and dressed without thought, her buttons misaligned. Last night's clothes lay in a heap on the floor of her bedroom. She wanted to burn them, but she kicked them under the bed instead.

She made the coffee, taking no pleasure in the scent as she spooned it from the Arbuckle's tin. Her mind felt asleep, and she aimed to keep it that way. She would walk softly and whisper throughout the day. She would not look back to the events of the previous night. She would not consider tomorrow or even one hour into the future. *Shhhh*, she hushed herself, setting the water to boil. She recalled the sound her mother had made on the rare occasions Jessa had been ill, a sort of clucking sound, a rhythm meant to soothe. The most Cherokee thing about her mother, this almost-song. It always made Jessa think about the long past, how if certain things hadn't occurred, her mother would be dressed in deerskins, living in a longhouse. Time was like a current: it pulled you along, spun you in its eddies. Jessa felt caught, suspended like a leaf in a whirlpool. She wished for her mother, for the feeling of her mother's hand smoothing her hair, pressing against her scalp, over, and over, and over again. But the longing started to rouse her, to wake her, so she pushed it away. *Shhhh*, she said to the oats as she stirred them in the roiling water.

For supper, Jessa peeled and cut potatoes into quarters for boiling. She sliced an onion and welcomed the burn. Her eyes watered. She cut twice as many as she needed. She wished for an arm full of scratches and a lemon slice to rub into them. She hovered her palm over the hottest part of the stove.

That night, after everyone else had retired, Jessa went to the cabinet that held the liquor. She bypassed the sherry the missus drank from tiny glasses and went for the whisky. She cared not for the taste but appreciated how it felt once it got to her belly, like a single life-giving coal in the midst of a great blizzard. It had allowed her to go somewhere deep inside herself the night before. She craved that refuge now. It burned her throat when she first swallowed, and she coughed a little, using her apron to muffle the sound. She took another pull to recapture the feeling of swallowing fire, but the feeling was not as intense. Like the hidden-ace card trick Will had performed for the boys, it had lost something in the repetition. She took a third swig and did not cough. She only stopped so there'd be whisky left for another day.

Despite the drink, sleep eluded her. Onions, lemon, poison, on loop. She tried to recite the twenty-third psalm, a trick for sleep her grandmother had taught her when she was visiting Albany one summer with her father. Even though she knew the psalm backward and forward, it kept getting tangled. Her brain latched onto only one part: "I shall not want." *I shall not want, I shall not want.* With the influence of the whisky, it turned into a slow, languorous song. A promise of freedom in not wanting. But it was a lie, she did want. Wanted to go back. To undo and undo and undo. She buried her face in the soft down of her pillow and wept bitterly.

15

Tap, tap at her bedroom window. The sound that had previously brought such joy felt like stones landing in her belly. She dreaded even seeing his face. *I shall not want. Shhhh.* The tapping was as urgent as a tea kettle, and then—sweet relief—it would stop. Each time he went away, she felt relief and prayed he wouldn't come again. She imagined the shame she'd feel if she had to see him face-to-face. A shame that'd sear her, a shame so hot she might combust. *Go away, go away, go away.*

By the end of the month, though she still nipped at the whisky— and learned the trick of adding water to hide what she'd done—she started to wake from her daze. It literally made her sick to think about what she'd done. All day, this feeling of unrest in her body. But what had happened had happened. No going back. Like her mother put it, you can't unmake soup. No putting the carrots whole, no sticking the bones back in the chicken and returning it to the yard.

16

It was after midnight. Jessa lay in bed, tossing from one side to the other. Sleep dodging her. She'd stopped the whisky when it was too weak to water. Moved on to the sherry until it made her queasy. Then quit drinking entirely. Only the queasy feeling hadn't ceased, and her monthly was late. For days she'd been telling herself maybe, maybe, maybe it was something else. Maybe, maybe, maybe. Tired of looking at the walls and ceiling, she slipped out of bed, out the kitchen door, and into the wide world. The sky so big above her, countless stars. Nellie said looking at the sky made her dizzy, to be shrunk down to the size of a grain of sand, but it made Jessa feel lighter, like she might just float up and become one with the sky. She closed her eyes, breathed in the chill night air. She could smell the juniper trees beyond the shed, the sand sage near the gate. After a moment, goosebumps sprouted on her arms. She crossed them for warmth, tucking her hands into her armpits. That was when, hands partially resting on her breasts, she knew. Her fingers detected the change, the tenderness. In this moment of knowing, she felt herself leave her body. Felt herself float, hover above, not as far as the stars, but far enough to look down on herself, cold in her nightgown. *You know how it works, Jessamine, the animals copulate, and the babies come. How did you not think it'd be as true for you as any living creature? How did you think you'd escape?*

•••

Jessa prayed and prayed, every day, throughout the day, ducking into her room between chores, getting on her knees like Grandmother Campbell had taught her. The grown-up part of her knew it was a too-little-too-late action unworthy of the Lord. God hadn't rescued her that night, so why would he pluck what was growing now? Still, it was something to do. *Please.*

When another week had passed, and still no sign of Providential rescue, Jessa decided she'd have to save herself. That meant, above all else, the baby needed a name. She wouldn't think about those other men, names she didn't know, didn't care to know. Will Keyes would have to make good on his promise to wed. In spite of her shame. In spite of her complete loss of faith in him.

• • •

Dawn in the kitchen. *Tap, tap* at the back door. She'd been waiting. She reached for the door. Will looked rode hard and put away wet. The pleading look in his eyes made her think of the word "beseech" from the Bible. "I beseech you . . . that you present your bodies a living sacrifice." He appeared to be offering himself, beseeching her to forgive, and contrary to what she had feared earlier, the shame in this moment belonged to him. That he had asked her, begged her, coerced her to do such a thing.

She held her position at the door. He could not come in; she would not go out. She studied him, trying to recall all they'd been to one another. So far from that day at the river, leaning against him, the setting sun on her face, his hands on her belly, the scents of cedar and skunkbush.

Will had bags under his eyes, but he smelled of soap, as if he'd just washed.

His voice low, he said, "Come outside."

She shook her head. It didn't feel safe to take a step.

"To hell," he said. "Tell me . . . you still mine?"

It came to her that she didn't belong to anyone anymore, not her parents, not the Martins, and not to him. To belong meant to be protected, kept. Nellie was right in her fears when she asked, "Who takes care of you?" Jessa felt like she might cry at this, so she didn't answer.

"Jess, I didn't mean for . . ." His words trailed off. "There's the life that I . . . I have, but when you talk about building a place, out on that Shinnery, I can see it. I don't remember a lot about my daddy, but I remember he loved his land. Put me up on his shoulders to where I could see the whole spread. 'Gonna all belong to you boys someday,' he'd say. Course that weren't true, but he didn't know it. All of us, we get what we're handed, and we do the best we can, see? We move on. Don't think about it, Jess, and you'll be all right."

Move on, don't think about it. Is that how he lived? Even without the child, she didn't know if that would be possible for her.

"I done things too," he said.

What things, she wondered, what terrible things? They were both mockered, dirtied, and defiled. Was it possible to meet in this new place, nothing to hide? She felt her resolve against him weakening. Oh, how she'd once loved him.

He reached for her hand, and she let him take it. "What I mean to say is, I didn't set out to . . . to hurt you."

But you did, she thought. *You did.*

"I love you, Jess. You believe me?" He had tears in his eyes.

She didn't know what to believe about him or his motives. Still, she felt a catch in her throat. She wanted to be held. But that was a girl's want. It brought to mind a verse she'd been made to memorize in Sunday school the year she'd turned thirteen. "When I was a child, I spoke as a child, understood as a child . . . but when I became a man, I put away childish things." Put away childish things. Had her love for him been childish? It was childish the way she'd gone around her family. Childish the way she'd been so set on never marrying before she'd met Will; a woman would have at least entertained the idea of a Grover Scott, or a nephew of a neighbor. It did no good to look back. She was going to be a mother; the important thing was a name; they had to marry. Once the child was born, its name recorded, she'd see about the rest. "You said we'd do things proper."

"Sure."

"Take me to Haskell. Or Aspermont or Clairemont or Abilene. I don't care. I want to marry."

His dimples flashed and relief washed across his face. "I was worried you hated me." He leaned in to kiss her. She let him but didn't kiss him back, at least not in the way she used to. "Levi wanted me to tell you—"

Jessa spit, the spittle grazing Will's dusty boots, hanging from her mouth in a silvery thread. "If Levi was here, I'd spit in his face. I—I don't want to speak of him. Or that night. Understand?"

"Course." Will took his handkerchief from his pocket and dabbed at her lip gently like her father might have done when she was young. "But you didn't do nuthin' other girls haven't—"

"Stop."

"Sorry." He shoved his handkerchief back into his pocket and pulled out something else. "Look, I brought you something." Will dug a pin out of his pocket, the type of jewelry a lady might wear at the top of her blouse. The silver pin held two blue enameled circles; a small pearl perched in the center of each. A distinct piece. Jessa realized she'd seen it before; it had reminded her then of a pair of eyes. One of the Martins' party guests had worn it . . . the pretty red-headed girl, Oneida.

"It was my mama's," he said. "I want you to have it."

She took it from him, turned it over. The clasp was broken, suggesting the pin was more likely lost than stolen.

"We can fix it," he said.

"T'aint the time for sentiment," she said. "Take it to Aspermont and see what you can get."

Will looked taken aback, like she'd tossed a bucket of dirty water on him. "You don't like it?"

"I know it's not your mama's."

They stood for a moment in a silence that felt weighted.

"I just wanted to give you something nice." *Beseeching.*

Part of him did seem to want that, but part of him was undoubt-edly a pole cat.

Haskell Free Press, JUNE 1, 1895

LARGE POOL OF JURORS SOUGHT

Judge Hammer opened District Court Mon-day . . . ordered a special venirie [*sic*] of 70 jurors in the _____ murder case, set for trial next Tuesday.

17

"Good morning, Mr. Martin." Jessa had the mister in her sights, like looking down the barrel of a gun. It had taken her a week to formulate her plan. Will had revealed to her what Goodsite was doing, and now she'd reveal it to the mister, being sure to highlight Levi's role, though she wasn't exactly sure what it had been. Once Levi was out of the way, she had to believe that Will would follow his better nature.

Mr. Martin sat at the dining table. His cotton shirt, silk tie, and wool pants all said St. Louis shopkeeper, but his leather vest told a different story—and not the one he was aiming for. The leather was so fine and soft it'd be torn at first brush against a post-oak or a downed fence line, but there were no such hazards walking to and from the store. He liked it so much he'd unconsciously move both hands down it, chest to belly, as if smoothing out wrinkles. It was almost more a companion than a garment. Jessa presented the mister with a plate of warm scones, his mother's recipe. She'd never made scones before, but the missus baked them every so often, usually when she wanted to put him in a good mood. The mister took hold of a scone, broke it in half, and inhaled deeply.

"My father sends his regards." Jessa tried to keep her voice steady, casual.

The mister looked up from the newspaper he was reading. "You received word from him?"

"Uh, yes. My brother-in-law had some, uh, business in town. Left a letter up at Mrs. Posey's."

"So he's feeling better?"

She had forgotten her fib about why she didn't go home for Thanksgiving: Papa was ill, and they wanted to make sure it wasn't catching. "Yes, much. Thank you for asking."

The mister took another bite of scone. "Heard he's our representative to the state cattleman's convention again."

"Yes, sir, third year in a row." Jessa was nervous about this next part, and she felt her voice crack a little but pushed through: "I guess, um, there's been some cattle trouble though."

"Hmmm?" he said, not looking up.

"Papa, or someone, said something about a cattle swindler gone missing."

"A swindler?"

"Took a whole lot of money from good people, I heard."

"Around here?" He took another bite of scone.

"Not sure. All's I know is some cattle king with a herd of five hundred has mortgaged 'em several times over, in different names. Now the cheat's on the dodge. They think he might be in Old Mexico."

"What's the fellow's name?"

"Umm . . . I don't recall exactly?"

The mister leaned forward. "Goodsite?"

"Sounds familiar . . ."

"Goodsite is the man I'm in with." The mister tugged at his vest, as if it suddenly didn't fit right.

"Oh, then it couldn't be. They say this man had, uh . . . ringsters working for him that'd prey on shavetails, get a cut of what was brought in."

"Shavetails?" His voice seemed to go an octave higher.

"You know, inexperienced men, men new to cattle." She could see the mister reddening. It made her stomach clench.

He said, "So let me get this right: this cheat hired scoundrels to drum up 'shavetails' for the scheme?"

Now was the moment when Jessa needed to point the finger at Levi, without pointing the finger at Levi, words she had practiced. "I understand the ones who did the recruiting profited handsomely . . . but who knows?"

"You seem to."

"Oh," she said, a bit taken aback by his tone. Was he eyeing her with suspicion? She shoved her hands into her apron pockets in case they started shaking. "I'm . . . I'm just the messenger . . . and well, really, this here, umm, borders on gossip, Mr. Martin." She turned as if to go but did not take a step.

"It wasn't a chastisement, Miss Campbell."

She faced him again, trying to look as innocent as she could. "'Whoever keeps his mouth and his tongue, keeps himself out of trouble.' Proverbs twenty-one."

"Whoever helps his fellow man with important information shall be appreciated."

"That a proverb?" she asked, though she knew it wasn't.

"It should be," he said. "Now what else do you hear?"

She took a deep breath. This is where the story took an invented twist. "Well . . . it seems maybe these ringsters cooked up the whole scheme, could be *they brought the cattle baron into it*'stead of the other way 'round. Anyway, it's a good thing we don't have filchers like that in Rayner."

"You'd be surprised." The mister wiped his mouth with his napkin, but he didn't fold it into fourths and place it neatly on the table, as he usually did. Instead, when he stood he let the napkin and a shower of crumbs fall to the floor.

Her mouth felt dry. She worried about what she had put in motion, but nothing could be worse than what had already happened, she reminded herself. "Your eggs?" she said.

The mister pulled his favorite hat off the rack, bypassing the natty bowlers. A wide-brimmed felt number, authentically dusty and a little frayed. "No eggs this morning. I've lost my appetite." With his hat on, he did look—briefly—like the man he aspired to be. Gone was the fussiness, and in its place was a grim determination. "I have an idea who one of those filchers might be."

Jessa reached for a scone after he left and took a bite. Then she undid the top button of her skirt, arranging her apron to conceal it. The beginning of her body's great change. She ate the scone slowly, right there in the dining room, her crumbs joining his on the floor.

•••

Within a week Mr. Goodsite's cattle scheme was the talk of the panhandle.

Mrs. Posey laid it out. "One of these shavetail investors—name of Luckly if you can believe it—he'd been waitin' almost six days in Wichita Falls when news of the scheme broke. Waitin' for Goodsite to bring in his herd. Thought he'd be shipping 'em out, but there wasn't nothin' to ship." The post office was busy, but Mrs. Posey acted like Jessa was her only customer. She could not rush a story. "To believe Mr. Martin helped break the thing open! Got the law on it. Turns out, the scheme ranged across five counties—and that's just so far."

Jessa felt some relief that word was out. She hoped it would make the question of how she knew about the scheme fade away. Mr. Martin would only be too proud to have the skinny without crediting a girl. Still, she felt a little shaky thinking about what would happen if Will learned she'd told Mr. Martin about Goodsite's scheme—and how she'd exaggerated Levi's involvement. It'd raise sand.

"On top of that, the herd's gone," said Mrs. Posey. "Crew made tracks to Utah, they say."

Jessa envied Mrs. Posey's independence. She spoke loudly, too often, and about any topic she pleased. As far as Jessa could tell, the postmistress had no parents, no husband, no children, no employer—at least not directly—to please. Even her body seem to proclaim her freedom. The way her hips jutted out from underneath her corset, the way her chin appeared twice, and how her hair sprang loose from its bun—and always a little bit damp. She struck Jessa as the happiest woman in Rayner.

"All told," Mrs. Posey continued, "sixteen fools laid claim to that herd. And Goodsite, he's on a ship to Spain."

"I heard Old Mexico," said a fellow behind Jessa.

Jessa turned to look at him then turned away. His hair was red. She steadied herself at the counter, felt as if she couldn't catch her breath.

"You all right?" Mrs. Posey asked.

Jessa nodded even though she didn't feel all right. Nausea threatened to overtake her.

"Thing we gotta do," said the red-headed man, "is get the rakes and the rascals out of this town."

You'll never see 'em again, Will had promised her. *Out of towners.* Jessa felt trapped between the counter and the man. She wanted to leave but didn't yet have the mail, which she'd been sent for.

The man went on. "That no-account Keyes fella, he's where it started. I hear Martin's commenced a campaign against his lush-crib. About time, the People's Party is calling for temperance all across the South. I, for one, will not step foot in there."

"Quite a vow, Mr. Fox." Mrs. Posey stepped away from the counter to riffle through a mail sack. "But I'll bet you didn't step foot in that saloon *before* this hornswoggle."

"No, ma'am. You got me there."

He'd never been in the saloon? Was that right? Jessa made herself turn again to look at the man. His pale skin was in full blush. She realized she'd never laid eyes on this particular man before. *Thank you, thank you,* she repeated soundlessly.

Mrs. Posey returned to the counter, her large bosom resting on top. "Let's see how far Martin gets on his crusade. I fear what comes next for Rayner."

Jessa left the post office. It was almost time to get Matthew at the schoolhouse. She didn't want to see anyone, and she didn't want to be seen. How did folks do it, she wondered, every day, surrounded by others? Every day in their little wooden boxes, traveling from one box to the next for visits and goods. It'd been so long since she'd been out on the prairie, far out where you couldn't see a thing made by the hands of man. She'd avoided going home for Thanksgiving. Too tired to pretend to people she loved. She held a distinct guilt regarding Nellie. Nellie had known better, could see it a mile off. Jessa, thick headed and childish, had pushed her away. More than that, she'd silenced her little sister rather cruelly in front of their sisters. That was the scene Jessa often replayed in her head.

18

Mr. Martin was stomping around the house, snapping at everyone. Levi had claimed complete ignorance of Goodsite's fraud, and the sheriff didn't have enough evidence to prove otherwise. Mr. Martin railed against both brothers. Every time he mentioned "those Keyes boys," Jessa's shoulders tightened as if she were pulling a heavy pick sack. She wanted to jump in, correct Mr. Martin, cut Will's name from his brother's, but she didn't dare.

Jessa put on her coat to go outside. The sky was overcast. It'd take forever to dry the laundry, but Jessa appreciated how all the colors looked richer in the dull light. Even the dusty earth looked pretty, the few shrubs and trees revealing dozens of shades of green and silver, variations that were normally washed out in the full rays of the sun. Transferring Gabriel's wet britches from the washtub to the willow basket, Jessa spotted a folded piece of paper. Since she figured it belonged to Matthew, part of a game he'd been playing—a treasure map, a ransom note—she opened it without trepidation. It read: "Dear Miss Campbell, W is boogered up bad. He said not to fetch you, said you wouldn't step foot in the saloon—" *What? What is this? Is "W" for Will?* Fear rose from the soles of her feet. "And I don't like to go against him, but I thought it only fair to tell you, if you wish to see him in this life, you should consider coming." The letter was unsigned, but she knew Levi must have written it. She looked around to make sure no one was watching then read the letter again, this time more slowly. She would have Will's name, even if it meant dragging a preacher to the saloon.

•••

The Martins turned in early, so she was able to steal away just after ten. She walked with urgency. Please, Lord, she prayed, don't let him die. She adjusted the shawl on her head, worn like a scarf. She was on a nursing mission, she reminded herself, no need to be ashamed. Still, it wouldn't look right if she was discovered out so late, alone. She felt queasy when the saloon came into view. A voice in her head said, Don't. Loud and clear. But was it the Lord or her fear talking? She peered through the dusty window into the room with the bed, dark and empty. The Worst Conclusion came to her: *He is dead. The room has been cleared of his body.* Her legs started to give way; she gripped the sill. Stop, you don't know, she told herself.

Using the back door, Jessa entered the unlit hallway of the saloon. It was warm inside, the scarf hot on her head, but she dared not take it off. She heard murmuring, glasses clinking, men coughing, wood creaking, chairs sliding. Hugging the wall, she peered around the corner. The place was busy. A man and a woman were behind the bar, a few patrons leaned against it, and a couple of tables held card games. A gathering of men at a table, some sitting, some standing, and Will. He was alive. She took a moment to thank God for deliverance. In the low light, it was hard to make out his injuries: a gash on his cheek, an abrasion on his forehead, his left arm tied in a sling. Bad, but he didn't appear to be on death's door as Levi had made out.

Jessa stared at Will intently, hoping to pull his gaze to hers. Animals didn't need words. They picked up signals, whatever the skin was radiating, whatever the taut muscles warned of. The way her dog Red's line of sight would follow Jessa's—two sets of eyes on the hawk, the quail, the errant cow. The way the horse would slow down before the rein was tugged, or the rabbit dart before the trigger was pulled. She found herself counting, *one, two, three, four.* Then it happened, he raised his eyes to hers. His eyes scanned her, like he was trying to make out who she was. Finally, he came toward her in recognition, hobbling, as if each step were a trial. As he got closer she could see one eye was blackened and his lip split.

Will took her hand and headed down the hallway toward the back door. Relief overtook her. It crossed her mind that maybe now was the time to tell him about her condition. Maybe he'd understand how vulnerable she was in this state, how important that piece of paper. She'd take inventory of his condition outside, make sure his wounds had been properly treated. Jessa was going through her mother's remedies in her mind, wondering what would be best for a black eye, when someone grabbed her free arm, and she was whipped in the opposite direction. Levi Keyes had a hold of her.

"I knew you'd come," he said.

"Will?" she called. Everything seemed to shift. Instead of looking at her, Will's eye was on his brother.

"C'mon, missy," Levi said.

Levi's legs were long. In three steps they were on the saloon floor. Jessa could feel all eyes upon her, the assembled drinkers taking her in, up and down. Though fully clothed, she felt naked. She wondered if any of them recognized her as J. R. Campbell's daughter. She prayed not.

"Drink for the lady," Levi said.

Someone chimed in, "Here, here."

The hair on the back of her neck stood up. What was the point in parading her around the saloon, she wondered. She kept her head down, scanned the floor for Will's shoes.

"Levi, come on," Will said.

"What you havin'?" Levi said.

She held her chin tightly to her chest. Levi countered by stooping low and looking up at her. His eyes were red, cheeks bloated, a man to steer clear of, and then he proved it by stumbling. He laughed and the assembled laughed with him. He clamped his hand on her shoulder. "You're gonna want a drink," he whispered.

Her legs felt as wobbly as a newborn colt's, but she could not fall. They'd pounce like a pack of wild dogs. Bloodlust lay underneath the alcohol, the laughter. Where was Will? He had to be close by, but she did not see him, just the tableful of men.

"So what's it gonna be?" Levi said.

"Rot gut," said a man, "that's all you serve."

"Miss Too-Good likes her whisky, don't ya?" Levi said.

Had Will shared with Levi the details of that awful night? How she had kept sipping from the dirty glass, kept sipping until finally the room spun, the men were gone, and her body emptied itself of everything but the memory? Will had held her hair away from her face as she vomited, wiped her brow with his damp handkerchief. Where was he now? A wave of nausea went through her. The room was hot and stuffy, her shawl stifling. She felt like a beetle in a schoolyard, and Levi, the boy with the looking glass. But what about Will? Where was that decent part of him? She lifted her head and found him. He was only four or five feet away, watching. A moment ago he'd been leading her out, away from these people.

"Will!" It came out louder than she'd intended. Still, he made no move toward her. Had he been in on the ruse? Her guts twisted. To keep from crying, she squeezed the skin between her thumb and forefinger, something Mama had taught her.

Will said, "Get her out of here."

Levi ignored his brother. His hand traveled from Jessa's shoulder to her buttock. She started shaking.

"Play us something, Big Jim." A fiddle started up, and Levi pulled her away from the group, pretending to dance. "I know what you did," he said. "You sicced ole Martin on me."

She tried to pull away, but he used the momentum to spin her in a circle.

"Now I got a bunch of rake-rattlin' yokels to deal with on top of the Galveston fellas. Used to be the good townsfolk would help run the unwanteds out of town, but that protection has been newly denied me."

She couldn't figure how he'd discovered the part she'd played. "I didn't . . . I don't know what you're talking about." She tried to plant her feet, but he kept her moving.

He moved in close, his breath in her ear. "You trying to get your sweetheart killed? We need money. Gotta get to California."

California? The first she'd heard of it. Was Will planning to duck out of Rayner without a word?

"You wanna get outta here, you gotta get workin'."

"I will not," she said, low and as steady as she could manage.

Levi brought her face-to-face, his hands holding her scarf, one on each side of her chin. His voice was a whisper. "You want I tell everybody who comes in that door about you? Mr. Martin thinks he's got a tale on me. Boy, won't he be surprised! Probably start with Nosey Posey, don't need no newspaper advert with her around."

The blood rushed to Jessa's face. She could hear her heart beating, her blood pumping, amplified in her ears, while other noises receded. *Whoosh, whoosh, whoosh.*

"And your daddy, such a fine upstanding fellow," he said. "County cattlemen rep, ain't he? Some kind of rebel hero?"

Jessa felt like a child. A stupid, stupid child. She would not be free of this man until he was dead.

Levi shoved her toward the hallway, toward the room at the back that held the bed. She lost her balance and fell hard on her knees. A clap of laughter echoed behind her. Then a hand reached down for her. Will's hand. He helped her to her feet, a protective arm around her shoulders. He was ushering her out of here, away from Levi. He had taken a stand.

As they moved down the hallway, she anticipated the relief she'd feel in the night air, but instead, as she reached for the knob, they veered to the left, toward the room. No, she thought, no, no, no. *What is happening?*

"I'm going," she said, pulling away from him. Despite his injuries, his grip was tight. "Let me go."

"C'mon, honey," he said, now dragging her.

Why was he doing this? She couldn't make heads or tails of it. Her skin felt clammy. If she cried out, she'd only draw attention to herself. "What are you doing?" she said. "Will?"

He didn't answer, so she kicked him as hard as she could. His eyes and mouth opened wide in surprise, but he said nothing. Then he lost his grip on her. She dove for the door, but Levi caught her. She raked at Levi's face with her hands, trying to gain purchase on his eye sockets. She was quick and he was inebriated, his reaction slow. She made deep gouges on one side of his face, but he twisted her arms behind her back so she could not get free.

"Bitch," he said. Levi's mouth was set in a straight, tight line, bright bubbles of blood flowing up and down his face.

She turned to Will, but his face was expressionless, like a corpse. Everything was twisted, wrong, like sour milk, a deformed calf, a dry well. She knew then there would be no building a little cabin on the Shinnery. Not ever. Not with Levi alive or dead. Her value was in one thing. How could she not have seen that coming?

"Them boys want their money, and Will here's wearing the warning." Levi indicated Will's injuries.

"You can both go to hell," she said, looking at Will. She wanted to weep for all she'd lost, but injured animals were vulnerable to being torn apart by the pack. Weakness begat destruction. "I'm not doing nuthin'." She turned to Will. "Tell him."

Arms crossed, he stood as silent as the moon.

"You owe me, Will Keyes." Tears streaked her face, but he was immovable. She calculated the steps it would take to reach the door.

"He's not gonna save you," said Levi. "Go ahead, Will. Get it out."

Will moved slowly to the dresser and opened the rickety bottom drawer. Out of a jumble of what appeared to be clothes, he pulled a perfectly folded white cloth, a sheet maybe. Then she saw it: a bloodstain, dried to the color of a rotten plum. Before she could wonder why he'd saved a bloody cloth, she knew. That cloth was their cloth, the marriage bedsheet without the marriage. He muttered something that could have been "sorry."

"You wantin' we should take this to your daddy?" asked Levi. "Tell him what a bad girl you've been. Tell everybody that old man Campbell's got a Jezebel for a daughter."

She wished them dead. Both of them. Had Levi instructed Will to save the bedsheet, or was that something he'd come up with on his own? Who was this man that she had loved beyond reason? He held the bedsheet at arm's length, his face unreadable. Behind him was the bed. She glanced at it and was hit by the full force of what had occurred, of what Levi was demanding now. Jessa vomited. She didn't try to stop it or contain it, didn't even bring her hand to her mouth. She let it spew, up and out, hitting the floor and splattering.

Levi jumped back. "Goddammit!" he said. "What the hell's wrong with you?" Everything, she thought, every goddamn thing is wrong.

Will set the sheet down on the bed and reached into his pocket for a handkerchief. His eyes softened as he held it out to her. She wanted to gouge them out. She used the back of her hand to wipe her mouth, eyes locked on his.

Levi banged on the wall. It must have been a signal because a boy came in. "Opie, clean up this mess, and then send in that cowpoke from Kansas." He turned to Jessa. "I'm either gonna get back to business or I'm gonna go see your pappy and tell him and everyone else about you. Which is it?"

"Which is it" sounded like "whichisit." Levi was knockered. Would he really go to her Papa tonight if she refused? And would refusing even protect her? A building full of drinking men against a girl from the Shinnery. "A cowpoke from Kansas." A man just down the hall, who'd be followed by another man, and another. At least before, she'd had the illusion of love, of sacrifice. She looked at Will, who was sitting on the bed, running his hand absentmindedly over the sheet.

He raised his head. "I'm sorry, Jess, but you already done it once." He pinched his nose like he was trying to stop tears.

How dare he. Will had no idea what that had cost her and, worse, he didn't care, not really. Had he ever had any feeling for her? What had turned it? Had she done something? Failed to do something? She felt utterly betrayed. Her shaking started again. A sob escaped.

Opie entered with a bucket and a rag. He wiped Jessa's vomit then left without a word. "This ain't easy on Will either," said Levi. "We all gotta do things we don't wanna do."

Was Levi really trying to maintain the illusion his brother cared about her? Continue to use her love as bait? It made her sick. She wanted to scream how much she hated Will, kick him again, tear his hair out, but it would do no good to be forthright. He had schooled her in the art of lying and misdirection.

"I didn't want to say anything, since *theMartinshavebeengoodtome* . . ." She was having trouble getting the words out in the tumble of shaking and crying.

Levi interrupted. "Can't make out what you're saying. Slow down."

She took a deep breath. Her body shuddered. They couldn't see how desperate she was, how terrified. "I said, the Martins have been good to me and all, but . . . well . . ." Jessa pretended that what she was about to say would come at a great personal cost. "The thing is . . . there's money. Martin keeps it hidden, in the nursery, where no one'd think to look."

"Why's it at the house? That don't make no sense," said Levi.

"If you're hiding it, it does."

"Hiding it from who?"

Jessa was at a loss but had to say something. "I don't know. Maybe his family in St. Louis?"

"How much?" said Levi.

She was afraid to name a number, worried that it'd either be too low to entice him or too high to be believable. "A lot."

"That store's a gold mine."

It wasn't, but they needed to think it was. "It is, and I can get some." She racked her brain for any idea beyond this enticement.

"When?" he asked.

"Um . . . Sunday." Her head throbbed; she wished for hot black coffee. "I'll beg off church."

"Can't wait that long. They're here for their money."

They. The Galveston boys. She wondered if they were in the saloon right now, if she was part of the settling up. She had to get out of there.

Levi shook his head. "We need it tonight."

"I can't." She needed more time to set her half-formed plan in motion.

"Tomorrow?" said Will, from where he sat on the bed.

Levi turned to his brother. "How do we know she's gonna bring it off?"

"She'll bring it off," said Will.

"Bird in the hand, brother," Levi said, indicating she should do what she had been summoned to do.

Will sighed. "I said she'd do it."

Jessa took a deep breath and looked straight at Levi. He was the gateway to getting out of the saloon tonight, and he did not trust her. He'd be duped only if he thought she was the sucker. "I am promised to your brother and he to me," she said. *Promised.* Her words were painful to her ears. She felt like she might be sick again, but she pressed on. She had to get out of there, had to escape the cowpoke from Kansas. She used her scarf to wipe her face clear of tears and snot. "It's clear you've roped Will into this. I will get your money if you swear to leave us be after that. We're getting married."

Levi smirked. Her stupidity appeared to be confirmed for him, that she would still champion Will after everything that had occurred.

"Course of true love never did run smooth." Levi picked something out of his teeth.

Will's eyes were half closed. Did he believe her, that she still swallowed his lies? Jessa wondered how much he'd had to drink.

"Do you promise?" she said, knowing that any promise from Levi would be as empty as a beggar's pocket.

"Sure," he said.

"All right, but I need to go now," she said, backing up toward the door, across the back room's threshold.

"How we gonna get the money from you?" Levi said.

"I'll hide it somewhere."

Levi shook his head. "What kind of chicanery is that? You gonna make us a treasure map?"

"No, that's good," said Will, eyes open now, sitting up straighter. "The cottonwood. Hide it at the base."

Levi made a dismissive sound.

"Brother, it'll work."

The cottonwood was one of Jessa and Will's meet spots, near the spring close to the Martin house. She thought of how she'd stood against it, her body pressed between the tree and Will. It flashed in her mind to chop the tree down.

"Tomorrow," she said. "By midnight."

The men nodded, their chins bobbing in the very same way, and she realized, for the first time, just how alike they appeared.

She took another step backward. Nothing between her and the saloon's side door but distance. Hard to appear nonchalant with her feet rattling in her shoes.

"Hang on." Levi saw what she was trying to do. "I got that sum bitch from Kansas. He's been waiting all night."

"If I'm caught out, Martin'll send me straight home, and you'll have nuthin'."

"My fella's half twisted. Won't take but a minute."

"Nuthin'," she repeated, "if I don't leave now." She would not lie with that Kansas man. Not while she still had breath.

Levi moved in closer, close enough to grab her. "You'll get back." He motioned toward the bed. "Just five minutes."

She wished him dead. A hundred times dead. Scalped, shot, dragged.

Gathering her last thimbleful of courage, she told the brothers to get out. "I need a few minutes to clean up, collect myself. And then only him. The cowpoke. No more. Understand?"

They nodded. She waited less than ten seconds after they left to slide open the window and slip outside. She ran. Fear made her fast. She considered running all the way home. Ten miles back to the Shinnery. But then her father would know everything, be crushed by it. Up to her to clean the mess she'd made, so she headed for the Martins', dogs barking in her wake.

19

Jessa laid out the tea things. She'd knocked the sugar bowl over, and her hand hurt from where she'd splashed boiling water on it. Last night had rattled her. Will had chosen sides, no confusion on that, and she'd barely escaped the back-of-the-saloon business. Most pressingly, though, she'd promised Levi money that didn't exist. She'd racked her brain all morning trying to think of something she could leave him. Something valuable, identifiable, so that when she tipped off Mr. Martin to the "thievery," Levi might be caught red-handed, and then punished, banished, killed. She didn't know exactly how that would unfold, how she'd tell Mr. Martin without incriminating herself. Her head started to ache. First things first, she told herself: steal something. She placed the silver teapot on the serving tray and considered its worth—something she didn't know much about. The pot was heavy, but likely too bulky for Levi to slip into his coat.

"You can pour now," Mrs. Martin called from the parlor.

Mrs. Garrett and her daughter Oneida, the red-headed beauty who'd been to the Martins' end-of-summer party, had come to tea. The trio was planning the menu for a Twelfth Night party, the last of the Christmas celebrations, which would christen Rayner's town hall. Jessa was too distracted to follow their chatter. She'd heard the girl speak French when they'd come in the door—at least that's what the missus called it. Since words often failed Jessa, she wondered if speaking two languages would increase the odds of being able to find the right ones or if it would make one's failure to grasp them twice as humiliating.

"And how fares your sister Nellie?" asked Oneida.

"Uh, she is well," she said, pulling three starched white napkins from the sideboard.

"Such a lovely girl. We must have her over—oh, and you too of course."

Jessa couldn't imagine being a guest in the Garrett home, sitting to tea and having another girl, a Jessa, wait on her.

Oneida continued, "She must be in the thick of preparing for her teacher's exam."

Jessa remembered Oneida and Nellie chatting at the Martins' party but hadn't realized they'd become fast friends. Jessa felt bad; she hadn't even inquired about Nellie's studies the last time she'd been home. "She must be," was all she could muster.

"*Maman* thinks young ladies don't need a vocation beyond wife and mother, but I, for one, admire your sister's ambition."

"So do I," Jessa said sincerely. Then she put out the saucers.

Mrs. Garrett leaned over to Mrs. Martin. "We send her to finishing school and she returns speaking of suffrage."

"*Toujours en évolution, Maman*," said Oneida. "The world is changing, always."

Jessa felt the truth of this in her bones, and her belly—just this morning, the top button of her skirt had popped off under the strain and skittered across the floor.

Mrs. Martin stepped in as the diplomat. "Party talk is so much more pleasant."

"Twelfth Night is dreadfully old-fashioned," Oneida said. "*C'est démodé.*"

Jessa placed the delicate cups on their saucers. She considered the china as a lure for Levi: valuable, but not easily transportable.

"Tradition, young lady. Don't dismiss its importance."

Jessa poured the tea into the first cup a little too quickly, splashing it into the saucer. Perhaps she could take the silverware to Levi. The missus had said it was "Tiffany" in a tone that suggested Jessa should know what it meant. Probably a fancy St. Louis silversmith, she reckoned.

"Don't you think a New Year's dance would be more fun, Jessa?" Oneida said.

Jessa was startled. She had no idea what to say. Parties? Dances? Her world felt so removed from that of this beautiful girl with the red hair and white teeth and creamy skin talking about king's cakes and bonfires. She had the urge to take Oneida's hands and unburden herself, tell her every last thing about last night, about what she carried in her body, the things she could not tell her sisters. She pictured Nellie's face taking in the news, how her face would collapse, her shoulders round over, as if to protect herself from the words. She'd be so afraid for Jessa that she'd shake as if the fate were her own. Maggie would be speechless. Wouldn't even be able to discuss it, would cup her hands over her ears, *Enough, enough!* Maggie needed the world to be nice. Bad things happened, but the Campbells didn't *do* bad things.

"And music," said Mrs. Garrett. "Wouldn't it be lovely to have a quartet?"

"We'll be lucky to hire a fiddler," said the missus.

"There must be another piano player somewhere," said Mrs. Garrett.

Jessa paused at the mention of the piano player. No longer eager to flee the parlor, she doled out the sugar slowly.

Mrs. Martin said, "It's a shame that boy got caught up in his brother's machinations."

"His brother?" said Mrs. Garrett. "He's got machinations of his own."

Jessa froze. What were they saying about Will? Machinations? She wasn't sure what the word meant. Sounded like "schemes."

"*Maman*," said Oneida curtly. She seemed to want to halt the conversation. "This tea has wonderful flavor, Mrs. Martin."

"It's from Ceylon—"

Mrs. Garrett interrupted. "We have a duty to protect members of this community."

"Gossip," said her daughter.

Gossip? Did they know about Jessa and the saloon? But they'd have said something straightaway—or, more likely, wouldn't have come at all. Jessa stopped all pretense of serving. She had to know what they were talking about.

"It's not gossip if it happened to you," said Mrs. Garrett.

"But nothing *happened* to me," said Oneida.

"He conspired to see you in secret, kept coming 'round the house even though he was forbidden, and then . . ." Mrs. Garrett looked around the room as if to make sure no children were present. "He wrote the most scandalous note."

"A poem, *Mère*. He copied a *poem* out of a book."

"Who did?" asked Mrs. Martin, who'd scooted to the edge of her seat.

"Mr. Will Keyes." Oneida sounded exasperated.

Will? thought Jessa. Will sent this girl a poem?

"Well," said her mother. "Either way. It was ill advised. He'd been warned to stay away."

Oneida looked at Jessa as if seeking a companionable nod, the young girls in alliance against the old, crotchety mother, but Jessa stood frozen. Though she knew this news was a trifle in the face of what she'd endured, it gutted her. How many ways could she be a fool? Her eyes burned. She fought to hold back tears.

"Oneida's brothers put him straight though."

"They didn't have to throttle him," Oneida said. "Three against one."

Jessa could hardly take the words in: This girl's brothers beat Will? Not the men from Galveston? He had been beaten for his own actions, not Levi's? Beaten for attempting to woo a girl?

"I'm so sorry," Mrs. Martin said to her visitors in the polite, noncommittal way she said most things. But when she caught sight of Jessa, she repeated herself. "So sorry." Her expression was tender, which made it worse. Jessa's mouth went dry and her cheeks burned.

"A real Belvedere. He deserved every lick," said the mother.

Every lick. He was whupped for showing up at Oneida's window, conspiring in secret, coming 'round, sending scandalous poems. All for this girl. *This girl he sought while claiming a true heart for me. This girl with the milky face, who went to school in Austin and speaks French and would never debase herself with strangers.* Suddenly her limbs weighed a thousand pounds. She wanted to sink through the floorboards and into the hard, dry earth. Disappear forever. And the thing that was left, the silly, stupid part, was the poem. *He never gave me a poem. Girls like Oneida get poems. Girls like me get nothing. No, that's not right. We get bloody sheets. A baby.*

"The sweet loaf? Jessa?"

Language had left Jessa. She felt like a mouse in a hawk's shadow. *Flee! Flee!* She dropped the sugar tongs and flew out the back door. Once outside, she didn't know where to go. Every nook and cranny within a mile of the place was somewhere she'd been with Will. She longed to be home. She wanted to walk there right now, and she could. She wouldn't tire, and she wouldn't look back. Home to Mama and Papa, to Nellie and Agnes, and dogs and cows, home to Sunday suppers. Home to church and field, and barn and bed. What was she without these things? Who was she here but a fool and a sinner?

Even as she longed to go, she could not. She dropped behind a boulder. Lion Top, the boys called it, climbing and roaring from its peak. She sat cross-legged in the sandy dirt, elbows to her knees, face in her hands, and tears plopping on the ground like raindrops. "Help me," she said aloud. She almost didn't recognize her own voice, childlike and soft as a finch's. She fell asleep leaning against the boulder and woke with a lap full of ants. She climbed Lion Top and looked out—one way home, the other back to the house, back to the Martins'. She'd never felt more tired. Then she thought of her father, how he'd been so broken and exhausted when the war ended. He'd been captured by the Federalists, a prisoner of war taken to Kentucky and then Ohio. At the war's end, he spent two months recovering in a Virginia hospital. Grandmother and Grandfather Campbell, along with a brother, too young to fight, brought him home to Tennessee in a pushcart since he was too weak to walk. Papa called it the longest, saddest journey of his life, his parents almost not recognizing their bag-of-bones son, and the family walking past the ruins of their country. Scorched earth and blackened rubble. He told her that many folks had burned their homes and barns rather than let the enemy have use of them. Their house was too modest to be commandeered or even attacked, but all the horses, mules, and cows had been taken, and the fields had gone to seed. As Papa told it, it wasn't until he saw his wife that he believed life had anything good left to offer, that he might enjoy days when the war never crossed his mind. Something that seemed impossible in the moment but was hinted at in the circle of Mollie's arms. As long as Jessa had her family, there was something good left for her too—there had to be. But would they turn her away? Being with child was perhaps forgivable, but what she'd done in the saloon: no. It was beyond the pale. They must not know. No one could. She hopped down from the rock. Time to steal something.

•••

By the time Jessa returned, the ladies were gone, and the missus and Gabriel were nowhere to be seen. Jessa figured that the missus had accompanied Oneida and Mrs. Garrett back down Main Street. Jessa had to act quickly, find something of value to take. Since Jessa had fled the house in the middle of serving tea, the missus might well discharge her. Now or never to enact her plan. She looked in the parlor at the walnut china cabinet with glass birds and pewter candlesticks, scoured Mr. Martin's desk with the ivory pens and calfskin ledgers. It didn't seem like these items might be easily traded, or even valuable. She went upstairs into the Martins' bedroom. Jewelry, she decided, was her best option. From the cedar chest, she took a wool wrap. She laid it on the bed and piled an assortment of jewelry in the center: chokers and pearl chains, hat pins and cameos, bracelets and rings, tie pins and cuff links. When she came upon the box that held the secret locket with the photograph of Mrs. Martin's true love, she resisted. If she left the box behind, it might seem suspicious. But if she took it and it were recovered, the missus could suffer greatly. She slipped the locket from its hiding place, wrapped it in a handkerchief, and made a plan to keep it safe. Jessa tied the corners of the wrap into a firm knot. The sun was beginning its descent, now shining directly into the bedroom window, the bright light momentarily obliterating her vision.

"No."

Jessa heard the voice of the missus behind her. Where had she come from? How had Jessa failed to hear her and Gabriel? Jessa turned. Mrs. Martin appeared wide-eyed, almost frightened. Jessa had been caught red-handed. She would be arrested.

"No," said the missus, almost pleading.

Jessa was surprised by Mrs. Martin's reaction. "I'm sorry. It's not—I plan to get it all back to you. I promise."

"You." She pointed. "You're with child."

Jessa looked down and could see the light's glow through the low window penetrating her muslin skirt, her waistband unbuttoned, as it had been all day. In this light the circumstance of her body was clear. Clear, too, why the missus had reacted as she did, a mix of fear and horror.

"How could you?" said the missus.

Jessa didn't know if the question referred to her condition or her theft. Neither was answerable. How could she have done any of it? How could this be her life? It could not. Tears spilled again; she wiped them on her sleeve. She didn't know where to begin with the missus, how to make her understand.

"Stupid girl," the missus said, almost under her breath. "This cannot fall on us, do you understand? It is not our fault." She surveyed the scene: a bundled shawl, emptied jewelry boxes, open vanity drawers. "What on earth is going on?"

Everything rested on this moment. Jessa would lay her cards on the table, as Will might say. She went to the bundle on the bed and untied it, revealing the jewelry.

"What'd that blackguard talk you into? He's turned you criminal!"

"No, ma'am," said Jessa. "This was my idea, and I don't think it's criminal."

The missus ran her fingers over her belongings. "You're attempting to take my things." She grabbed a handful, necklaces dripping through her fingers like candle wax. "How is that not criminal?"

"Borrow, ma'am. You'll get it all back."

"I've half a mind to walk you to the sheriff myself."

"Please. I didn't . . . I don't know what else to do."

The missus dropped the jewelry. "Explain yourself." The missus sat down on her vanity stool like a judge taking his seat at the bench. "Two minutes before I hand you over to my husband."

As rapidly as she could, Jessa laid out her scheme to get Levi out of town and out of their lives. The mister was already out of his mind over the cattle swindle and his subsequent failure to have Levi arrested. Wouldn't having the chief culprit gone greatly improve things for the missus? Jessa explained that she was merely borrowing the jewelry, would plant it at the cottonwood for Levi to pick up, and would set the trap for him getting caught. She also spoke of a great looming threat to her own person.

"And the child?" the missus asked. "That should be your first concern."

Jessa didn't want to discuss it with the missus, especially after they'd just heard how Will had pursued Oneida and how he'd suffered for it. But if she was to enlist Mrs. Martin's help, she had to share. "It's Levi that doesn't like me. With him gone, I believe Will will at least give the child a name." Jessa stood up straight to deliver the last part, the most important part as far as her employer was concerned. "And spare your family any scandal."

"He's promised this?"

"No, ma'am, but only because of Levi." Only because of Levi. Jessa used to believe this was true.

"You must have that, his name, do you understand?"

"Yes, ma'am." It seemed like such a paltry thing for her to have to content herself with. Five measly letters to append to her name, to pass down to the child.

"You cooked this up all on your own?" asked the missus, her hand sweeping over the bed and the spilled contents.

Jessa nodded.

"How do I know you're telling the truth? What if your story is all part of a ruse? Maybe that beau of yours, or Levi, or I don't know, Billy the Kid, put you up to this and you're about to rob me blind."

"Please, ma'am," said Jessa. "I am not. I swear on my family's life."

The missus appeared vexed. "This is too much you're asking."

"It is, and I'm sorry. It's the only thing I can think to do. And we have to do it quick. Levi Keyes will smear my name and, with it, yours. Mr. Martin is most at risk. When house girls become with . . ." It made Jessa shudder to finish the thought, the idea so loathsome to her but also the most persuasive argument she had. "The baby, ma'am. Levi might spread the rumor that it's Mr. Martin's."

The missus went whiter than should have been possible. She stood and grabbed a fan from the drawer. Though the December air made the house cool, she fanned herself rapidly. Then she scanned the objects again, appearing to look for something specific. "What about my locket?"

"Wrapped tight." Jessa pulled the object from her apron. "I was gonna hide it downstairs in the cornmeal bin." She handed the locket to the missus.

"Thank you," said the missus automatically, then corrected herself. "Thanking you for not stealing everything! Holy Mother of God!"

"We need to get this stuff wrapped up and at the tree before Mr. Martin comes home."

"We?" the missus said, her eyebrows raised. She pawed the bundle once more and fished out two rings and a necklace. "My grandmother's," she said, fingering a chain of delicate gold garland. "Go on now."

Jessa secured the bundle.

The missus crossed her arms. "You think Levi Keyes is going to let himself get caught red-handed?"

"No, I think he'll flee when confronted with arrest. Too much danger here. He'll have to stay away."

"Sounds like an ending to one of those outlaw serials Elias likes. Nice, but not wholly plausible."

Jessa had never read such a book, but she could recognize how flimsy her plan was, how easily undone or thwarted, but it was all she had. "Levi already had to leave Galveston, didn't he? He'll go from here too."

The missus looked at her squarely. "I rue the day you crossed our threshold, Miss Campbell."

Jessa looked squarely back. "Me too, Mrs. Martin. Me too." Jessa didn't move until the missus broke her gaze.

When Jessa returned from planting the loot at the base of the cottonwood, she saw that the missus had further staged the "break in." She'd opened the wardrobe, tossed items about, and mussed the bedcovers. The delicate gold necklace now graced her neck, the two rings, her fingers.

"We need to be seen in town," said Mrs. Martin. "That way, it's at least possible we could have been burgled. And if we happen to walk Mr. Martin home, we'll all discover what happened here at the house together."

"Thank you," said Jessa.

"Don't thank me. This is about protecting my husband. You and Will Keyes can go to blazes."

•••

When the Martins and Jessa returned to the house, the missus made it a point not to go upstairs. She went over Matthew's lessons with him in the parlor. Gabriel was kept busy in the kitchen with Jessa, who hurried to throw together a soup. When Jessa heard the mister mount the stairs, she froze. The whole house seemed to hold its breath.

"Charlotte!" hollered the mister. "Get up here!"

Jessa heard the missus comply, Matthew and Gabriel trailing after her. All three voices were muffled, but Jessa could make out shock and agitation. Then she heard her own name called.

As Jessa entered the bedroom, the missus spoke. "The most awful thing has happened. We've been robbed."

"Are you sure?" Jessa's hands shook at her sides.

"Of course we're sure," said the mister. "Are you blind? Look!"

Jessa took in the mess; the missus had staged a compelling scene.

"She's in shock is all," said the missus. "Poor girl."

"I'm shock," said Gabe. Matthew put a protective arm around his little brother.

"We're all shocked," said his mother.

"When did you leave?" said the mister.

"Maybe three? I was expecting a letter from Fanny, and Gabe wanted to walk, so I asked Jessa to accompany us to town. You don't think someone was watching, waiting for us to leave?"

The room was silent as Mr. Martin appeared to ponder the possibility. Jessa tried to keep her breathing slow and steady.

"That thought just scares the wits outta me," said the missus.

"Keep your head. They wanted your jewelry, not you. Else they would've come when you were home."

"Are they coming back?" said Matthew, his eyes wide.

Mr. Martin put his hand on his son's head. "No, son. You've nothing to fear."

The missus said, "You'll go to the sheriff?"

"What sheriff? We have two volunteer deputies: Cox, who's gone to Fort Worth, and Macmillan, who's older than Methuselah. It's not like St. Louis, Charlotte, with the rule of law. This place is one step removed from wilderness, and ruin."

"So what is it you're going to do?"

"Stop him or them."

"But how, Elias?"

The mister fished in his chest of drawers and brought out a pair of silver pistols, the stocks with bone-white inlays.

"Boys," said the missus, "why don't you bring in some more wood? Looks like it's going to be chilly tonight."

"But what about the bad guys?" said Matthew.

"You father will figure something out. He's a smart man."

"With guns?"

"Only for protection," said his mother. "Go on." The boys tromped out of the room. "Who's even been here to know about my jewelry?"

"You don't have to come here to know such a thing. I own the mercantile, one can assume we have assets."

"Of course, Elias." The missus fingered her necklace.

"You're wearing jewelry right now!"

"You don't want me to wear it?"

"Don't be daft. The fact that it's on your neck saved it from the thieves!"

"I don't know if I'm remembering this correctly, but didn't someone comment on my necklace, Jessa? A tall fellow. We were on the sidewalk by the milliner's. Right when we came into town, I believe."

"That was Levi Keyes, ma'am. 'A fine necklace on a fine neck,' I believe he said."

"He didn't!" Mr. Martin's face darkened.

"A crude comment from a crude man. I paid it no mind, dear."

"You should have paid it mind. That's your clue."

"I don't understand."

Jessa marveled at how innocent and naive the missus could appear to her husband. Instead of puffing himself up and lecturing her, he stepped closer and took her hand.

"I'm on the brink of running that son of a gun out of town. Besides his part in the cattle swindle, there's the gambling debts, the trading of stolen horses, and other things I cannot name. I've exposed him, sweetheart. Because of that, no decent man will come to his aid. If there's anyone that crook would target, it'd be me."

"Will you be safe?" said the missus. The weight of what she and Jessa were doing seemed to settle on her face, her forehead wrinkling in true concern.

"Of course." The mister kissed her on the forehead.

In all her time at the house, Jessa'd never seen the couple show anything close to affection. For some reason, this line crossing gave her a deep sense of foreboding.

"I'm gonna round up a posse; don't need Cox."

Jessa cleared her throat. She was exhausted by the seemingly endless lies, but she had to press forward. "Mr. Martin, this probably doesn't mean anything, but one time—"

"Speak up."

"This one time the other Mr. Keyes, Will, he told me a story about bandits who . . . Oh, never mind. Just a story. Probably nuthin'."

"Go on, Miss Campbell. Let me be the judge of that."

"Will said he knew a bandit once from San Antonio, and his secret to not getting caught was to never leave the scene with loot. This thief would hide what he'd stolen somewhere close by, a big tree was best."

"Needle in a haystack."

"Not just any tree. A tree that stood alone and grew near water because the soil would be softer there, easier to dig."

"He said all that?"

It didn't sound like something Will would say, but she was trying to point the mister to the correct tree. "Uh-huh."

"An oak?" said the mister.

"Maybe," said Jessa. "Or maybe a cottonwood."

"Hmmm."

Jessa dreaded this next part; it was the least plausible. "Anyway, under cover of darkness, the bandit would come back at midnight and pick up his loot."

"You don't say."

The key to misdirection, Will had said, was to make sure the person felt like he or she had free will, even as you were drawing attention where it needed to be. If Jessa expressed skepticism, the mister wouldn't have to. "It's probably a tall tale."

"Or something he learnt from his brother."

"I don't know about that. He also told me a good one about a horse that could fly."

"Thank you, ladies. I can take it from here."

Jessa watched him head out the bedroom door, wondering what on earth she had set in motion.

20

Jessa woke from a dream, one that evaporated as soon as she opened her eyes. The room was still dark, but a look out the frosted window revealed a just-lightening sky, the strike of a match on the low horizon, neither night nor day. The sounds of heavy footsteps must have triggered her waking. She heard them now like hooves across hard-packed earth, along with deep, muffled voices. It reminded her for a moment of the sounds of the saloon, flooding her with a momentary sense of panic. They were in the dining room, this posse of men. She heard chairs being scraped across the wood floor, glasses set hard upon the table, the jingle of spurs, an errant chuckle, and a "Here's how!" But what news? she wondered.

Here, on her side of the door, whatever happened was suspended, unknown to her. Perhaps they had run Levi off and he was now halfway to wherever would have him. Perhaps Levi saw through her fishy scheme and never showed to retrieve the promised stash. Perhaps they'd apprehended him, and he was sitting in the very Rayner jail cell her father had helped build. That would be the most worrisome outcome since he could still tell tales on her. Her guts roiled. She did and did not want to know but took a speck of comfort in the fact that it was over and done, whatever the result. The men's energy was palpable, the house vibrating with their presence. The missus must feel it too, she thought, and was probably standing on the other side of her bedroom door. But where it would be unseemly for the missus to come down in such company and circumstances, Jessa knew she may well be summoned. *Clink, clink.* She could hear glasses meeting, a host of *saluds* and here-here's. A winning outcome, but for whom?

She pulled her dress over her head, her braid catching on a button. It would do no good to hurry. She took a deep breath, unhooked her hair, finished dressing, and slid her feet into her cold shoes. Hand on the doorknob. No going back.

She entered the dining room. "Put on the coffee, Mr. Martin?"

"Don't give him an excuse to put away the whisky!" said one of the men.

She turned to see the red-headed man from the post office, and possibly the saloon. She felt herself blush and looked away. It's not *that* red-headed man, she told herself.

"Vittles!" said another. "I's hungry."

"Yes. How about eggs, Miss Campbell," said Mr. Martin. "And whatever else you can muster."

Jessa knew she should nod and continue into the kitchen, but she had to know the outcome. "Success, sir?"

"Triumph!" said the mister.

"The jewelry?" she said.

"Recovered."

"How 'bout you, Martin? You recovered?" This was an older man, the one they called Rider for his days with the Texas Rangers. She'd seen her father talk with him a time or two and sensed he didn't like him much. He was short but full of swagger, even in his old age, with one shoulder on permanent droop. His face was brown as a saddlebag and covered in gray stubble.

"All's well that ends well," said Mr. Martin.

Jessa still didn't know how it had ended though, and she couldn't ask outright. "That's good news," she said mildly.

"Good news for the undertaker," said Rider.

She froze. Someone was dead. "I'm sorry it came to that." Her words were even and calm even though her breathing felt shallow, difficult. Who's dead? she wanted to shout.

"Self-defense," said the mister.

"Sure as shuck," said Rider. "Defense of this piss-poor town."

"Shut your trap," one of the men said. "It's a fine town."

Jessa scanned the room; there were almost a dozen men gathered.

"Rayner's gonna rival Austin someday," said a man in new chaps and a freshly pressed shirt.

"I'll drink to that," said Mr. Martin, who appeared eager for another shot of whisky. He had stripped down to his shirtsleeves, his collar was detached, and his hair was mussed. For the first time, Jessa could imagine him as handsome, a man who could get things done.

"Too bad Martin missed all of it," said Rider.

"Not all of it," argued Mr. Martin.

"If that don't take the rag off the bush," said a bearded man Jessa didn't recognize. "Man down! Man down!" he said, waving his hands and giggling like a schoolgirl.

"Martin, I told you when I sold you that mare, she likes to puff up like a prairie chicken. Gotta give her the knee so you can tighten the girth strap, otherwise . . . Well, now you know the otherwise." Rider slapped the table to punctuate his mirth. He laughed until he went into a coughing fit.

Jessa sprang into action and retrieved a cup of water from the crock, anything to prolong her time among the men. She handed it to Rider. He took it without thanks.

"That mare was kickin' mad when she showed up, saddle underneath her like an extra pair of tits."

"That's enough," said Martin.

Jessa almost felt sorry for him. No wonder he wanted to drink. He'd rounded up his posse only to fall off his horse. Some men didn't seem to belong out here no matter how badly they wanted it, she thought. Like her in stiff shoes and making small talk, it would never come naturally.

"Who gotcha after you tumbled?" said one of the younger men, a fellow Jessa vaguely recognized from the Martins' church.

"My assistant," said the mister, gesturing to a young man who helped out at the store a few days a week, the one who'd been at the house the first day she'd arrived.

Patrick looked wide-eyed, excited, like he was eager to spring again into action. "Horse came right to me. Happy to return her to you, Mr. Martin."

"Caught that son of a bitch red-handed," said Rider.

Which son of a bitch? Jessa wondered. She needed confirmation it was Levi.

Martin set his glass on the table, a gesture that garnered attention. "You shoulda waited." He slurred, just a slip.

"Waited? Devil's balls we shoulda waited. 'Pardon me, Mr. Keyes, our esteemed proprietor requests the pleasure of your incarceration,'" mocked Rider. "'He'll be 'round soon.'"

The church fellow raised his glass. "Well, you got your jewelry back, and he got his eternal reward."

Eternal reward. A body lies somewhere, she thought. "Which Mr. Keyes?" She heard herself speak the words aloud. Not evenly, not mildly, but with unmasked concern, desperation even. Her heart pounded so loudly in her ears she was afraid she wouldn't be able to hear the answer.

"Levi Keyes," said the mister.

Relief swept through her. Perhaps she was safe. "Just as you suspected," he continued.

"Me?" said Jessa. All eyes were on her. "I didn't . . ." She didn't know what to say, how to distance herself. Her name couldn't be associated with this. Any feeling of safety evaporated. Will could not get wind of this. "You, sir. You put it together. You stopped him, and I, for one, feel better for it. Thank you."

"Here, here," said the dark-haired man. "Let's drink to that."

As she left for the kitchen, Jessa could hear their voices rise again in a kind of manly sing-song. They were telling the story: "over the ridge," "spotted him first," "son of a gun." Jessa knew they'd spend the dawn telling it ten different ways, each man a bit of a hero in his own version. She wondered for a moment which version Will would hear. As she plopped drippings into the cold skillet, she pictured Will's face crumbling with the news, his shoulders heaving with grief. The phrase "blood of the Lamb" came to her, how one could be cleansed by loss, sacrifice. Perhaps he would be all new or restored. Restored to his highest, best self. The self at the lip of the Brazos, the self on the shoulders of his father, looking out over acres of corn. Or maybe not. Maybe all she could hope for was a man broken and lost enough to agree to marry her, a man willing to give her child a name. She cracked an egg into the pan.

Haskell Free Press, JUNE 8, 1895

WITNESSES FLOOD HASKELL

Haskell has been full of Rayner and Stonewall County people all this week. Fifty or sixty of them being witnesses in the _____ murder trial . . . They have been an orderly and well behaved crowd as far as our observation has been extended.

21

Three days after Levi's death, Jessa entered the nearly empty saloon through the rear door. The missus had thrust a tin of biscuits into her hands. "Take this as a condolence," she'd said. "You won't look suspicious going in."

Alone at a dirty table, Will barely looked up when she arrived. She indicated they should step down the hall for privacy. He was unmoved.

"What do you want?" Arms crossed, eyes as red as ripe currants.

"I'm sorry, Will. I know—"

"You know. You don't know."

"What don't I know?"

"Anything. Levi was . . ." Tears streamed down his face. "You didn't know him. I tell you how my mama's husband broke my arm? Cracked my ribs? Meanest drunk you ever met. And he was harder on Levi than he was on me. He woulda killed him. My mother scraped up three dollars for Levi and sent him away. Fifteen he was, *fifteen*. He had nobody. Then later, he come back for me. How many brothers do that?" He used his sleeve to wipe the snot from under his nose. "And you got him kilt. Goddamn stupid whore."

"I had to fight back. I couldn't . . ." She stepped closer to him. "What he wanted me to do. What you wanted. I'm—I'm not . . . I only did it that one time because . . ." Words, words, trapped. "You saved that sheet. Why'd you save that sheet?"

He shrugged.

Jessa had done what she'd done, though she couldn't believe any of it now. Not the love, not her willingness to debase herself. *How was I so convinced?* Will had been as false as a peddler hawking bottle cures. "I'm with child."

"So?"

So? Did he care for nothing but that goddamn brother of his? "So we need to marry. You don't have to—"

He started laughing loudly enough to draw the attention of Opie, who was tending bar, and the saloon's two patrons. "I don't hafta what? Hafta listen?"

"*Shhh . . .*" she said, but he didn't pay her any mind.

His laugh was loud and bitter; he'd been drinking. "Don't be a bally fool." He went up to the bar. "Another shot of that oh-be-joyful." Opie poured. Will downed the glass and took his seat at the piano. He played "O Lamb of God," the first song they'd sung together. One of the patrons booed, but he kept going.

Jessa felt like she was watching him from miles away. If she lay on the ground, he'd step over her without a word. She slipped out the side door and collapsed against it. The sounds of the piano thrummed through it, into her body. "Because thy promise I believe, O Lamb of God, I come, I come." How dare he play that song. She hated that song. She threw the tin of biscuits on the ground. *Bam, bam, bam, bam, bam.* She stomped the tin like she wanted to stomp the piano, stomp Will, take a stick to the tables and chairs, smash the bottles, and light that goddamn bed on fire.

●●●

After another three days she was back at the saloon with Mrs. Martin. A grace period, the missus called it, believing that given a bit of time, Will would come to his senses. Jessa stood behind her. A fool's errand, but desperation trumped any pride Jessa had left.

"Mr. Keyes," called Mrs. Martin, tapping on the back window of the saloon with her Belgian lace parasol. The day was cold but bright.

No one seemed to be around to witness their visit, but Mrs. Martin had practiced what she called her "cover story" anyway. "The postmistress has asked that we check on you." She paused for a moment, listening. "Mr. Keyes. Mr. Keyes, please come to the door so that we may offer our condolences." The missus flipped her parasol to the handle end and knocked even more loudly on the window frame. She wasn't used to being ignored.

They could hear the side door opening and walked around the corner of the building. Opie stuck his head out. "He ain't gettin' up. You wanna see 'im, you come inside."

"We have business with Mr. Keyes, and if entering the premises is the condition of conducting said business, then we shall proceed. But note, my friend," Mrs. Martin said, "it is under duress."

Opie appeared confused, but he cleared the doorway for Mrs. Martin, who charged through. When they entered the back room, the air was fetid like a farrowing room, overwarm and skin scented. Jessa was struck by a deep homesickness. Walking across this threshold five months earlier had been the first step toward an exile she couldn't have fathomed.

Will leaned against a pair of stained pillows, his face sprouting eight-day whiskers, his hair so dirty it appeared wet.

"While I wish to give you time to grieve, Mr. Keyes, the clock is against us here. This young woman of my employ is, as she has informed you, with child, a condition that cannot be concealed much longer. I fear a grievous outcome if you are not wed immediately."

Will laughed like he had before. "That bastard could belong to ten different men."

Jessa's face went hot. It was Will's child. It had to be. That day against the shed. That was when it happened. That's what she'd decided. That's what she could live with. She turned to Mrs. Martin. Will's words had caused the missus to step back as if suddenly avoiding quicksand.

"I beg your pardon," Mrs. Martin said.

"No need to beg, sweetheart."

He sounded like Levi now. She had made a mistake in coming with the missus. "Please," she said, gently placing her hand on Mrs. Martin's arm. "He's drunk and he's hurtin.' No sense in talking to him 'til he's sobered up."

The missus pulled her arm away. "You are not the father? Is this your claim, Mr. Keyes?"

"Yep," Will said.

"You deny relations with Miss Campbell?"

"No, I fucked her, but so did a lot of fellas. Probably even your husband. A soiled dove in your employ."

The missus's face went white. Jessa feared she might faint. The missus grabbed the edge of the dresser to steady herself. When Jessa took a step toward her, Mrs. Martin raised her parasol as if to ward her off.

"Never Mr. Martin," Jessa said.

The missus gave a sharp intake of breath, and Jessa realized what she'd done.

The missus fled.

Jessa flew out the door and caught up with her. "Will Keyes is a liar."

Mrs. Martin stared hard. "Maybe, but either way, you are poison."

Poison. Jessa couldn't think of a worse thing to be called. *Would such a thing seep into the child?*

"You will pack your things immediately. Don't say one word to my sons." The missus turned, her skirt flaring once more, parasol opening like a fist. Jessa stood there in the middle of Main Street. A lark in a tornado. What in God's name was she to do? She felt faint. She hadn't eaten anything. Babies needed sustenance. She couldn't walk home in her present state. It was too far, and she didn't know how she would explain having none of her things. She sat on the bench in front of the courthouse. What if she couldn't return home? What if Mr. Martin, when he heard about the pregnancy, and maybe the other part too, went to her folks' place and poisoned them against her? "You made your bed," Grandmother Campbell might say. But what did a girl do when the bed was stolen?

She thought about the highest cliffs of the Brazos, how it might be to jump off one. Was that what was expected of a girl in her position? No one would voice it, of course, but maybe a girl who'd been where she'd been, done what she'd done, maybe that's what folks would secretly hope. Maybe the only way to clear her name was to leave it behind.

She wouldn't know until she got back to the Shinnery. Arms open or doors shut. First, she needed to clear out of the Martins', and she needed to eat. Mrs. Posey. Mrs. Posey was the town crier, but she was also its gathering bosom. Jessa had seen lonely young brides in the post office, wrapped in the comforting embrace of the postmistress when they'd not received an expected parcel from home or, worse, gotten bad news. What Jessa wouldn't do for a lost package of handkerchiefs or a bedridden grandmother.

•••

Mrs. Posey offered to collect Jessa's things from the Martins', but Jessa didn't want her hearing any more details of the story than necessary. Jessa had told her a bare-bones version of events: she was pregnant and Will Keyes was the father. She did not consider that he wasn't. Would not. As for that other night, she pushed it out of her mind as best she could, as if it had happened to someone else, someone she wasn't particularly close to.

"Ain't that a ducker," Mrs. Posey had said. "I'd of thought Will woulda done right by you. He's awful chewed up over his brother though. Maybe he'll see his way to sense once he's done grieving."

"Maybe," Jessa had said. She'd thought of her father. He was the only person who might be able to persuade Will to give the child a name. Everyone respected J. R. Campbell. Her whole life she'd witnessed folks seeking his advice on all kinds of matters, from land buying to animal doctoring. While he was humble he spoke with authority, something Will might respond to now that his brother was dead. A man must own up went the unwritten rule, if not for the woman's sake, then at least for the sake of decency. She tried to picture it, the two men shaking hands, a deal struck for a quick in-name-only marriage, but then another image popped into her head: Will at the piano, drunk, sloppy, and wishing her dead.

Jessa was startled out of her thoughts by Mrs. Posey's hand on her

151

arm. "Sure you don't want me going in with you?" They'd arrived at the Martins' in the little wagon Mrs. Posey had borrowed that morning. The roan horse had a swayback and was said to balk at water, but the livery owner had let them take the rig without charge.

Jessa had spent the previous night with Mrs. Posey in the big room behind the post office. She'd eaten two bowls of porridge and fallen into a dreamless sleep despite Mrs. Posey's bed-rattling snore. Morning brought a shock, as it had done every morning since she'd discovered she was with child, but this time she was at least comforted by the fact that Mrs. Posey knew her circumstance and welcomed her anyway. She'd been expecting a litany of questions, but the postmistress didn't pry.

"I can manage," said Jessa, climbing down. "Thank you." She looked at the Martin home. She remembered how it'd seemed so perfect in every way when she'd first arrived, how out of place she'd felt, like the Martins were better than her because their house smelled new and was filled with pretty things. How silly she'd been to compare this household to her own and to think, for a moment, that the Campbells came up short. She didn't regard anything here as pretty anymore, except the children. She would miss Gabriel, and even Matthew.

Jessa walked around to the back of the house and entered quietly without knocking. She hoped to gather her things quickly, leave without being detected. Her heart hurt thinking how she wasn't allowed to say goodbye to Gabe. She could hear heavy shoes behind her as she went down the hallway. When she reached the bedroom door, she felt a rough push. She turned to see the mister. His face was ugly set, lips pulled tight, nose flaring like a bull. He came at her, shoving her to the floor, her tailbone flaring in pain. His foot rose and half-kicked, half-stomped her thigh. She was a girl, and no matter what she'd done, a grown man had no right to set upon her like this. She locked eyes with him. Not a word was exchanged as he kicked her again, the toe of his shoe making contact with her backside. She thought of the baby and pulled her knees in tightly to her chest.

"You're a liar and a sneak, and you have whatever's coming to you," he said. "To think of how you exposed my wife to this, how she, a pillar of virtue, tried to help you."

Jessa pictured the missus, eyes misty, speaking of her long-lost Mr. Broussard. *He must know he is only the consolation prize.*

"Have you nothing to say?"

He had kicked her like a dog; she would not lick his hand.

"Get out of my house."

When he left the room, she pulled her valise from under the bed and quickly packed it. She thought of leaving the clothes the missus had given her, but she realized they'd only be thrown out or burned if she left them. She had earned the clothes. She dug for the worn envelope she kept under the mattress. Four dollars. Seven months of work, and this was all that was left. This and a baby. A cry escaped her mouth, or a laugh, a bark. Press on, she thought, press on. She latched the valise and spotted the hand mirror on the dresser. The missus had loaned it to her, saying her hair was messy in the back and instructing her on the proper use of pins. She picked up the mirror and smacked it on the dresser's corner. The glass cracked, half a dozen lines shooting through it like caught lightning. She placed it back on the dresser, mirror side down, and hoped it would give the missus a little shiver. A token of bad luck.

Bag in hand, Jessa approached the wagon. She tried not to hobble, but soreness was rising through her legs. She must have winced as she lifted the bag, because Mrs. Posey noticed her discomfort.

"Any problem?" asked Mrs. Posey.

"No." Climbing into the wagon, Jessa purposefully bit her lip, an effort to counteract the pain in her side.

"Fiddle cakes," said Mrs. Posey. "Got a hitch in your step."

"It's over," said Jessa. "I want to go home."

They rode on for a while in silence in the cold and clear day, only the sound of the harness and Mrs. Posey's breathing. Jessa cried, but silently. Her body ached, and she wondered if the kicks could've harmed the baby. Women lost babies for less. All the girls knew Mama had lost a child at almost nine months after an ill-advised ride on a rough horse. It would be best, she knew it would, if she did lose the baby, but she worried that praying for such a thing would push her even further from the Lord.

"You're not the first girl," said Mrs. Posey, after a time.

Jessa turned. Mrs. Posey's cheeks were as red and wrinkled as crab apples, her eyes squinting against the sun. Did Mrs. Posey mean to suggest she'd been pregnant without benefit of a husband? Surely not. She was the postmistress, trusted, respectable.

"Mine went to my sister," she continued.

"Your baby?" Jessa was shocked, but suddenly Mrs. Posey's companionable silence the night before made sense.

"I was fourteen, and not a willin' participant in any of it. My sister came and got her."

Jessa pictured her sister Maggie—Maggie of a dozen miscarriages and a line of four tiny headstones. She felt an empty space inside to think of someone taking her baby, and yet moments before, she'd half-wished the Lord would do so.

"And my daughter became my niece."

"She never knew?" Again, a feeling of loss washed over Jessa.

"Nope. Part of the reason I married Mr. Posey and lit a shuck to Texas."

"Did you have any more?"

"Children? Nope. Never did. Mr. Posey was an old goat when we got married. Think he got hitched for the washing and chow. Three years in he died, and I took over his postal duties on a forged recommendation. This is my—" Mrs. Posey scrunched up her face while she appeared to count. "Third post in twenty-five years." She looked up to the sky. "Thank you, Mr. Posey."

Mrs. Posey's story joined the growing list of things Jessa had never imagined about the world. She thought back to that May morning when Papa had first brought her to Rayner, how naive she had been, stupid even.

"Saw my daughter again at my mama's funeral. She was eight, smart as a whip and just sassy enough to keep it interesting. We took a little stroll out to the orchard, my sister watching us from the porch, but I didn't say a word about who I was. I was a distant aunt." Mrs. Posey adjusted herself on the unpadded wagon seat. "Her name's Violet. Almost thirty now. Got three of her own."

Jessa didn't know what to say. "Violet's a pretty name," she offered. "It is."

In the distance, the Shinnery. Jessa felt suspended between worlds. What is and what was. She felt shaky, like she'd had too much coffee and not enough bread.

"You know what you're gonna tell your folks, about your . . . uh, 'hitch'?"

"I'm thinking on it."

"Looks to me like maybe you took a fall. Better to rest up at home."

"Yes," she said, after a moment. "I fell hard."

"You won't mention the boot to your backside though," said Mrs. Posey.

Jessa wondered how she knew. Mrs. Posey must have met a boot of her own in her day. "No, ma'am, I won't."

"Shame about his mail."

Jessa looked at Mrs. Posey, the reins loose in her lap, her face giving nothing away. "The way it might start disappearing," she continued. "A letter for every blow. How many do you reckon?"

"Four," said Jessa.

"Four," repeated Mrs. Posey. "I'll make 'em good ones."

22

The animals, as was their practice, announced the women's arrival. Papa and Agnes emerged from the barn, and Nellie and Mama from the house. All but Agnes looked a little puzzled. She was just excited.

"Look what the dog drug home!" said Agnes. "Whadya bring me?"

"Not a thing," said Jessa.

"She took a fall." Mrs. Posey handed off the reins to Papa, who tied the nag to the post.

"Off a horse?" said Agnes.

"Stairs."

"I'm so sorry," said Nellie. "Let me get your bag."

Jessa handed the valise to her sister. Papa came 'round to Jessa. "You sure you're all right?"

"Nothin' broken," she said.

"Get the kettle on for your sister," said Mama to Agnes.

"I really wish you'd brought candy."

"Agnes," chided Nellie, "don't be a beast."

Agnes growled then hightailed it to the house.

Papa raised his arms to help Jessa down; it reminded her of being a tiny girl, of her father carrying her in when she'd fallen asleep in the wagon after a long day at church. So close to him she worried he'd notice her thickening waist. "I got it, Papa. It's easier if I do it this way." She climbed down with her back to him. As she stretched to reach the ground, her sore spots flared like new kicks. Red sidled up next to her. Looked up and held her gaze, as if he sensed some kind of trouble.

"Go on," Mama said to the dog, shushing him away. "I'll fix up some bark tea."

No greetings or sweet words, but Jessa felt her mother's love acutely as she watched her shuffle to the cabin, her back as small as a child's. Both her mother and their home seemed to have shrunk even more since she'd been home last. If she was sent away and couldn't come back for years and years, she wondered if this place would disappear altogether. The Shinnery, with its go-forever shin oak roots, taking the homestead back.

When Mama was halfway to the door, she turned around. "Pardon my manners, Mrs. Posey. You'll come in. Some coffee and stew."

It wasn't really a question, but Mrs. Posey answered as if it had been. "I'd be most grateful."

A cedar bough decorated the door, tied with one of Nellie's favorite ribbons. Crossing the threshold Jessa felt like she was bringing a Christmas curse. After a few questions about how she'd fallen, the family did not appear to think on it again. Except Nellie. Nellie watched, nervous as a cat in a room full of rocking chairs, but she did not confront her sister, and Jessa would give her no opening. Jessa drank the tea, had a bite to eat, and excused herself to bed. She pretended to be asleep when her sisters came in, but Nellie knew better. Nellie lay beside her and took Jessa's hand. She hadn't put in her braid yet, so her golden hair spilled across Jessa's pillow.

"You didn't fall, did you?" Nellie whispered.

Jessa opened her eyes but didn't answer. One word would be too many.

"Are you home for good?"

Jessa didn't know how to answer that one either.

"I'm glad if you are," said Nellie. "I've sore missed you. Maybe you'll be here for my birthday. Only fourteen days."

"Then you take your exam?"

"Exactly. Just think, by spring, I could be a schoolmistress."

It made Jessa shudder to even consider what her own life could be like come spring.

•••

The next morning, Jessa explained to her father that the Martins no longer had need of her services. Papa lifted an eyebrow, so Jessa felt compelled to elaborate. "Mrs. Martin called me clumsy when I fell down the stairs. I think it was the last straw. I'm sorry, Papa." Jessa hoped he wouldn't want to humiliate her further by pressing for details. She prayed, too, that the Martins would keep tight lipped, wanting to avoid having anything to do with Jessa.

This turned out to be the case. For three weeks, while Jessa lay low at home, Papa made trips to town with nary a word about the Martins. She was grateful for the cold weather and the layers of clothing it afforded, grateful for the hard work that made sleep come in spite of worry. Christmas was celebrated with food and a three-day visit from Minta and her family. Solon and Maggie brought Grover Scott—the "beanpole suitor," as her sisters had teased. An interesting fellow, he knew a lot about horses and a little about dry farming on the plains of Texas. Instead of reading a Bible verse on Christmas Eve—"Unto you a child is born"—he recited a poem about grass and bees and giving thanks. Nellie and Agnes had to stifle their mirth, but Jessa admired his earnestness. The holidays concluded with Nellie's birthday dinner, which marked the new year. Jessa felt like she'd play-acted her way through the whole thing. For brief moments she'd get caught up in activities or conversations and forget, but then the truth would hit her like a bitter wind.

•••

December turned into January, the days grew short and cold, and the water troughs froze overnight. Though Jessa dreaded cold weather, it aided in her concealment. She was careful to turn away from Nellie as she slept, explaining she'd hurt her hip in her "fall" in town and had to sleep on her side.

By February the fluttering feeling Jessa thought she'd felt presented itself as a sure thing. She snuck outside to the barn with a needle and thread and relocated the top two buttons of her skirt, buying herself some time. Luckily, she wasn't a tiny thing like Nellie, who wouldn't have anywhere to hide a pregnancy. Jessa's height and sturdy frame gave her more cover. But she knew eventually her body would give her away. Every day she'd tell herself: this is the day you tell Papa. "If you're ever in trouble," he had said. She wondered if he'd had a sense then, months ago, of the things that could go wrong for a girl. Surely not his girl. The bloody sheet, the dirty bed, the men. Everything she worked to push out of her mind. The only way to get up in the morning, move through the day, was to misdirect her own thinking. She had trusted the wrong man. She was with child. Those were the truths she would tell, both to herself and to her father. But how? How would she begin?

After an hour of walking the border of the Shinnery in the cold March morning, her nose running, her cheeks burning pink, she'd found the will to tell him.

She entered the barn with purpose, two hounds following. Papa was working on the mule's feet, trimming his hoof. "Papa," she said. The next word stuck in her throat, like a boiled egg.

"Hand me that file," he said.

She did. He moved the rasp up and down, up and down. She couldn't swallow. Papa finished and untied the mule.

"Go to it," he said, patting Beck on the rear. Without the mule nothing stood between father and daughter. "You all right?"

"Fine," she said, and regretted it. How could they ever talk about the Big Thing if she kept saying "fine"?

Papa put the file back into the wooden chest his father had made. They'd hauled it from Tennessee by wagon, carrying Mother's few tea things and the family's Bible, in which all the family's names were written on the day of their birth. Would her child be listed there? Her older sisters' names now had their husbands' names written beside them, their children's names tucked below them, like baby chicks. If a child was born outside the covenant of marriage, could that child go in the Book? The thought crossed her mind that maybe she and the baby would be erased altogether, a tiny strip of cloth pasted over her name like they did with significant mistakes.

"I'm not fine," she blurted out.

"What is it?" he said, his eyes soft but wary.

"I'm with child, Papa."

He looked at her in confusion, as if he couldn't quite place her. "What?"

She'd said it clearly. If she tried to add to it, she'd just start bawling, so she merely repeated the part she could get out. "With child."

"Jesus God," he said. "Who's the father?"

"Will Keyes." When Papa didn't seem to recognize the name, she added, "The piano player."

Papa's face drained of color, his eyes wide and uncomprehending. She hated herself, what she was doing to him.

"The one whose brother was kilt? The salooner?" he said.

"Yes, sir."

"How?" He held his calloused hands out to his daughter as if she could fill them with answers.

From there to here, how, how, how? The most basic question, yet she couldn't answer it.

He covered his face with his hands. "God Almighty."

Shame pulled on her like a wet skirt.

"So why isn't he here?"

"He won't have me."

"What?"

"That's what he said."

"By God, he will marry you."

"I tried, Papa." Jessa fought her urge to cry. "Mrs. Martin tried too."

"The Martins know about this?"

"Yes," she said. Jessa didn't think his pallor could go any whiter, but it did. She feared his heart might seize. "And Mrs. Posey."

This time, his face turned red. Jessa had disgraced him.

"Of all people," he said.

Jessa wanted to assure him that Mrs. Posey—of all people—understood her plight, would be discreet, but she didn't want to break Mrs. Posey's confidence. "I needed help after . . . after . . ." She didn't know how much more to say. She felt no relief in the telling, because she was leaving the worst parts out. This part, the beating, he seemed to grasp without her saying it.

"So you didn't fall," he said.

"No, sir, I didn't fall."

"God damn!" he said. "God damn, damn, damn!"

She had never, ever heard her father curse like this, even when he was among the roughest of ranch hands. He was damning God. Jessa's stomach lurched. Then she knew she had to tell the worst. Otherwise, he'd hear it from someone else, and they might not tell it right. They might make it sound like she was willing.

"I haven't said the worst of it."

He looked like a feather could have toppled him, but she plowed on and told him about the men in the back of the saloon. How she'd been coerced.

Silence filled the barn after she finished. It felt like being held underwater; here they were, caught in an eddy, unable to breathe, held in the swirl, while the world waited silently above them. Then boom! Papa turned from her and kicked a tin pail. It flew toward the hounds, who yelped and scattered. Then he grabbed the thing closest to him, a saddle on a peg, and hurled it, making a guttural sound. Jessa had never seen him act like this, wild-eyed and out of control. Even when he'd shot the goat, he'd never outwardly lost control. He grabbed the rake. *Will he swing it at me?* Instead, he turned to the corn crib. Splinters flew until the tines caught in the soft wood. When he tried to pull the rake out, the board came with it. He flung the rake then leaned against the damaged crib, head in his hands. Jessa took a step toward him, but he held his palm up. She knew to stay back. Animals told when they'd had enough: the horse with the set of his head, the cat with the twitch of her tail, the dog by baring his teeth. She moved a few steps away. When she sank to the ground, Red sidled up to her, but she didn't touch the dog. She didn't deserve the comfort. The fact that her father hadn't immediately sent her away filled her with hope. Perhaps he'd speak to Will and they'd marry. Then Will would light a shuck for god-knows-where, and that would be the end. But just as soon as she allowed herself to think she'd be all right, her father spoke.

"Go!" he said, his blue eyes as bright as wet stones. "Go." His shoulders shook, and he cried like he had cried when Newt died.

Go? He was sending her away? First Will, then the Martins, and now her father, her protector. Where would she go? If her own father wouldn't allow her to stay, what were the chances that one of her sisters would take her in? Or Grandmother Campbell; surely she would refuse Jessa if Father did. What did a girl do in this situation? She had no earthly idea.

She stood, dazed, and made her way to the house, go, go, go echoing in her head. As she came into the house, Nellie called to her: "Help me with the potatoes." Jessa pretended she didn't hear her and went straight to the bedroom. She pulled the valise out from under the bed and began to pack. Let her father explain. She couldn't bear to say it again. She was a loathsome creature. She might infect her sisters, like mange going through a herd. Better not to say goodbye. The thought of never seeing them again brought her to her knees. She laid her head on the bed and sobbed into the quilt as soundlessly as she could. Bam! The sound of the front door slamming, a sign Agnes had come inside. She wiped her face with her sleeve.

She shoved two pairs of drawers into her valise, along with her best skirt and waist from the missus. She was already wearing her warmest coat and a scarf, which she tied snugly around her head. She reckoned she could reach Rayner before supper if she walked quickly, and she prayed Mrs. Posey would welcome her again. Tiptoeing, she crossed the front room without alerting her sisters and mother in the kitchen. The last scent of home was the smell of boiling cabbage, usually something she disliked. Now, the familiar scent was as dear to her as one of her mother's roses.

Jessa concentrated on the horizon, one foot after the other. One hand dug deep into her pocket against the chill while the other gripped the valise. The low clouds in the distance were a deep smoke gray, and the air was slightly moist. Everything felt unreal to her. She had lost her father's love. The cold bit her throat. She wondered if she would ever feel truly warm, truly safe, again. She walked on.

At Tonk Creek cows were clumped together for warmth. Soon, they'd have calves and would circle up for protection, babies to the inside. Though she didn't exactly love her baby yet, she felt what every animal felt, an instinct to protect it. Behind her Jessa heard a horse trotting in the distance and fear shot through her. The roads were sparsely traveled, and she wondered, a moment too late, if she should try to hide.

"Jess!" her father called.

She turned. His hand was raised as if signaling to her in a large crowd. Had she forgotten something? Was he bringing provisions for her exile? Surely, he wasn't giving her the mule he had tethered to the horse. Unless he wanted her to go farther away than she could on foot.

Papa came off his horse before Dan had even come to a complete stop. His mouth was set in a tight, straight line, eyes on hers. For a moment she wondered if he was set to finish what Mr. Martin had started. He'd never struck her before, but he was coming toward her with great intensity. He swung his arms and she flinched for a second before realizing they were open to her, an invitation, an act of grace. Jessa threw herself into his embrace. They both wept, for all that was lost, and all that was held in this moment.

"Why'd you leave?" he asked, his breath warm in her ear.

"You told me to go."

"From *the barn*," he said.

Jessa sobbed again, something like a laugh riding beside it. Stupid girl, she thought.

Stupid, stupid girl.

"A man can't hear news like that and take it in unless he's got some time to himself. Couldn't have you standin' there watching me blubber. A man—a father—is supposed to know what to do, Jess, and I . . . I needed to think on it. Needed to pray on it." He took a half step back. "How can you think I'd turn you out? You think your mama or your sisters'd let me do such a thing? You're my child, and you've been sore wronged."

I have, she thought. I have. Her teeth started chattering, whether from cold or relief she wasn't sure. Papa ran his hands up and down her arms to warm her. That's when Jessa noticed his sidearm.

"Are you going somewhere?" she asked. The sidearm made her nervous.

"To town."

Papa never wore a sidearm into Rayner. He tucked his Colt into a saddlebag, a coat pocket, or under a blanket on the wagon seat. Why did he need it now? "What are you going to do?" she asked.

"Talk to him."

Papa had said Will would marry her. Did he mean to enforce it? Would Will heel to her father's command? The gun made her nervous. It looked strange on him. Strapped to his side, the pistol made him look unbalanced, unnatural. Unlike other men her father never seemed to enjoy talk centered on guns or war. The old men from church liked to jaw about Union companies they'd evaded or battalions they'd struck down, but Papa never joined in. "It was a bloodbath," he'd once said, "and a miracle of the Lord that I came home. No glory in killing men." Her father was a man of peace. She knew this to be true. No cause for worry, she told herself.

"Take Beck home," he said.

Jessa lifted her skirt and stepped into the stirrup, swinging her right leg over the mule. Papa secured her valise. "Does Mama know?"

"Yes, and the girls. Mama told 'em some part."

Jessa couldn't imagine looking Mama in the face again. She took up the reins, though no one ever had to urge Beck home. Papa mounted his horse, and when she looked over to him, she noticed what she'd missed before, a rifle scabbard tied to his saddle. In it, the Winchester. That chill feeling came again. Her teeth danced in her mouth. She wanted to say to her father, Will's grieving something awful. Warn him of the precariousness of things. But she knew her father wouldn't much care about Will's grief. And what did she know about it anyway? Everything she'd thought had turned out wrong. She was exhausted and longed to return home, climb into bed, her sisters and her mother now in the full know.

"Tell your mama not to wait up on me," her father said.

24

Papa didn't come home. Not that evening, and not when the hands of the clock shifted into the next day. Not when the sky began lightening and the cows were milked. Not when the sun rose enough that it made long shadows of the barn. Not when the women ate their breakfast in a tightly wound silence, listening, like the hounds, for the sound of approaching horses.

Papa's absence loomed larger than his presence. Every clink of a spoon and scrape of a knife across day-old bread was amplified. The clock had never been louder. *Tick, tick.* Even Agnes knew to keep her tongue. Mama had prepared cooked oats, including a bowl for Papa, as if such an act might summon him. After a time Mama got up from the table and picked up the untouched serving. She held it over the tin pail they used to collect scraps for the animals, but instead of scraping Papa's breakfast into the bucket, she paused. Her daughters watched her.

Jessa had never known her mother to be indecisive, yet Mama hovered, spoon in hand.

"May I?" said Nellie.

Mama obliged, handing Nellie the bowl. Then she headed outside without a word, the back door smacking loudly into the frame.

Mama had embraced Jessa when she'd come in the night before, an odd sort of embrace. Mama was so tiny, and so obviously rattled, that when they hugged, Jessa felt she was comforting her mother. Nellie and Agnes knew about Jessa's condition and the reason for Papa's trip to Rayner, yet neither said a word. Agnes's only acknowledgment was a series of searching glances, as if trying to gather evidence of Jessa's new state. Even now, at the table, Agnes stared openly at Jessa, mouth slightly agape, silent as a trout.

"Stop it," Nellie said finally.

"Stop what?" said Agnes.

"Looking at Jessa like she's grown another head."

"That's all right," said Jessa.

"No, it's not," said Nellie. "The whole world's gonna look at you like that. Least we can do here is not gawk."

"I wasn't," said Agnes.

"She's the same sister."

But I am not the same, thought Jessa.

"Ladies have babies all the time," said Nellie.

"She ain't got a husband," said Agnes. "How d'ya have a baby without a husband?"

Nellie's face went flush. "It happens."

Agnes looked genuinely distressed. Her world no longer made sense. Jessa understood why her little sister was staring. "We were promised, Agnes. He—Will Keyes—well, he was gonna be my husband. He may still be if . . . if . . . There's a lotta ifs."

"You want him to?" Agnes said.

"I'd best be married if I can."

"Because of the baby," she said.

"Yes, because of the baby."

"Can I see it?" said Agnes.

"No," said Nellie, aghast at the idea.

Jessa had shown no one her changing body. At almost five months along, it fascinated her, like watching the peaches grow from blossom to small, hard green fruit to ripe, yellow, fuzzy splendor. Her body was producing a fruit. She pictured it as something forming around a stone. Something, someone. Jessa glanced out the window to make sure Mama wasn't about to come in. When assured she wasn't, Jessa pulled up her blouse and lowered her skirt, her flesh on display. Agnes hopped out of her chair and immediately placed her hands on her sister's swollen belly.

Nellie looked on in controlled horror. "Stop that," she said.

"What?" Jessa and Agnes uttered at the same time.

Nellie balled her fists at her sides. "Fix yourself this minute." She motioned to Jessa's clothing.

Jessa would not. Agnes wrapped her arms around Jessa as if to protect her from Nellie. "You can at least *act* like a lady," Nellie said. "If only you had . . ."

There, thought Jessa, the thing Nellie wanted to say. Say it. "If only I had what?"

"Everything!" Nellie said, in a girl's bubbling fury, her face bright and hot. She went out, door banging behind her, just like Mama.

"Jessa, is there a way you can give the baby back?" Agnes's arms were still wrapped around her, so Jessa couldn't see her face.

"No, lamb, only God can undo a baby."

"Like when God took Newt?"

"Yes."

"Nellie won't like it, but I will. I'll help you take care of it. Even if it's a boy."

"Thank you, Agnes," she said. They stayed in the embrace for a long time, Jessa's blouse askew and skirt falling down, the oats growing cold, and time flowing as slowly as molasses.

•••

By night mother was pacing. No one cooked supper. They ate salt pork and some pickled summer cukes. Nellie had gone over to Maggie and Solon's place to see if they'd heard anything about Papa. She didn't want to be the one to share what had happened, the reason Papa had left in a hurry, but Maggie sensed something was up and Nellie ended up telling her and Solon everything she knew. At least that's what Jessa deduced, seeing her sisters walk in together, eyes swollen and red.

"Solon's gone into town," Maggie said. "He'll straighten this out, Mama. Let's get the chores done."

Agnes didn't move.

"I'll fetch the eggs," said Nellie, leaving.

"They should all be home by nightfall," said Maggie.

"Don't seem like it," said Agnes.

"Hush." Maggie looked over at Mama, who seemed to be somewhere else. "You don't know."

"I know plenty," Agnes said. "Jessa's got a baby growing, and God won't take it back."

"Enough," said Maggie. She was trying to keep from crying, but a tear or two escaped. She wiped them as fast as they fell. Jessa wondered if Maggie's tears were partly over the injustice of Jessa's pregnancy.

She wondered if she was supposed to give her baby to her sister and brother-in-law, like Mrs. Posey had, though she wasn't sure they'd want a bastard. Then she chided herself for such dark thoughts. Maybe her father had prevailed, and the delay was in rounding up a preacher. Maybe they were on their way back now, her child would have a proper name, and her family could wear theirs without shame.

25

Mama's hand flew to her mouth. Maggie collapsed into Solon's arms and Nellie sobbed. Jessa was too shocked to move. Will was dead. Papa was locked up. She didn't know which of the horrors to settle on, so she bounced between them. *Will. Papa. Will. Papa.* She grabbed the back of the chair to steady herself.

"Did you know?" said Solon, looking straight at Jessa.

"Know what?" she said. *Father shot Will. Father shot Will. Dead. Shot him dead.* Solon had said it; they'd all heard it. Yet it didn't sit with her. Not as a true thing.

"What was gonna happen," he said.

How could she? Her father was not a violent man. The guns though. He had the guns. What did she think those were for? Should she have followed him into town?

"Jessa!" Solon said sharply.

"Solon," said Maggie, "she's in shock."

"We're all in shock," he said. "I'm trying to figure this thing out."

Jessa thought of Will's lifeless body. Where did it lie? Unbidden, her mind's eye recalled how beautiful he'd looked that night they lay together.

"You should of come to me," said Solon.

No, she thought. Papa had wanted it handled as quietly and as quickly as possible, the circle not widening beyond their home until the thing was done. "He'll marry you, by God," he'd said. The guns were there to see it done. How had it gone from that to a body on the ground?

Nellie was taking deep hiccuping breaths. Mama looked so old suddenly, her face like a raisin.

Solon turned to Mama, took her hands in his. "We're gonna get him a solicitor, but we need money."

"There's a tin near the firebox. Twenty-one dollars in it," Mama said.

"That's a start. Jessa?" he said.

"Four," she said.

"All those months and you've only got four dollars saved?" said Maggie. "How is that?" Jessa looked down at her empty hands. A pathetic result of her labors.

Nellie said, "I bet she gave it to him."

"Who?" said Maggie.

"Will Keyes. She gave him everything," said Nellie.

Mama spoke, just above a whisper. "It don't serve to fight."

"She's a liar." Nellie practically spat the words.

"Nell," said Jessa. She could tell by the set of Nellie's jaw that no amends would bridge the rift between them in the moment. Her sister was as bitter as raw dandelion. Jessa hadn't considered the full implications of what her actions might cost her sisters. She had been closer to Nellie than anyone else in the world, but their bond had turned to ash. She was grateful Agnes was asleep in the other room; she couldn't stand to lose the easy love of Agnes too.

"I can think of half a dozen families I can go to for funds first thing in the morning," said Solon.

Solon let go of Mama's hands, and Maggie moved in with an encouraging arm around her shoulders. "Papa knows everyone in Stonewall County, and most of Haskell and Shackleford—"

"No!" Nellie interrupted. "You can't tell everyone."

"Nellie," Solon said gently, "there's no stopping that. Ya'll should know that Mr. Harder, the one that runs the newspaper, he was on scene before the body was even . . ." Solon stopped, glancing at Jessa. "He was there. It practically happened outside his office. It'll be on the front page of the *Lasso* tomorrow. Harder says every paper within a hundred miles will cover it, and the rest of Texas will republish those stories."

Nellie was beside herself. "It can't be."

J. R. Campbell. Jessa pictured Papa's name printed on all those papers, all those eyes taking in what had been so personal, so secret. The Martins reading it aloud in the parlor. It made her head spin.

"What did John Reese say?" asked Mama.

Mama hardly ever used Papa's Christian name; it unnerved Jessa for some reason to hear her call him "John Reese," like everything familiar had vanished.

"His main concern is you and the girls," said Solon.

"Is he hurt?"

"No, ma'am."

"I don't understand what happened in town," said Mama.

"I don't either," he said. "Deputy Hicks rightly told your husband to hold his tongue until he met with an attorney. What I do know is that there were eyewitnesses to the shooting itself. Apparently, what J.R. said to those assembled was he'd shot Keyes on account of the man's ruin of his daughter."

Shot. On account. His daughter. Will had been the ruin of her. She had been the ruin of him.

"Wait," said Nellie, eyes wide. "*That* part will be in the paper?"

"They won't mention Jessa by name," said Solon.

"That's worse, don't you see? They might think it's another daughter then." Nellie's breathing went shallow, her voice slid an octave higher. "They might think it's me."

"Harder knows to be discreet. The *Lasso's* a family paper."

"But is he privy to the nature of Jessa's . . . condition?" said Nellie.

"I suspect everyone in Rayner's privy to it by now, Nell."

"We have to go," she said. "Leave." She moved about the room like a trapped squirrel, all action, no purpose.

Mama made no move to calm her, so Maggie stepped in. "Nellie, sweetheart, Mama's only got twenty-one dollars, and Papa needs every penny. Besides, you passed your teacher's exam. You'll be gone soon enough."

"But until then, we can go to Grandmother's in Albany."

"And who would run the place?" said Jessa. The ranch, the orchards, this was what kept them alive. She couldn't imagine the Campbells anywhere else in the world but here, on their hundred and sixty acres of rough prairie. Jessa saw it as the proof, and perhaps the source, of their strength. *Where else in the world would this baby be welcome?*

"The Shinnery can overtake this place for all I care, let it eat up the fields and pull the house down." Nellie practically spat the words.

Mama stood. "You stop that. I mean it, not another word."

"Then what?" said Nellie. "We just stay here?"

"Yes," said Mama. She pulled her spine straight, and though shorter than her second-to-youngest daughter, she managed to give the appearance of looking down at her. "That is exactly what we will do."

Jessa felt momentary relief. Mama had spoken as if she were in charge, as if she could see a path through. Jessa wished she were little and could crawl up in her mother's lap. She tried to call up a memory of it but could not. She could remember Papa carrying her, and her older sisters, but not Mama. She was not yet two when Nellie was born; perhaps that was why.

Mama took a seat at the table. "I would like some whisky now," she said.

Maggie gave a nervous laugh. Nellie looked on in disbelief. The girls had never known Mama to imbibe. Ever.

"There's a jar under there," said Mama, pointing to the basin. "Wrapped in burlap. It's your father's. I'd like a nip."

"Yes, ma'am." Solon knelt under the basin and pulled out the jar, something the girls had seen but thought was one of Mama's stinky remedies. Maggie set a glass down in front of Mama and poured it as if it were lemonade.

"Whoa," said Solon.

Watching Maggie pour, Jessa knew her sister had never had whisky. Mama took a big sip. Then another. She shuddered slightly.

"Medicine," Mama said. "If any of you are to sleep tonight, you'll do well to take a sip."

"Whisky, Mother?! You want us to drink whisky?" said Nellie. "If Papa were home—"

"But he's not," said Jessa. She took a drink, the promise of reprieve.

Nellie watched Jessa drink. "You're going to hell in a handbasket."

Mama said, "Go on to bed, Nell." And she did.

Maggie took the whisky glass and tilted it back into her mouth like Jessa had done, only instead of a smooth swallow, she choked and sputtered as soon as the alcohol hit her throat. Solon put a hand on her back as she collected herself. "Guess that's why they call it fire water," she said, her eyes going liquid. She managed a little smile.

Solon took a hearty gulp and returned the glass to Mama, who drank again. "What happens next?"

"I don't reckon I know exactly. That's why we gotta get him a good attorney."

"But he already owned to the killing," said Maggie.

Killing. Jessa still couldn't absorb the words they were speaking. *Jail, trial, killing.* They spoke as if this were a situation with which they were all well versed.

"A deed done with good reason, with cause," said Solon. "A jury will understand that a man has to protect his own. They're gonna see Keyes as the wolf he was."

A wolf, thought Jessa. I lay with a wolf. What does that mean for the child I'm carrying? Please, be a girl, she prayed. A boy might be mistaken for the father, marked in a way a girl might be able to escape.

"That's what will happen." Mama stared off, talking to no one in particular.

"What?" Maggie's face was already flush from the drink.

"My John will come home to me, just like he did from Greensboro, worse for the wear maybe, but returned. Mark my words, girls, your father's coming home."

Morning spilled across the bedroom. Solon would arrive in less than two hours to take Jessa to town to meet with Papa's lawyer. She couldn't think of anything she'd like to do less. She fished around for the woolen socks she'd kicked off in the night and spotted one on the floor. When she threw her feet over the side of the bed, she noticed that dust had painted every surface. The boards had been laid when Jessa was just learning to walk. When the family first arrived, they'd lived in a dugout with a dirt floor carved into the earth, its chimney rising from the ground like a tree stump. According to Papa, Mama had swept it at least a dozen times a day. "You like your dirt clean, don't you, Mollie?" he'd still tease. Now, they used the dugout for storage and as a summer kitchen, rendering fat for soap and canning and pickling. As the house continued to settle, dirt kept rising between the floorboards. Mama seemed to have lost her appetite for sweeping—and for order in general. Unwashed bowls were left for the girls. The eggs Mama collected got stranded on the porch, the slop bucket showed up in the hen house, and the whisky jar went empty. If Papa were sent away for years, the dirt might overtake the floor; the great sands might swallow the house.

The bulk of the care of the livestock—feeding, watering, checking on the cows and first spring calves—was falling to Jessa. The buds of the shin oaks had broken the last week of March. She'd had to move the cows out of the pastures that bordered the shinnery to keep them from eating berries that were toxic to the cattle for a few weeks each year. Solon had sent Grover over to help. She'd noticed how light Grover was on the rein, using his legs to signal to his horse what needed to be done. Seemed a lifetime ago she'd met him at that picnic. He was still a beanpole, but he looked more rugged than when he'd first come to the Shinnery. They worked efficiently together, ensuring the Campbells wouldn't lose any livestock to the berries. A lot of ranchers destroyed their shinneries for this reason, but Papa had taught Jessa better. Without the expanse of the low-growing thicket of shin oak, the sandy plateau it occupied would eventually collapse and blow away. They'd lose all the tall grass that took root in the shinnery—big bluestem, switchgrass, and drop seed—food for many creatures, from cattle to cottontails. The thicket's fall acorns fed the hogs, and the deer and pronghorn—and, before they were driven out, the Comanches. It also provided shelter to prairie chickens, turkeys, bobwhites, and quail. All that Jessa loved about her home was held by the roots of the shinnery, roots said to go on for miles. Its budding was a danger, but only if you didn't take care. To eliminate the danger was to lose the vitality of the place.

Jessa reached under the covers, searching for her other sock. Agnes was her bedmate now, splayed across the bed like something spilled. Nellie had moved to Mama's bed. She'd made a big fuss about having to take care of "dear Mother," but Jessa knew she'd moved out to spite her. Nellie had passed the teacher's exam, and she had put in for a position in Colby, Kansas. Jessa hoped there'd be some semblance of reconciliation before her sister left. She thought a lot about the night they'd learned Papa wouldn't be coming home, how when Jessa finally made it to bed, Nellie was waiting.

"You lied to me," Nellie had said. "I knew you were with Will after that party. If you'd told the truth then, none of this would have happened."

Jessa was silent. Her sister had a right to be indignant.

"Now Solon says I can't even go to town. Not for the mail, not for anything. Not 'til this 'business' settles down. Business," Nellie repeated. "As if Papa is away arranging some cattle sale and not sitting in jail." A deep furrow appeared across Nellie's forehead. "And the thing is, you could have stopped it."

It hadn't felt like it at the time, Jessa thought; it had felt ordained. She'd raked over events a lot in the past month. How painfully naive she'd been to believe God Himself had guided her steps toward a piano player. She'd always been so sure of God on the Shinnery. She heard Him in the thunder and wind, the screech of the red-tailed hawk. Found His blessing in the sunshine and rainfall, in the spring grass and the night sky. But she saw now, how in moving to town, she'd reduced Him. A God she could fit in her apron pocket that concerned Himself with the matters of her heart—that told her to go this way or that, that cared one whit about her and Will Keyes. She'd gotten God wrong, it was clear to her now, and although prayer was a reflex, she vowed never to ask God for anything again. The only prayer worth the Almighty was thanks. This morning, socks on her feet, preparing to don her too-tight skirt and stiff shoes, she took a deep breath. She would have to get through this day, and the next, and the next, on her own power.

•••

Solon and Jessa walked side by side down the center path to the courthouse. The big stone planters were filled with dandelions and petunias, and something that looked like a lily that Jessa couldn't name. The courthouse looked forbidding to her now, like the building itself was waiting for an answer, an accounting. She told herself that was silly. Papa had made it clear to Solon he didn't want Jessa near the place during the trial. She was only coming to talk to the lawyer.

Mr. Stanhope met them in the hall. He had large brown eyes and a salt-and-pepper beard, neatly trimmed. His belly strained against a bright blue brocade vest. He didn't seem too much younger than Papa. They followed him into a room off the corridor. Although there were three chairs, Solon stood at the threshold. When Mr. Stanhope motioned to the door, he left.

The lawyer explained to Jessa that he served clients in the surrounding five counties but lived in Haskell, some twenty-five miles away. "But this being a 'high profile' case," he said, "Judge Hamner's allowed me the use of this office for the duration."

High profile? Jessa didn't like the sound of that.

The lawyer pored over some papers. "We're just waiting on a transcriptionist."

Jessa didn't know what a transcriptionist was, but it sounded vaguely medical. As she waited, she felt her baby stretching—at least that's what it had looked like the times she'd witnessed it, a hand or foot traveling across her belly, like the path of a prairie vole moving just under the surface. At six months along, she almost always felt the baby when she was still.

She looked down over the square through the room's big, tall window and was glad no one could see inside. Maybe today, after she confirmed her father's story, they'd let him come home. The judge had said no bail, but if she could bear out the facts, perhaps the judge would reconsider her father's release until trial. But what exactly were the facts? Her father had said Will would marry her, his aim in going to town—everyone knew the old jest of a shotgun as a persuader. That's what she knew.

The door burst open and in came Mrs. Posey. She nodded to Jessa in a formal way, making no indication of their friendship. Jessa was surprised to see her, but then she remembered one time Papa had needed something notarized and they'd gone to the post office to do it. Introductions were made and Mrs. Posey settled into a chair. As she scooted closer to the desk to arrange her papers and uncap her ink jar, her bosom practically rested on the table. Mr. Stanhope seemed distracted by it.

"Gotta get the date and time recorded," Mrs. Posey said. "Make sure it's all according to Hoyle."

Mr. Stanhope eagerly pulled out his watch. "Ten fifteen."

"Ain't that a fancy one!" she said of the timepiece.

"Harvard Law, Class of 1875."

"Land's sake! A Yankee lawyer," she said. "Might want to consider bringing in someone from south of the Mason-Dixon with you on this case."

"You are schooled in jurisprudence, Mrs. Posey?" said Mr. Stanhope, no longer gazing at her bosom.

"I'm schooled in Texas. The shooter is a father of five girls, and a thrice wounded Confederate. The seducer, a northerner by birth. A case of southern frontier justice, whether you intend it or not."

"I appreciate your opinion," he said, when clearly he did not. Jessa'd seen this when she had first come to Rayner to live with the Martins: townsfolk saying one thing when they meant another.

Mr. Stanhope gave Jessa a smile, though his eyes contradicted his lips. "For the record now, dear—name, age, and relationship to the defendant."

"Jessamine Campbell, seventeen, daughter," she said. Strange to be reduced to three small facts.

"Now state the nature of your relationship with Will Keyes, twenty years old, male, formerly residing in the city of Rayner, Stonewall County, Texas. Now deceased."

Deceased. She took in the word: *deceased.* Where had he been buried, she wondered. Who had come to mourn him? Probably not his mama, far off in Indiana with her bad husband.

"Miss Campbell?" said Mr. Stanhope. "Your relationship?"

She aimed for simple. "I loved Will Keyes. We were—we planned to marry. At least he led me to believe it."

"You met him in June, correct, when you moved to town, boarding with the Martin family?"

She nodded.

"You need to affirm it verbally," he instructed.

"Yes," she said. "June."

"And when exactly did he propose marriage?"

She shrugged.

"For the record," he repeated, less patiently.

She didn't know, for the record or not for the record. "I'm carrying his child, isn't that enough to know?"

"We need a timeline. When was the promise made? The date?"

"Umm . . . I can't say."

Mr. Banks sighed. "If we are to defend your father, we need to make the strongest case we can. And since your father cannot testify, you're going to have to—"

"What?" Jessa interrupted. "Solon said Papa doesn't want me to talk in court."

"That is correct. He does not," said Mr. Banks. "But we cannot have your father incriminate himself on the stand."

Mrs. Posey set down her pen and crossed her arms. "So you expect this child to save him?"

The lawyer appeared agitated with Mrs. Posey. "Do we need to call another scribe?"

"Good luck, darlin'," she said. "There ain't no one else in this two-bit town 'til next Wednesday, when the county's part-time secretary makes his bimonthly visit." She pushed her chair back from the desk.

"Let me explain something, Miss Campbell." He spoke slowly, deliberately. "You must convince the jury that Mr. Keyes obtained carnal knowledge of you *after* he made the solemn promise of marriage. And paint, for the jury, the picture of how, after breaking said vow, he threatened you with disgrace."

"Your plan then," interjected Mrs. Posey, "is for Campbell to enter a plea of innocent and remain silent, while you extract some salacious tale from his barely growed daughter in front of everyone?"

Stanhope stood up, as if he were actually in a court of law. "Without her testimony, Mr. Campbell is a villain. *With* her testimony, he's an avenging angel."

Mrs. Posey was not swayed. "She'll have to move to the Yukon when you're finished with her."

Her protest seemed to inspire him. He turned to Mrs. Posey theatrically, voice booming. "Without her testimony, he may never see his family again."

Now her voice boomed. "It's a manslaughter charge."

"Well, he's not a young man. *With* Miss Campbell's testimony, possible acquittal and a return home to take care of his daughter, this girl you so wish to protect—along with her bastard, I might add." Mr. Stanhope turned to Jessa. "Pardon the nomenclature, Miss Campbell."

Nomenclature? Villains and angels? Jessa's head was starting to spin. "May I please speak with Papa?" she said.

"No," the lawyer said. "The State *will* call you, Miss Campbell. I'm merely trying to prepare you for that. Now, continuing . . . your relationship with the deceased with dates, please."

"Well, we were sweethearts. Betrothed in August. The last Saturday, I think. Whatever that date was."

"Good. So, this was in secret?" he said.

"Yes. I know that wasn't right. That's why I'm telling you everything now." Jessa glanced over at Mrs. Posey on "everything," to indicate she was doing no such thing.

"Very good," said Mr. Stanhope. "So, you had—and excuse me for such indelicate questions—intimate relations with Will Keyes." The lawyer sounded out each syllable of "in-del-i-cate" and "in-ti-mate" like he was competing in an elocutionary contest.

"Yes, sir."

"As a result of this in-ti-mate relationship, you found yourself with child, is that correct?"

"Yes, sir."

"And how did Mr. Keyes react?"

Not my bastard, bastard, bastard. "He was . . . uh, caught off guard."

"Caught off guard?" he repeated. "Do you mean unhappy?"

"I suppose a little." Will was dead and could not dispute her. "We were gonna elope, but then his brother got kilt. Grief ate him. He was drinking. Papa went to talk to him, to help him, you know."

"So, it is your testimony that John Reese Campbell went to Rayner to help Mr. Keyes, not hunt him down."

"Yes, sir." Papa had been angry. He wasn't a killer, yet he had pulled the trigger. Was it in rage? In grief over Jessa's condition, like the grief that had turned violent against the unruly goat? Or did Papa do "what had to be done," a righteous act, as some were claiming, to maintain order on the front porch of the frontier by avenging the wrong done to him? Reading some of the headlines, her father was portrayed as the victim. Was that right?

"So, next . . ." Mr. Stanhope stared down at the papers on the table as he spoke. "Were there any other men with whom you were in-ti-mate, Miss Campbell?"

Where had that come from? She felt clammy. "No."

He looked up. "And you will testify to that under oath?"

Jessa clasped her hands together in her lap to steady them. "Yes, sir." Surely, no one would say otherwise. What could anyone hope to gain in testifying to such a thing but bald shame? Besides, she thought, those men had long since vanished. Strangers. Drifters. She'd never have to see them. They were as gone as Will. Gone as Levi. Ashes to ashes. Dust to dust.

What a fool-headed girl she'd been.

Haskell Free Press, JUNE 8, 1895

TRIAL UNDERWAY

The J.R. Campbell murder case . . . was taken up. The examination of witnesses occupied the time until Wednesday afternoon, including night sessions, when the attorneys began their addresses to the jury, the eight speeches being concluded about 3 p.m. Thursday.

27

The Campbells' church community immediately rose to Papa's aid; folks donated their precious hard-earned dollars to the cause of his defense. It was moving, everyone agreed, the way the community rallied to the cause of a righteous man, acting in the only way expected when a scoundrel violated the innocence of a daughter. "Protecting the sanctity of hearth and home," the editor of the *Lasso* had written, and Agnes haltingly read, until Mama asked her to put it away.

Two months after the shooting, the women of the family were headed to church, their first public outing—save Jessa's visit with the solicitor, Mama's to the Rayner jail, and Agnes's to school. The schoolhouse, where they worshipped, was not more than a half-hour's stroll, nothing between but cows, prairie chickens, and scrub brush. It felt good to be doing something regular, even without Papa there. Smatterings of wildflowers appeared in every direction: Blackfoot and chocolate daisies, white yarrow and Indian paintbrush in bright scarlet. The bee balm was just coming into bloom, yellowish, purple-spotted flowers on long spikes. Its leaves smelled like minty oregano—Mama used the leaves in teas for backaches and fever. Nellie held back a few steps behind them and didn't say much. Jessa hoped seeing friends again, after so many weeks, would cheer her sister.

The Wainscotts joined the path at one of the several crossroads. Normally, Mrs. Wainscott would stop so the families could catch up on the latest happenings as they walked. But they did not. When the youngest boy turned around and waved at Agnes, his mother yanked him forward. This gave Jessa a bad feeling about going to church. "Mama," she said, stopping. "I'm not feeling too good. Maybe I should . . ."

Mama didn't say anything but pulled Jessa's arm in the manner of Mrs. Wainscott with her little boy. Jessa looked back at Nellie, her face still, eyes wary. Agnes didn't seem to have registered the slight. She was hunting for verbena, picking tiny blooms of lavender. Agnes wore two braids; Jessa noticed her crooked part and how mismatched the braids were in size. She wondered who'd fixed her hair, who had paid so little attention. It could have been any one of them, the way they lived in their heads, wondering, wondering, wondering what was going to happen. Nellie was biding her time. She'd signed a contract to teach in Colby and was waiting on confirmation of her boarding; she hoped to leave by midsummer. Jessa hoped the distance would offer some space for, if not forgiveness, at least a thimble's worth of understanding. Let Nellie come face-to-face with a beautiful man, one who might touch her earlobe and call her pretty. Let Nellie's body betray her with a hunger for a thing she'd blush to name. Perhaps she'd know something then that she couldn't know now.

Agnes held up a miniature bouquet. "The flowers are for Mary," she said. Mary was her only doll, passed down through all the sisters, its cloth body stained, its plaster limbs and round face chipped. The girls had sewn clothes for it, but Agnes never seemed to keep them on. Jessa had seen the doll that morning in a ditch. Agnes had explained she was hiding it from Indian raiders.

When no one responded to Agnes—they were all focused on the Wainscotts ahead—Agnes repeated herself, adding, "Look."

Nellie responded with false cheerfulness. "How nice. Mary will like that."

"It's for her grave," said Agnes. "She got kilt."

No one said anything after that. The women trudged up the path, the schoolhouse in sight. When they arrived Mama said good morning to several worshippers, but none responded. Jessa reasoned that perhaps they hadn't heard Mother's quiet greeting, so she took a deep breath and loudly wished the Sinclair family a good morn. That wasn't returned either, though Mr. Sinclair nodded. When her family sat on one of the long benches against the wall, the Browns rose from it and crossed to the other side of the room. Again, without a word. She slid closer to Mama and noticed Nellie, on the other side, doing the same thing. A herd move, instinctively protective. Jessa hoped maybe she'd misread the situation.

Between hymns Jessa glanced around, searching for a friendly face among the forty or so people she'd known her whole life. Not Mrs. McGunigle, who'd tended Mama when she'd been so ill the previous year; nor Aunt Vida, the childless woman who'd taught the Campbell girls how to tat; nor even Ida Lynn Weber, Jessa's old school friend—none would return her gaze. So this is what it is to be shunned, she thought. She'd heard the term before but had never seen it in practice. No one had announced the shunning, of course. No vote taken. Brother Bielby led the morning's service as he'd done a hundred times. The hymns were the same, no emphasis on Sodom and Gomorrah, or Jezebel, or God's Almighty Wrath. In fact, the shunning was the opposite of hellfire. It came as a chill frost.

Not one person, during a full hour of worship, met her eye. While Papa's plight brought out sympathy, hers seemed to breed disgust. And what if they knew the whole story? Would they stone her? She glanced down the room's narrow aisle trying to figure out how she could leave unnoticed. Though no one was looking directly at her, she'd never felt more watched in her life. She knew who she was: a plain girl, hair braided and wrapped into a neat bun, wearing a hand-me-down woolen dress the color of smoke. They were looking for signs of another girl, one who had defiled herself with a piano player, a saloon girl perhaps in a silky dress, a comb of feathers in her hair. The girl they imagined.

Jessa felt tears threatening to well. She looked over to see if Nellie had registered the shutout, and sure enough, she had. Spine plumb straight, an imitation of a person concentrating on the most important service ever, but Nellie's red neck gave her away. Jessa knew that under her light blue calico, her chest was covered in patches of red, and soon it'd extend to her cheeks as well. The color of shame.

Mama's face wasn't red, but leached of color, as if she'd given all her blush to Nellie. Mama's head was down and would remain so until the benediction.

Once they were down the steps, Agnes grabbed Mama's hand and started jawing about a frog some boy had smuggled into worship. She described its color and general attributes in mind-numbing detail. Unlike most of the times Agnes had recounted such things, this time all three women were absorbed, grateful to learn of the frog's warts, its bum leg, its slick skin and its possible extra toe. When Agnes ran out of things to say about the frog, Nellie asked what its name might be, prompting the young girl to make suggestions for each letter of the alphabet. After listing a dozen or so prospective names, Agnes got bored and ran ahead, hunting for rabbits. The women walked the rest of the way home in silence, wiping the occasional unremarked tear.

Approaching the main entrance to their property, Jessa could see the small wagon Mrs. Posey had been regularly borrowing from the livery. The dogs surrounded her as if she had cargo just for them.

"Miz Posey!" said Agnes, skipping toward the wagon.

"Don't go askin' after anything, Agnes Mae," said Mama.

The postmistress had been coming out to their place once a week, bringing mail and a variety of newspaper articles involving Papa's arrest and impending trial, sometimes clippings and sometimes whole pages. Mama never picked them up. Agnes read them aloud to her, while Nellie went off by herself to read them.

Mrs. Posey was patting each hound on the head when Agnes flew up. "Can I help you, Miz Posey?"

"Sure you can," she said, pulling parcels from the wagon. She gave Agnes a couple to carry.

Once they were all in the kitchen, Mrs. Posey explained that she'd brought a few extra supplies. "Folks are always giving me stuff. How much sugar can one person use?" she said, making sure Mama didn't feel like she was bringing alms for the poor.

"Awful kind of you," said Mama. "I have butter and cream you can take with you."

"Happy to share. Happy to take." Mrs. Posey did look happy, Jessa thought. Genuinely pleased to be in their company.

Since Mrs. Posey had brought her home and watched out for her at the solicitor's office, Jessa had come to regard her as an earthly angel. Jessa would never tell her that though. Mrs. Posey, with her big bosom, slightly wrinkled clothes, tainted past, and too-loud laugh, wouldn't think it possible. "Land sakes, child, that's a tall one," she might say.

Nellie quickly unwrapped the items Mrs. Posey had brought and folded them into the family's existing stores, as if to erase the charity. At one time pride might have made Mama beg off accepting such gifts, but after the morning's shunning, Mrs. Posey's kindness was something to be especially treasured.

"We can have sugar in our coffee now, Mama," said Agnes.

They'd used the last of the sugar two days earlier. Jessa was eager to have a cup too.

"Miz Posey, you'll join us?" Mama put the pot on the stove. "I've got biscuits and gravy."

"Miz Posey brought molasses. Can I have that on a biscuit?" Agnes asked, already helping herself.

"Is there mail?" Nellie asked.

"Of course," said Mrs. Posey, pulling mail from her bag.

Papa's letters always said the same thing: faring all right; hope you are well; may God keep you; please write. Jessa couldn't muster the will to answer those shallow missives. Her father felt a stranger to her now. She remembered that last time on the road, the way he'd embraced her so fiercely. She'd felt held in the palm of God's hand. But had he looked out for her? It felt blasphemous to think such thoughts, but she sometimes did. The papers said Papa had gunned Will down in front of the saloon, barely a word exchanged. Had he even tried for that paper, a name for the baby?

Mrs. Posey handed Mama three envelopes. Mama looked at all three and handed one to Nellie.

"From the Thomas County School Commission." Nellie's face lit up like Jessa hadn't seen it do in weeks. Holding the envelope, she looked as she had at seven, giddy over ribbons or candy. Jessa's heart ached over how she missed this sister, and she hoped good news might restore them to one another.

"Thought this would never come," Nellie said. It had been a month since the offer had been made and she'd sent in her official certificate proving she'd passed the teacher's exam.

Jessa smiled. "About time something good happened."

At this, Nellie's face took on a more neutral expression, as if trying to act grown up, but her hands shook as she opened the envelope.

"What's it say?" said Agnes. "You going to Kansas?"

Nellie read the letter, eyes scanning the lines, back and forth, back and forth.

"Are you?" said Agnes.

"No." Nellie's eyes filled with tears. "I'm not going anywhere. None of us are." Nellie ripped the paper in half, and in half again. She turned and faced Jessa, thrusting the scraps of paper into her sister's face. "You stole everything from me!"

Jessa felt slapped. Worse than what had happened in church. A stranger's disapproval ran cold, but this was hot. Nellie's hate a living, irreconcilable thing. She regretted that Mrs. Posey had to witness it. But just as she thought that, Mrs. Posey offered her a hug. Her open arms were inviting; Jessa wanted to be wrapped in them, feel the weight of Mrs. Posey's thick, soft hands on her back, lay her head on her warm, ample bosom, experience a smothering kind of love. She hesitated though, looked to her mother at the table, small as a child, hands folded in her lap, watching. She wondered why Mama wasn't offering such comfort. Was it out of loyalty to Nellie? Or did she carry a kind of bitterness toward Jessa too? Jessa didn't move. She wouldn't take from Mrs. Posey what her own mother clearly didn't think she needed or deserved.

Mrs. Posey's arms dropped, and she smoothed the front of her skirt with her hands, as if that had been her intention all along.

"She'll be a teacher somewhere else," said Agnes. "Kansas ain't nothing but sod-busters and mush-heads anyway."

"Ain't that the truth," said Mrs. Posey.

"Please read the school letter, Agnes," said Mama.

Mrs. Posey helped Agnes lay the torn pieces on the table.

Agnes began. "Dear Miss Campbell, we regret to inform you that we must res . . . res . . ."

Mrs. Posey leaned in to help Agnes. "Rescind."

"Re-send our previous offer of a teaching position. The words of the esteemed educator Horace Mann best explain our position: 'The school committee are sent . . .' Sent-nells?"

"Sentinels," said Mrs. Posey.

"'Sent-tin-nills stationed at the door of every schoolhouse to see that no teacher crosses its threshold who is not clothed, from the crown of his head to the sole of his foot, in virtue.' Huh?" Agnes took a breath. "Recent events . . ." Agnes bit her bottom lip and turned to her mother. "I don't want to read it anymore."

Jessa felt bad for her littlest sister, only nine years old and shouldering grave responsibilities.

Mrs. Posey took up the letter. "Recent events in Stonewall County give us great pause. As the adage goes, one bad apple spoils the others. One must not show quarter to sin or sinners. Though you, Miss Campbell, may be a model of upright living, we cannot take that risk with our most innocent citizenry, namely our children. Sincerely . . . nonsense, nonsense, stuff and nonsense."

"What's that mean?" said Agnes.

"It means I don't want to give those spineless weasels the credit of their own names," said Mrs. Posey.

Mama took out her handkerchief and blew her nose.

"Mama, I'm sorry," said Jessa. Mama didn't acknowledge Jessa's apology, and she felt stupid for offering it. Like spit on a barn fire, it did nothing.

"Nobody write a word of this to Papa," Mama said. "It'll only pain him." With that, she left the kitchen, though not in the same direction as Nellie. It wasn't in Mama to comfort anyone.

Mrs. Posey went to the stove for the coffeepot and filled three cups. Agnes stirred in five big spoonfuls of sugar, but no one said a thing.

"I feel like I'm pulling the house down on everybody's head," said Jessa.

"I know, darlin'. You just gotta weather it is all."

"Nonsense, stuff and nonsense," said Agnes quietly, looking out the window.

"Nonsense, you sugar fly." Mrs. Posey playfully reached over to tickle Agnes, who laughed. A high, light sound the house hadn't heard in weeks. Agnes must have registered it too, how long it had been, because in an instant she was sobbing. Mrs. Posey pulled Agnes into her lap and rocked her until she caught her breath.

I haven't just pulled the house down, thought Jessa, I've set it afire.

After Papa's supporters flooded Rayner's courthouse during his arraignment, the district attorney requested the trial be moved to more neutral Haskell County. Although Papa's attorney, Mr. Stanhope, fought it, the move was granted. Soon after, Stanhope added a Texan to the defense team, just as Mrs. Posey had advised.

With Papa's move to Haskell, twenty-five miles away, visiting him was an ordeal. He'd been there two weeks, and this was the first time Mama would be calling. Solon had taken her that morning. They'd have to sleep over at the boarding house, an expense not easily covered. Mama had left Jessa in charge of her sisters and the place, though in truth Mama had relegated the running of the place to Jessa the day they'd learned of Papa's arrest.

By evening Jessa was in the kitchen scraping bits of egg into the slop bucket and washing up. She struggled to get everything done. The weeds were overtaking the peach orchard. The window for cotton planting was closing. The floor needed mopping. And Agnes required attention. Nellie's bad-news letter seemed to have struck Agnes almost as severely as Nellie. She'd stopped making up silly songs and chattering about the animals; her doll, Mary, sat untouched. But by nightfall Jessa's bones cried for rest, and she couldn't minister to anyone.

Nellie had fixed the eggs for supper, though she didn't seem to eat any. As Jessa gained weight Nellie seemed to lose it. She had a look of desiccation to her, reminding Jessa of a dead bird, dried flat with raisin eyes. Jessa wondered if her sister could be sick, but when on occasion she'd tried to bring it up, Nellie had shut her down with a terse "I'm fine." Mama didn't seem to notice Nellie's changes, but she never inquired over Jessa's health either. Never a "How are you feeling?" or "How's that baby faring?" Thank goodness for Mrs. Posey, who asked both those questions every time she visited. Mrs. Posey was the only one Jessa didn't wish to apologize to for her bulging figure.

Drying the plates, Jessa wondered where her parents spent their visit in Haskell. She pictured them both behind bars, but that didn't seem right. Jessa couldn't believe that in two short weeks she'd have to testify. She hated speaking in front of people about anything, but to speak about Will and the baby . . . She wiped the dutch oven Mama had used to make biscuits that morning. Mama had wanted to take Papa a fried chicken dinner, but they'd been low on fryers. They'd had to sell some birds—a second lawyer didn't come any cheaper than the first—and none of the spring batches of chicks were big enough for eating yet. Mama made do with an old laying hen, slow cooking it in broth until the meat fell off the bone. That, along with the onions and carrots, would hopefully mask the age of the hen.

Jessa heard Red scratching at the kitchen door. Since Mama wasn't home, and Nellie didn't seem to care about anything, Jessa let him in. He followed her toward the bedroom. Nellie was still staying in Mama's room. Under the door was a slip of light. "Good night," she said. Her sister did not respond. The dog plopped down on the floor of the bedroom. When Jessa was sure Agnes was asleep, she pulled up her nightdress and ran her hands along her stretched belly. Her time was nearing, maybe six weeks, maybe seven. Every night when she settled down, the baby seemed to wake, kicking and turning, shifting into her like an animal rooting in straw.

JUNE 1895

Two weeks later, at daybreak, Solon came for Jessa and Mama. Nellie followed them outside, carrying Mama's satchel. Agnes, still asleep. The air was still, wisps of fog over the Shinnery, birds beginning their day. In addition to peeping finch and the buzzing, chirping dickcissels, Jessa could make out the trill of the Cassin's sparrow, always ending with those two isolated notes, as if the bird had more to express but not the song to do so.

The three travelers climbed into the buckboard, Mama in the middle, with little more than a word or two exchanged. Even the mule seemed reluctant, requiring several slaps of the reins to get him going. As they headed out, Grover Scott headed in. He'd be helping on the place while they were gone. Hopefully no more than a few days.

Grover said, "Morning."

Jessa could see he wanted to say more, but what would suffice? "Have a good trial"? Her life was a vexation to so many people. Words tangled; eyes averted. But she'd be on display in Haskell, permission to gawk. Strangers with no sense of personal embarrassment regarding her condition.

As the trio started down the lane, Jessa looked back at Nellie, standing alone. Neither girl waved nor smiled, but they held one another's gaze. Perhaps when the trial was over, and their father came home, they could rebuild what was broken between them. When she could no longer make out her sister's features, Jessa faced forward. Her back ached, and she wondered how she'd fare over the long day. The baby was active now, and she was afraid it'd start moving in a way that her mother, sitting beside her, would notice. She adjusted the thick wool lap robe high over her bulging middle then felt a tickling pull, a foot or an elbow traveling underneath and across her flesh.

Soon she'd meet this creature inside her. How soon she wasn't sure. A month? She wondered if the baby would look like Will, would have his dimples. She still couldn't quite believe he was under the ground, a box of bones. Mrs. Posey said his people had ordered him a stone with a rosebud carved on it, and some words too, but Mrs. Posey couldn't recall what they were. His grave was next to Levi's. She would see it for herself one day, no matter what anyone said. Not to mourn him, but to mark his passing.

For a moment the thought crept up that the trial might uncover

Levi's story too, the way she'd pretended to conspire with him to steal the jewelry and tipped off the mister, who had eagerly formed the posse who'd shot him. *Shot down.* Two brothers, same ending. It always came back to this: Will had been her undoing, but she had been his as well. From this point of view, she was the danger. She breathed through her nostrils, a long breath. Levi had been in the ground since December. No one was poking around about his death. The trial would unfold as she'd practiced with the lawyer: *Falsely promised. Seduced. Abandoned. Ruined.*

The sun was high in the sky when they reached the Double Mountain Fork of the Brazos. The river flowed between red sandy banks, splitting off around gleaming sandbars—a braided river. Jessa longed to wade into the river, minnows and shiners dashing around her ankles. The baby was pressing on her insides in a way that made her need to relieve herself more often, but since she didn't want to impose on Solon, she hadn't mentioned her discomfort. Seeing the water flow brought a new urgency. She clenched her teeth and sort of jiggled her thighs so as not to wet herself. Mama must have picked up on Jessa's misery, because she said, "I'm needing to stop for a bit."

Solon directed his mule to a stand of cottonwoods. Jessa practically leaped out of the wagon before it rolled to a complete stop.

Behind her she heard Solon chuckle, the first time she'd heard a family member acknowledge her condition in anything but solemn tones. His reaction, small though it was, gave Jessa a thimble's worth of hope that perhaps all could be well in time. In the last week Mama had directed Solon to get the cradle down from where they'd stored it, high up in the barn. Mama then rubbed it with linseed oil, and she sewed a fresh bed sleeve, stuffing it with wool and finely chopped straw. Jessa wondered if the act of preparing the cradle was her mother's language of love or simply a matter of practicality, crossing a chore off the list.

As Jessa climbed back into the wagon, she heard wild turkeys boggling on their roost in the elm and hackberry grove just down the river a pace. Solon heard it too.

"We'll nab a few on the way back, huh?" he said. "Celebration supper?"

A couple of hours past the river, the prairie flats were covered in nee-dle grass, acres and acres of grass. In the distance a stand of giant mes-quite trees; the largest were twenty feet tall and forty feet wide. They'd been killed in a prairie fire; only their skeletons remained.

Haskell's only boarding house sat in the middle of the block on the main square. Two stories tall, it sparkled newness. The floor in their nar-row room shone; the scent of cut wood and lacquer permeated it. From their single window Jessa and her mother could see the courthouse, the jail, and half of the town, all built around the square. The courthouse was constructed of thick blocks of gray granite. Two stories high, the second taller than the first, giving it the appearance of being top heavy. Jessa thought it grand, but in a way Mama might deem flashy or "put-ting on airs." A clock tower marked the time.

Jessa had never traveled anywhere with just her mother, and she was worried about how it would be to share the small bed. To change into her nightdress, Jessa used the water closet down the hall. Though Jessa was at least eight months pregnant, her mother had never directly mentioned the baby. In the small room the baby felt as big as a water-melon, and its weight pulled at Jessa's lower back. Her mother patted the bed, and Jessa gratefully lay down. Mama sat in the stiff chair near the window and watched the clock.

•••

They'd been in session all day. Like a dog whose hackles shoot up in alarm, everything in Jessa went cold and prickly when the red-headed man took the stand. He was from the post office. He was from the saloon. He was from the room at the back of the saloon.

"Do you solemnly swear . . ."

Her teeth started chattering, her lower jaw rapidly clacking against the upper. *Clack, clack, clack, clack.* Her mother was beside her but didn't react to the chattering.

"I swear," he said.

What is he doing here? What can he possibly have to say?

"You are here, Mr. Kelly," said the prosecuting attorney, "to help us establish the nature of the relationship between the deceased and the defendant's daughter . . ."

Noooooooooooooo. Jessa felt ambushed. Better to have her ankle caught in an iron trap than to sit here. *Clack, clack, clack, clack,* those teeth. She felt as if they could snap off. Defendant's daughter, defendant's daughter. All parties had agreed to leave her name off the court records, even the news-papermen, eager for a story. She was "the defendant's daughter," but here, in this courtroom, she felt no protection—even stripped of her name.

"The defense has posited that they were sweethearts. Mr. Campbell went to town to collect his future son-in-law, no premeditation of killing."

Jessa was sitting behind Papa and his attorneys, but none would turn to look her way. She still hadn't been allowed to meet with Papa face-to-face, and this morning she'd been excluded from what the lawyers called opening statements, as Mr. Stanhope wanted her entrance to be as "stirring as possible." He'd also asked her to take her hair down from its bun. Mr. Aames, the Texas attorney, handed her a new blue ribbon. "Here, darlin'. Try somethin' more . . . girlish," he'd said. With his curly blond locks and two-toned boots, Mr. Aames looked better suited for a Buffalo Bill Cody traveling show than a courtroom.

The prosecuting attorney's voice boomed across the chamber. The red-headed man kept his eyes on him, like a dog waiting for his mas-ter's signal. "Sweethearts," the prosecutor continued, "implying monog-amy, fidelity—"

"Objection!" said Mr. Stanhope.

Yes, thought Jessa, I object to it all. Her breathing was shallow, going shallower.

"Sustained," said Judge Leggett. "Stick to the facts, Mr. Clark."

No. Stick to the story, please, she prayed. *Please let them stick to the story.*

"State for the record how you personally became acquainted with the defendant's daughter."

She was gasping for air. It wouldn't do to make a scene. But air! She tried to take in a deep breath, but her lungs stuttered. Mama took her hand.

"*Shhhhhhhhhh,*" Mama said soothingly, "*shhhhh.*"

"I need you to state for the record how you became personally acquainted with the defendant's daughter."

Personally acquainted. *Clack, clack, clack, clack,* Jessa's teeth marched in place. Was she dying?

Everything got quiet.

"As a prostitute," said the red-headed man.

Noise erupted like a flash flood. Cries and hollers and objections barreled through the courtroom. Jessa heard chairs scraping and skirts rustling, someone crying, and banging. *Bang, bang,* it sounded like a gunshot. She buried her face in her mother's skirts, sobbing audibly. *Bang, bang,* again. The judge's gavel. She wished for it to strike her. Bullet. Gavel. Flood. She longed to go down. *Bang, bang.* Sink under the earth. *Grant me a headstone with a single carved rosebud.*

Somehow, Jessa found herself in her father's arms. He'd reached over the low wooden rail dividing the courtroom and pulled her to him. She could feel all eyes on her but couldn't stop sobbing. The pale blue ribbon lay at her feet.

"Mr. Campbell!" Mr. Stanhope shouted. "You cannot touch the witness!"

Papa held tight. "You don't like it, tell the bailiff to arrest me."

Jessa could still hear the crowd, loud murmurs, a word here and there. Then the gavel banged again, twice. The judge said something about recess. For a fleeting moment Jessa thought maybe the trial was over and they could all go home.

"Bailiff," said Aames. "Get us a room. *Apurate!*"

As soon as the door shut, Papa spoke sharply, "Did you know about this? This witness?"

"No," said Mr. Stanhope indignantly.

"I heard a rumor," said Mr. Aames. "Hopie here thought the DA was above it."

Mr. Stanhope said, "Those brothers were scoundrels, and your daughter was—before encountering them anyway—an innocent. Never did I think the prosecutor would sink so low, move so far away from the pursuit of justice—"

"Enough," interrupted Aames. "Save it for our closing."

"No closing," said Papa. "I'm changing my plea to guilty. End of trial."

Jessa felt a flood of relief, but the attorneys would have none of it: "Mr. Campbell . . ." "Now, wait a minute . . ." "Hold on . . ." Then Mama spoke up, a small voice from behind the circle of men. They seemed surprised, but they opened the circle to include her, as if commanded.

"The cow's outta the gate, John. You have to fight to come home."

"Now, Mollie . . ." He moved to pat her arm, but Mama shooed him off.

"I've made things out to be easier at home than they actually are. I didn't want to trouble you." Mama's voice was as soft as a girl's. The room leaned in to hear her.

"What do you mean?" Papa said.

"Solon can't run two farms, it's mostly on Jessa and the girls and I . . . well, even with help from some of the neighbors—and not as many as you think—it's not enough. The peaches are in trouble. We sold most of the hogs. And I can't imagine how we'll get the cotton we somehow managed to plant harvested."

Papa's face went a little red. Mr. Aames looked up at the ceiling; Stanhope, down at his shoes.

"What about Jessa?" Papa said.

The room hushed. Mama said, "Will you excuse us?" The attorneys nodded and stepped outside into the hallway.

"John Reese, hear me: the damage has been done," said Mama. "That word. It's been said."

Prostitute hung in the air. Papa rubbed his face with his hand.

"If we don't let her try and explain, it'll be worse. They'll only have that awful man saying that awful word about her." Mama took hold of Papa's arm. "Keep to your plea and let her tell it. The jury will see how she was seduced, and threatened, and abused. They will see the true heart of our daughter."

Love flooded Jessa's heart. It was the most she had ever heard her mother speak about private matters of any kind, and she found the tenderness she craved there in her mother's soft words and pleading eyes.

29

The prosecuting attorney wasn't done with the red-headed man, but before he could resume his testimony, Judge Leggett spoke to the assembled crowd. "There will be no more outbursts such as what occurred in my courtroom earlier, do you understand?"

Jessa was grateful he didn't single her out but looked over the entire room. "At this time," he continued, "I'd like to encourage the more delicate of our citizenry, namely you ladies, to excuse yourselves. Otherwise, be silent." No one made a move to leave.

If only Jessa could excuse herself and run the twenty-five miles back home. She'd prefer bloody feet to what was coming, but Papa's attorneys said the jury needed to be able to watch her as she listened to the testimony. "If you feel tears coming, Miss Campbell," said Mr. Stanhope, "do not attempt to contain them." His voice lacked warmth or pity, as if hearing the word "prostitute" had set him against her as well.

The prosecutor stood. "So, Mr. Kelly, it is your testimony that the defendant's daughter is a sportin' woman in a bawdy house?"

The room sucked in its breath. No words spoken, save, "Objection!" Mr. Aames was on his feet. "Your honor, I think I speak for the entire community when I state that Rayner has no bawdy house." Some in the gallery started to clap, but a stern look from the judge stifled them. Jessa had never heard the term, but she was sure she hadn't been in one.

"Overruled."

"The defense posits the defendant's daughter was an innocent, a maiden coming into Rayner. Based on this, can we assume that you forced this 'maiden' to have relations with you?"

"Forced?" The witness seemed taken aback. "No, sir."

"Did you hit her?"

The red-headed man crossed his arms. "No, sir."

"Threatened her then?"

"No," he said defensively.

Jessa felt her anger rising. This awful man could never have coerced her. Nothing in the wide world he could have said or done would have made her lie with him. It was for love. For love, she was duped. For love, battered.

"Then how did you possibly get this young, unsullied girl to . . ." At this, the prosecutor cleared his throat. "Enter into carnal relations."

"I just got in line."

Again, an audible intake of breath from the gallery. Jessa's breath adding to it.

"A line, you say?"

Jessa felt her guts squeeze. She'd been drunk that night, had never considered what was happening on the other side of the door. Mama shifted on the bench. The prosecutor shook his head.

The prosecutor continued. "Mr. Kelly, what happens when it is 'your turn'?"

"I just come into the room, and she's lying there like it's nuthin'."

Like it's nuthin'. Nuthin'. That's what she'd aimed for. A nothingness. A disappearing. They'd only required a body, and that's what she'd given them. But she could see how now, in the courtroom, it read as indifference.

"She didn't cry out for help? Attempt to fight you off in any way?"

Jessa pressed her fingers into her eye sockets. She could see flashes of color in the black. "Nope. She took a swig of whisky and then . . ." The red-headed man let his words trail off.

"And then, Mr. Kelly?"

"Then she spread her legs."

The gallery wheezed. Jessa lifted her head. Some people were standing to leave, and others were standing to accommodate their leaving, an explosion of shuffling feet and "excuse me's" as they left the long wooden benches. The disruption rankled the judge, who used his gavel to call the courtroom back to order.

"Objection, your honor," said Mr. Aames. "Relevancy. She's not the one on trial."

What he said was only true by the letter of the law.

•••

After the day's testimony, Jessa, Mama, and the attorneys gathered in the small room again.

"You're not on trial," Aames explained. "In attacking you, they're trying to turn the jury against your pa. They want to erode public sympathy by making you out to be a harlot."

An idea came to Jessa, a way, perhaps, to cast doubt on the prosecution's version of her. It made her feel all hollow inside to think about it, like she was leaving her body again. She swallowed, then leaned over to speak softly into Mr. Aames's ear; easier to tell one person than the whole room. The attorney pulled back in surprise.

"Hot damn," he said, shaking his head. "And you know exactly where it is?"

"I don't think anybody would have moved it," she said.

"I'll have to let the judge know. See if he'll authorize someone to go to Rayner to collect it. Chain of evidence and all. Has to be done by the book. Prosecution won't rest 'til at least day after tomorrow. Plenty of time for retrieval."

The object of her greatest loathing was to be aired in court. On her invitation.

•••

Three days after the red-headed man's testimony, Jessa was on the witness stand for the defense.

"The night that Mr. Kelly talked about, at the saloon, Will made me believe that I was the only thing between his life and his death," Jessa testified. "It pained him to ask, or so it seemed, like it took as much from him as from me." She glanced at the twelve men who made up the jury. Many leaned forward in their chairs.

"The Galveston boys were going to kill him, you said?"

"If'n they didn't get their money. That's what I believed. I'm not sure now what was true."

"Why didn't you give Mr. Keyes the money you'd earned at the Martins'?"

"I did." The worst part about the witness stand was that she could see her father at the edge of her vision, even when she tried not to. "I gave him everything I had."

"Including your 'innocence'?"

"Yes, sir."

"The prosecution suggested that you were already a promiscuous girl when you went to Rayner, experienced in such ways."

"No, sir. I was a virgin when I met Will Keyes." The word seemed to unsettle the room as much as "prostitute" had. People shifted in their seats, cleared their throats.

Mr. Aames walked over to the defense table and picked up a parcel wrapped in brown paper. The jury watched closely as he unwrapped a folded white cloth. "Your honor, I have what has been marked for identification purposes as Defense Exhibit C. May the record reflect that I am showing counsel what has been marked."

Mr. Aames took the object to the prosecutors' table. After some murmuring and nodding and more formal words between him and the judge, he addressed Jessa. "I am now showing you what has been marked as Defense Exhibit C; do you recognize it?"

Too well. "I do. It covered the bed in the back of the saloon when—" She wanted to get this exactly right. All her muscles tensed, knowing in seconds everyone would see her ugliness. "When Will Keyes stole my virginity."

Mr. Aames unfurled the bedsheet and revealed the large rust-colored stain.

"That there's my blood."

The crowd erupted. A woman cried out, followed by a chorus of deep male rumblings. "No decency" was the only phrase Jessa could make out.

Even the jury appeared offended, looking away, coughing into handkerchiefs, turning to one another. Papa turned around, probably to make sure Mama was all right.

"I move Defense Exhibit C into evidence." Aames folded the bedsheet back up but did not put it down. "Mr. Kelly testified that it seemed like 'nothing' for you to lie with a stranger. Is that true?"

"No. It was . . ." Jessa's face crumpled, her chin quivered, and her eyes stung. "I . . . I don't have . . . I don't have the words. I know it's all about the words here, the testimonies. But I can't say how terrible. I was sold, Mr. Aames. Sold by the one I loved. It took something from me I'll never get back."

"By the 'one you loved,' you mean Will Keyes, the man who took your virginity under the solemn promise of marriage?"

"A broken promise."

"When did you know this to be the case?"

"The night I saw the sheet again." Mr. Aames held the sheet slightly aloft. She remembered how shocked she'd been to see it again in Will's hands. How confused, and the way her heart twisted when the confusion lifted. He'd saved it with purpose. She'd felt pushed off a cliff, arms and legs flailing in the empty air. "Will kept it hidden in the dresser. His brother Levi knew about it. Mighta been the one with the idea." She'd blamed almost everything on Levi back then, blindly excusing Will. "They said they'd bring it to my father, hang it in the town square, tell everybody what I'd done."

"Unless?"

"Unless I did it again."

"Prostituted yourself?"

"Yes." A tear rolled down her cheek. This is what the jury, the town, her father, her mother, and anyone reading the papers needed to understand. She'd been set up from the beginning, tricked, coerced. Her father was only trying to right a grave wrong.

"So you did?"

"No, I did not. I knew what Will was about by then. I fought like a hellcat and got away." Her voice got a little shaky. She would tell only what she had to. The witnesses were dead. No need to bring up how she fought and lost, how the only thing that got her out of the saloon was promising the Keyes brothers Mr. Martin's money.

•••

Maggie, Solon, and Mrs. Posey joined Jessa and her mother for closing arguments. She'd survived cross-examination; it'd been less brutal than having to listen to the red-headed man's testimony. Mr. Stanhope had explained that it didn't work in the prosecution's favor to directly attack a young, very pregnant girl.

After the defense rested the judge asked for final arguments. The word "final" set Jessa's teeth on edge.

The prosecution delivered its closing first. Jessa was relieved the Martins hadn't needed to testify. Mr. Martin had submitted a letter on behalf of the defense, testifying to their financial arrangement; he had also spoken of her character as being "decorous." Jessa's beating went unmentioned. According to Mrs. Posey he'd fled to St. Louis after Mrs. Martin, who'd decamped there with the children after Will had been shot. The romance of the frontier had worn clean off.

Mr. Aames, with his golden locks and southern drawl, was elected to deliver the closing. He wore a suit much like the other attorneys', only underneath his coat, he wore a vest of leather. It served as a nod to the assembled that this was not Boston or New York—or even St. Louis—lest anyone forget. He started off by listing Papa's credentials, facts known and shared throughout the trial: churchgoer, war veteran, civic leader, father of five daughters. Their case had been built on the idea that J. R. Campbell should not be penalized for killing a man who'd "crawled into the confidence of his family circle and debauched one of its innocent members."

Mr. Aames seemed at home in the courtroom, striding about in front of the jury box like a flashy colt. "As a general principle, we do not believe any human power has the right to deprive a man of his life, but there is one way in which a man may sacrifice his right to live, and that is when he defiles a pure young girl whom he has made to love him." He then recounted J. R. Campbell's steps the day of the killing.

Papa did not testify, so no one could attest directly to what, if any, words were spoken between the two men. Jessa tried to picture it: the dusty road, the wood-sided saloon, its single front window covered in a heavy shade, a wagon maybe, horses, men standing outside the mill-works across the way, the leaves on the pup trees moving slightly in the breeze, a bird calling, and Papa, lifting his shotgun, the bullet flying, Will turning away and then falling. Who would she have run to in that moment, the bleeding boy or the old man?

Mr. Aames came right up to the jury box, taking time to look into each juror's eyes. "Rather than be humiliated by wearing the stripes of the state prison, the father who kills without mercy the seducer of his daughter should be the recipient of civic honors. Great God, is his humiliation not sufficient without further punishment?"

His humiliation. It always came back to that, the way her father had been wronged.

"Amen," Jessa heard Maggie whisper from two seats away.

As soon as the jurors filed out, Mr. Stanhope turned to Mama. "A splendid closing," he said, as if speaking about a particularly good meal. Behind him Papa was escorted out of the courtroom by the bailiff.

"They're gonna find him innocent," Maggie said. "They have to."

They didn't have to, thought Jessa, and she wouldn't bother God about it either.

•••

The air felt charged like before a lightning storm. Jessa surveyed her family. Solon's knee was bouncing. Maggie chewed her cuticle. Mama, beside her, was as rigid as a carcass. Jessa held still, but inside the baby fidgeted. The bailiff cleared his throat before speaking.

"The jury finds the defendant guilty."

Murmurs rose from the crowd like the sounds of lowing cattle, distress without direction.

"Much obliged, gentlemen," the judge said. "The jury is hereby excused. Court is adjourned." He banged the gavel.

Adjourned? Wait, Jessa thought, *wait! I'll tell it again. I'll tell it better.*

Mama made not a sound but looked as if she'd been punched in the gut, slightly bent over and clutching her middle. Could bad news actually kill a person? Maggie moved in to care for Mama.

Mrs. Posey muttered, "No, sir, no sir."

Mr. Aames clasped Papa on the back. Men from the gallery approached. In the din of the room, she couldn't tell what was being said. To the devil with protocol. Jessa leaned over the rail. "Papa," she called. "Papa." He appeared bewildered, like he'd gotten on the wrong horse. Two reporters shouted questions as he was led away. Jessa felt a queer sensation. Had she leaned too far over the low rail? She felt a deep pull, like with her monthlies.

Jessa turned back to her family. Mrs. Posey had an arm around Mama's waist. Maggie's head lay on Solon's chest. Jessa felt as alone as if she were out on the vast prairie. Even in the midst of this worst thing, watching Solon and Maggie, she couldn't help but remember how it felt, in those first days, to be held by Will. To feel answered by a body. This was the one extravagant thing about her, she'd discovered. She'd held nothing back in love. Arms flung open, her heart proffered, again and again.

Haskell Free Press, JUNE 22, 1895

A PETITION: TO THE HONORABLE BOARD
OF PARDONS FOR THE STATE OF TEXAS:
THE CASE OF THE STATE OF TEXAS VS.
J.R. CAMPBELL

The jury would have been proud of an opportunity to acquit defendant but . . . [we] were compelled to follow the hard, cold mandates of the law . . . We do sincerely feel he ought to have his liberty, not only that in his old age he may remain as a protection to his wife and daughters and help them to bear the burden of the dishonor and disgrace . . . but too, that his discharge may serve as an example and rebuke to seducers and adulterers as well as all other enemies of female virtue . . .

30

Jessa struggled to push the infant out. Her water had broken on the trip home, over thirty hours ago. Above her now, the faces of Mama and Maggie radiated worry. Mrs. Krauss, who was serving as the midwife, seemed anxious. Jessa felt on the threshold of something, her feet planted in two different worlds, her thoughts lucid then dreamlike, the baby not yet born but no longer safely contained either. She heard the midwife tell Mama things were "stalled." Jessa thought of the ropes Papa would pull down from the rusted peg in the barn when a calf was breach or suffering some other impediment. How she felt a little sick when she saw them, the old bloodstains visible on the once-white lengths. Papa would tie a rope to whatever beam or limb was available and pull on the calf with each contraction. Sometimes, Jessa had to hold the rope while Papa used his hands to pull a shoulder or a neck. A brutal sight, but Papa always maintained a kind of gentleness, even when pulling with all his might. Where was he now? she wondered. Was he in the barn? No, that wasn't right. The ropes seemed to dance in front of her. She reached out to shoo them away, but instead caught Maggie's arm, sleeved in white cotton.

"You don't want the cloth?" Maggie asked.

"Go ahead with it," said Mama.

Jessa didn't know what they were talking about until something cool and damp was laid across her forehead. Another contraction moved through her. If she didn't know better, she would swear someone was sawing her in half. She didn't push this time. Just lay there and endured it.

She thought of the many animals she'd seen give birth, that glazed look in their eyes, as if a part of them were somewhere else. She allowed herself to drift off.

When the contraction ended, Mrs. Krauss spoke. "Too long. Time to move, Jessa."

Krauss, with her German accent, pronounced Jessa's name with a Y. It brought to mind little Gabriel Martin, and for a moment, Jessa felt a shot of panic thinking he was still her responsibility, only she'd lost him. "Gabe?" she said.

"*Ja*, the babe is coming. Can you turn?"

Jessa had changed positions a number of times to no avail. Maybe she'd take a nap, try birthing another time. She closed her eyes. She could hear water, the Brazos, feel the cool water trickle across her body. She was lying in the shallows, the sun on her face. Then someone stepped in front of the sun and was trying to pull her from the water. She could feel someone slapping her face, her eyes opening and closing, the lids so heavy. Let me rest, she thought but didn't have the energy to say.

"What's wrong?" she heard a voice say. "What's wrong with her?" The voice sounded alarmed. Whatever was happening was happening far, far away and didn't concern her. She felt a rocking motion. Perhaps she was on a boat.

"Smelling salts!" ordered the midwife. "*Jetzt!*"

Whoa! All at once, Jessa felt like she was inhaling a hundred piercing needles up her nose. The salts triggered a fierce intake of breath and delivered her back to the room where she labored.

Nellie was sitting next to her on the bed with a small blue jar of salts. They hadn't been this close to one another in months. When they'd come home without Papa, Nellie had continued to punish Jessa by barely speaking to her. "Pass the butter" and "Did you feed the hens?" had been the extent of their conversations. But this Nellie beside her said, "Oh, Jess, you scared me. Don't you dare die."

"And don't *you* talk of death," the midwife barked, swiping the salts out of Nellie's hand.

"I'm sorry." Nellie turned to Jessa, her voice low. "You can't leave me with it undone, you hear?"

It felt good to have her sister's warm breath in her ear, even though Jessa found herself only half-listening. "I'm sorry," she thought she heard Nellie say.

Maggie spoke next. "Give her some room," or something like that. Then Mama moved in. She brushed the hair off Jessa's forehead and grabbed a fistful of it in her hand. "Wake up," said Mama. She pulled on Jessa's hair as she spoke, twisting it. "C'mon, girl." The burning tingle pulled Jessa into her body and into the moment. "Ooow," she said.

"That's better," said Mama.

Maggie hovered in her sight. "You're so close to the end. Right, Mama? Tell her."

"Feel its head." Mrs. Krauss directed Jessa's hand to the place where the baby was emerging. She could feel its wet head and her own taut, slippery skin.

"*Gut*," said the midwife.

Jessa had seen enough animal births to know that bodies stretched open, but still, hard in the moment to believe hers would do the same. She pulled her hand away and saw blood. The scent of it made her afeared. "Is that still the bloody show?"

"Well past that," said the midwife. The midwife held Jessa's chin firmly in her hand. She made sure Jessa was looking into her pale blue eyes as she spoke. "No good for a baby stuck so long. You keep pushing, *liebchen*."

Jessa had been pushing for what seemed like days but must have been hours. Three or four by her foggy recollection.

"Drink some tea," Nellie said. "You're gonna be all right, Jess."

Jessa took the cooled cup of wild cherry bark. Mama had made a big jar of it, said it would speed delivery. She drank it down in one gulp. "More," she said. Nellie refilled the glass, but the midwife took it for herself instead.

"We'll see. That stays down, you can have more." The room was overheated. The women flushed and damp, hair sprung from their pins.

"Let's get her on her feet," said Mama.

"No, no," said Mrs. Krauss.

Mama laid a couple of worn quilts on the floor. "She needs to squat."

"This what your people do?" asked Mrs. Krauss.

Mama did not respond to the comment about "her people," but in the silence Jessa could sense the rebuke.

"Come on," said Mama, urging Jessa up.

"In a little bit." Jessa felt too tired to rise.

"Up, up," said Mrs. Krauss, now under Mama's direction. Mama and Maggie helped Jessa down off the bed and supported her as she moved into a squat. Her back had been aching something fierce. This position relieved some of the pain. But at the moment she recognized one kind of relief, another contraction hit.

"Push, push, push. *Gut* girl!" said Mrs. Krauss.

The contraction ended, and so did the intense burning. There were just seconds between the contractions now, or at least it felt that way.

"Almost," said the midwife, and the scene repeated.

The contraction gripped Jessa, but instead of resisting, folding into herself like a snail into its shell, she thought of herself opening: all the pain from the inside working toward opening, the baby's emerging head pushing her open, and the midwife's hands spreading her open. Open, open, open, it sounded like a song in Jessa's head, and she pushed with all her might.

"Yes, yes," the midwife said. "Baby coming."

The burning was like giving birth to fire and then, when she thought she couldn't take it another moment, everything shifted. She had opened; her baby's head was almost out. In another push, its head and shoulders were through. After that, the rest of the baby slid out, as slippery as a fish. The midwife caught the baby, and within seconds it cried, the bleating of a tiny lamb.

"It's a girl," said Mrs. Krauss, holding her up. The baby looked so tiny and hairless and vulnerable dangling from the midwife's large hands. "*Gut* job everyone." Jessa's sisters helped her back down onto the bed.

"We'll get her cleaned up," said Mama. As the midwife held the baby, Mama dipped a clean cloth in water and began to wipe her down.

Maggie hovered, eager to assist. "Here's a flannel," she said.

Mrs. Krauss had been with Maggie through two of her births. "Get this babe swaddled. I'll see to your sister."

Jessa wanted to hold her daughter, but Maggie's eyes were going misty over her. It would serve no one to rush her. Maggie cradled the infant and hummed a tune Jessa couldn't make out. Again, she wondered if she should give the baby to Maggie and Solon. "Take her," she could say. Just two words. It was wrong they didn't have a baby and, by the world's measure, wrong that she did. Jessa longed to be that generous, but she was not.

"A perfect baby girl," Maggie said. Nellie stood next to her, cooing at her niece.

The midwife was using warm water to clean Jessa up when, all of a sudden, she felt gripped by another contraction. The afterbirth. An easy push. The midwife caught it and wrapped it in one of the bloody rags.

"I want it," said Jessa.

"She needs the salts again," said Nellie.

"I don't need the salts. I want to plant it with a sapling for the baby."

"Eeeew," said Nellie.

"That an Indian thing?" said the midwife.

"Excuse me?" Mama said. The room went quiet. In spite of Mama's Cherokee features, "Indian" was not a term to be bandied about, and this was the second time the midwife had referred to Mama's heritage. Even though Mrs. Krauss and her family had immigrated in the last ten years, Mama was the one who was regarded as foreign. Mama stood as tall as she could. "It's a *Tennessee* practice, Mrs. Krauss. My daughter Jo has a dogwood and Minta, a maple." She stepped toward the midwife, holding a clean rag as if it were a silver tray. She would not be put down.

"Do I have a tree?" asked Nellie.

"A rosebush. You and Agnes. Maggie and Jessa have trees at your grandmother's place in Albany."

Nellie asked, "What about Newt?"

"A cedar elm," said Mama. "In Ellis County. We only lived there a year. Sometimes I think of that tree, how big it might be."

The room went quiet. Maggie rocked the infant, her eyes closed. Nellie was collecting the dirty linens.

"Can I see her?" said Jessa.

"Oh, course." Maggie brought the perfectly swaddled infant to Jessa, who immediately unwrapped her. The baby looked like a little frog, the way her head sat on her wrinkled neck, her eyes so big in proportion to the rest of her face, with froggy legs and a flat behind. Something not quite grown into a person. Jessa could feel herself smiling, her face stretched wide with joy. She put her lips to her daughter's downy head and whispered a prayer of thanksgiving.

"She's beautiful," said Maggie.

Jessa laughed. That's what people always said, thought Jessa, but without actually looking at the babies. They were strange. Nellie caught her eye, and she could tell her sister was also skeptical of the baby's immediate "beauty."

"She is miraculous," said Nellie, "that's certainly true."

Jessa had half a mind to lick the infant in her lap, like animals do moments after birth, but that was crazy. The force of her attachment to this helpless creature immediately felt greater than the sum of all her affection for every animal she'd ever loved, nursed, or buried. She untied her damp chemise and placed the baby, flesh to flesh, on her chest.

"Get her to latch," said Mrs. Krauss. She bent in close to Jessa, rubbed the infant on the side of her mouth until the baby took to rooting at the breast. The baby twisted her head around, mouth open, searching. Her lips alighted on skin, but not the nipple. Piglets and calves seemed to have an easier time finding a teat, and Jessa wondered for a moment if her child could be dim-witted. When the baby started crying in earnest, the midwife stepped in. One hand cradled the baby's head, the other Jessa's breast. Then she brought the two together like a cork to a bottle.

"There you go," the midwife said.

As Mama walked Mrs. Krauss out, Agnes quietly entered the room, apprehension on her face. Jessa called her over. "Come see your niece."

Agnes crossed to the bed, reached out to touch the baby, but Nellie moved in like a duck on a June bug. "Let me see those hands."

Agnes put her hands behind her back. "I'll wash 'em in a minute." She put her face close to the baby's. "Finally, something good's happened."

Jessa reached over and brushed the stray hairs from Agnes's face. Her little sister had been knocked sideways when Papa had failed to come home after the trial. No one had taken the time to explain to Agnes that Papa's release wasn't guaranteed—Mama had been unwilling to even consider it. She'd bawled as hard as if they'd told her Papa was dead. Grief and indignation ran through her like a fever. Agnes needed the "something good" of this baby. "So, what do you think, does she smell like Mrs. Krauss's pickles?"

Agnes sniffed. "Not even a little bit. She looks kinda squishy though."

"Uh-huh, she does."

"And her hair's as red as the dog's."

Jessa sat upright, jostling Agnes and the baby. "Her hair's not red."

"Why're you mad?" said Agnes. "I didn't say she wasn't purdy."

The red-headed man. Prostitute. He'd said the word.

Maggie spoke. "It's birth wet. It'll dry different."

"We're Scots-Irish," explained Nellie. "There's some on Papa's side with that coloring."

Jessa couldn't think of one.

"Who?" said Agnes.

"Who, who, who, said the owl." Maggie started ushering Agnes out of the room. "Wash your hands so you can hold your niece."

The air in a room could change suddenly when a person said something that ought not be said. She could feel it. Mama must have too, because as soon as Mama came back into the room, she said: "What on earth?"

Jessa was about to say, "Nothing," like she always did, keeping her troubles to herself. But Mama looked at her so kindly. She thought of how they'd held hands every day of the trial, how they'd learned to share that little boarding room bed, how she'd come to know her mother in a different way this past week. In this closeness, she spoke. "Agnes said the baby's got red hair." All the exhaustion of her labor suddenly felt laid upon her like a wet wool blanket, and she couldn't help crying.

"*Shhhhh.*" Mama was at her side, head-to-head. "Those Campbells make red-headed babies all the time. You go to Warren County, and you'll find your father's Tennessee cousins are as carrot-topped as can be."

Nellie wasn't lying then, thought Jessa. She felt some comfort, but she still craved reassurance. "Mama," she whispered. "Do you think she's Will's?"

Mama touched the baby's tiny hand. "Jessamine, I think she's the Lord's."

31

Jessa looked at their alfalfa field, ready for its last cutting. Her dog was at her side, and her daughter, Rose, in her arms. The only thing missing was Papa. Solon had asked her to come by their cabin after supper to discuss what he called a "serious matter." In preparation she'd been surveying their place to make sure she could intelligently discuss crop conditions and animal management issues, but there was so much she didn't know. Though she and her father had been constant companions since she'd left school, she could see now how she'd been his "assistant." Her father had depended on her, but he hadn't groomed her to lead, to one day take the reins. Solon's meeting had to be about money, about getting the last of the hay in, about picking the cotton when the bolls were ready, about selling some cows they'd rather hang onto, about how they'd go about feeding themselves and the animals through winter. The only hard money they had to their names was in a tin can behind the wood box: eighteen dollars, and Grandmother Campbell had sent that. Jessa had tried to talk to Mama about their situation, but Mama had deflected. "Papa will see to it." He couldn't see to it though.

The family was grateful for the way the town of Haskell was treating Papa. Haskell embraced him as a hero, "the avenger of a wrong done to his home," as one newspaper put it. Mr. Edward Habermehl, owner of the mercantile on the main square, had hired Papa to keep shop six hours a day. In the morning Papa let himself out of the jail and walked around the corner to the shop. He worked until late afternoon, whereupon he left, picking up vittles from the boarding house. He then delivered food and himself back to jail, sharing his supper with the only other inmate, a drunk by the name of Patch, who did not enjoy such freedoms as Papa. The shop pay was meager, but it had helped fund the appeal Mr. Aames was pursuing. Papa was also able to send a few staples home to the Shinnery by way of anyone from Rayner who visited. Mr. Barnes, Rayner's blacksmith, had delivered coffee just the week before. He gave it to Solon, who brought it around. Few folks, save Mrs. Posey, actually stopped by their place anymore. Informal visits, Sunday picnics, and dances hadn't been part of their routine since Papa's arrest. Since the trial ended, even occasional help from their worship community had ceased. With the urgency of "saving" Papa gone, they had turned back to their own affairs, weary of the family's plight. Jessa didn't blame them.

Things were different in the nearby towns of Haskell, Rayner, Aspermont, and Rule, and others even farther away. All over, people were signing petitions directed at Governor Culbertson, asking that J. R. Campbell be pardoned. Some even gave small amounts of money for his appeals case. Mr. Aames, on his own now, was willing to accept the family's small but steady payments. He'd been invited to Austin to speak on the topic of frontier justice; the notice of his talk had appeared in the *Haskell Free Press*: "Preserving the Sanctity of the Home in Lawless Environs: One Man's Tale of Evil Vanquished." Jessa wondered which man's tale of vanquishment the attorney would tell, her father's or his own. Mrs. Posey reported he'd had a new suit made for the trip. He'd told her if the lecture went well, he might go on circuit and possibly write a book. Jessa hoped Mr. Aames was all bluster and there'd be no book for Rose to read one day.

Also appearing in the *Haskell Free Press*, just days after the trial, was a letter Papa had written thanking the officers, citizens, and jurors for the kind treatment he'd received. This was met by the publication of a letter signed by all twelve jurors stating their belief that, although factually guilty, Papa should have his "liberty" so that he could protect his family and help them "bear the burden of dishonor and disgrace." The phrase stuck with Jessa. Bearing "the burden of dishonor," a lofty sentiment, silly in the face of the real work to be done. They needed Papa home for a hundred reasons more important than that.

Employment also helped Papa endure his time waiting on appeal. Though he had some freedom of movement, he was still held by the court and could not come home. Solon had let it slip that Papa had lost a good deal of weight and worried about his family to the point of sleeplessness. In contrast Papa's letters brimmed with "beautiful weather" and "kind citizenry." Never did he mention his incarceration. If you didn't know better, thought Jessa, you'd think he was on holiday. Agnes seemed heartened by the letters, and Mama grateful for any word. Nellie drifted off when they were read aloud, as if she'd come in the middle of a story she wasn't much interested in.

Jessa found it all so false. She still didn't know what had happened on that fateful day in front of the saloon. She'd labored over a letter to him, trying to say things just so, asking for an account of the shooting, wanting so much to know what had been said—did he at least try to persuade Will to give Rose a name? Papa wrote back, telling her about Mrs. Habermehl's excellent schnitzel and the weather in Haskell—the same as on the Shinnery, which made it even more galling—along with a request that she say hello to the hounds for him. She stopped corresponding. The girl who would do anything to please her father was gone.

Walking down the lane to her sister's, Jessa watched her long shadow bobbing in front of her, only the outline of her elbows indicating what she carried. She carried the world, heavier than lead and more buoyant than a cork. No matter what Solon said or didn't say, she had her ballast.

Red dove into the field after a bobwhite. A flock of sparrows burst forth. The noise of their wings made Jessa think of the sound Mrs. Martin's taffeta skirts made as she rustled down the stairs. She wondered how the missus was faring in St. Louis, wondered if she ever thought of Jessa. It seemed like a hundred years ago she'd lived with the Martin family. It struck her as odd how such a short period of time, a very small percentage of her life, if she reached a ripe old age like Grandmother Campbell, could have such an impact. Sometimes she tried to imagine a life where she didn't go to town, where she refused the call. "No, Papa, not this girl," she might have said. But it always came down to the little body she now held, this branch of her with its own limbs and heart.

The sparrows looped around and descended again a few rows over. The waning daylight infused the landscape with a touch of gold. The baby stretched one arm up and out in her sleep. It reminded Jessa of a kitten's paw, and she half expected Rose to move her tiny fist in half circles, washing her face like a cat. She put her lips to her daughter's and breathed in. She never tired of staring at her, her slack, milky mouth, the threadlike veins across closed eyelids, and her hair, just a touch of copper. Like their Scots-Irish kin. At Jessa's feet Red had his nose in the ground, his snout covered in dirt. Jessa adjusted her daughter in her arms, a dampness starting where she held her, and wondered what kind of sling she might make so she'd be able to work in the cool of the morning with the child swaddled to her. Mama and her sisters seemed content to care for Rose, but they had chores of their own, and it was almost time to pick the cotton, a task that demanded everyone's labor. They would need more hands if they hoped to get it in. Surely that was one of the things Solon meant to discuss with her.

•••

"Let me see my rosebud," Maggie said, flinging the door open wide. The baby was asleep, and Jessa was loath to disturb her, but Maggie's eyes danced like a drunk eyeing a whisky bottle; she would have that baby. Though younger by five years, Jessa felt the elder to Maggie now. Motherhood and the fact that she was, by default, running the family household had aged her. Maggie, by contrast, had moved directly from her sisters' bed to her husband's, a distance of less than one-half mile, and didn't seem to make any decision without first consulting Solon.

"Hand her over," Maggie whispered.

Rose started to mewl when Jessa passed her, but Maggie made the whooshing-hushing sound like Mama. *Hushhh-shhhhhhew, hushhh-*

shhhhhhew, all is well, all is well, and the baby quieted. Solon watched all this from the table.

"Take a seat," he said.

"I'm gonna take her to the swing." Maggie headed out to the porch. Jessa felt a little unbalanced without her bundle. She took a seat. Straightened her back, trying to exude a confidence she didn't necessarily feel. She looked straight at Solon and noticed bits of gray in his sideburns, shadows under his eyes like ashes. He'd aged since Papa's arrest. "What's on your mind, Solon?"

"I can't do it," he said. "I can't run your place and mine."

"I'm running our place." She laced her fingers together.

"And a fine job you're doin'."

"Thank you." She waited for the "but" that was sure to follow.

"But it's not enough. And you've no money to pay for help. We can't get everything harvested on good intentions and the steady labor of one girl."

Jessa wondered if he'd be giving this same speech to Newt if he'd been left in charge. She doubted it. "Liam Hale mentioned he could help with the picking. Came up to Mama during the trial."

"Liam Hale moved to Abilene. We won't be seeing him."

"Barton Applewhite?"

"As lame as the horse that fell on him."

"When?"

"I heard about it Friday."

Jessa hadn't seen Mrs. Posey in a week, so she was behind on the news. She couldn't help but resent how Solon was free to go to town, while she and her mother and sisters still felt unwelcome there. She wondered what would happen if she went anyway, ignored the looks and endured the unkind words. Mrs. Posey had promised there'd be more scandals to come, and hers would fade, like barn paint in the West Texas sun.

"It's not just me," she said. "There's Agnes and Nellie."

"And the child."

"Mama and Maggie can take care of her."

"Jess." He reached over and put his hand on hers, as if she wasn't understanding and this gesture would somehow help her to see.

She did see. Nothing to be done. They'd bring in what they could with the hands they had available, and the rest could go to rot. They either had faith or they didn't; the Lord would provide, or He wouldn't. What good was it to lament what they lacked? She pulled her hand away.

"Do you even know how to bale linen?" he asked.

"If you show me—"

"It's brute strength. Understanding a thing and being able to do it—" He stopped himself and let out a breath that was close to a sigh. He rubbed his chin. "It's . . ." He started to speak but didn't finish.

What would Solon have her do? Then it occurred to her that perhaps he was trying to tell her he was done. Solon was leaving the Shinnery, laying out his case for why it made sense to take sweet Maggie into parts unknown, free from the burden of four females who were only kin to him through marriage. Jessa stood. "Go then," she said.

"Go?" He got a funny look on his face. "You think I'm gonna quit you?" He laughed but in a weary way, not much sound underneath it. "I've too much love for this place, and that woman who just ran off with your baby. No one's going."

Jessa felt relieved but also a bit chastised. His tone indicated that a grown woman would never jump to such a ludicrous conclusion.

"I mean to add, not subtract," he said.

"What do you mean?" Jessa had never been good at riddles. "Add how?"

"Add whom," he corrected. "My cousin Grover. He was set to hitch up with Katie Barnes over in Aspermont, but she was sweet on someone else. He's batching it out at the Browns, in their old dugout, probably sleeping in a potato crib."

Jessa thought back to the day she'd met Grover, when her family had hinted at the makings of a match—Nellie was already worried about Will then. Jessa wondered if maybe her sister had the shine, the sixth sense that made you feel the future in your bones. One of Mama's aunts was rumored to possess it. Then Jessa put together what Solon was proposing. "You think he'd want me still?"

"No," said Solon. "Of course not."

Jessa's face went hot. His words stung. *Of course not.* What a ridiculous idea. Jessa was as turned as rotted fruit. A silver spoon could be restored but not a tarnished girl. *Of course not.*

"For Nellie," he said. "She's old enough. If she agrees to it, he'd take a stake. Like sharecropping. A percentage of the profits would go directly to him, irrespective of any family debts. And your father would deed him some acreage."

"Give away land?"

"He'd be family. With his help, I think you could come in the black."

"Black?" she said.

"The balance books."

Both terms were unfamiliar, but what she did catch was that Solon planned to give Nellie to the beanpole to save the rest of them. To eat, feed the animals, keep the place, and pay the lawyer, they'd trade Nellie. Nellie, the girl who wished nothing more than to flee. "No, she's got her heart set on teaching."

"And no contract. I heard about Wichita."

Jessa corrected him. "It was Colby, and there's other places."

"She's not been hired," he said.

"Next year'll be better."

"You might not have a next year if the appeal fails. Grover's a good man."

Jessa heard her voice growing louder. "I'm not saying he isn't, but she won't agree."

"Not at first, I'd imagine, but I'll bet she comes 'round."

"She worked for that certificate."

"And bully for her, I mean it. She can teach her children someday."

Jessa's anger rose, like foam in a boiling broth. It didn't matter what Nellie wanted, just like it hadn't mattered what Jessa had wanted when she'd been sent to town. "Teach her children? You mean like Maggie?"

A cruel thing to say, she knew. Solon was trying to help the only way he knew. Still.

Solon tapped the table with his thumbs, his jaw clenching and unclenching. "Gonna pretend you didn't say that." He stood. "Maggie," he called out the front window. "Give the baby to Jessa. She's leaving."

Maggie reentered the kitchen, her cheeks flush. "But I made cobbler."

"She's not hungry," said Solon.

"You're not?" Maggie looked a little hurt, the edges of her mouth downturned like a limp satin bow.

Jessa couldn't disappoint her sister. "On second thought, I am hungry. Very much so."

Solon made no move to interfere.

"Oh, goody, that will be so nice. I've coffee too." She set out three plates.

Maggie seemed so easy to please. Most everything was nice or pretty or fine or wonderful. But Jessa knew she was not a simple creature. She worked around the bad and terrible things, referred to them as merely difficult. She strove to be like water, moving with the current of her life, over and around her dead babies, her jailed father, her meager pantry, and her small life.

"Look, Solon," Maggie said of Rose, "she's dreaming." After staring at the child, they looked at each other, such sweetness in their eyes, their love a balm for all their losses. Though it was impolite to stare, Jessa did anyway. She puzzled at how Solon, so blessed in his own marriage, could plot to hand off Nellie, only sixteen and smarter than them all, to a skinny, landless farmhand. Jessa wouldn't let another Campbell girl be traded. It would be doom for Nellie. Jessa felt it in her bones. Maybe they both had the shine when it came to each other, sisters connected by ties, known and unknown. Jessa could not fail her sister again.

"I'm to do what?" said Nellie.

"He's a fine fellow," said Solon. "A hard worker."

Solon had laid out his plan right after a supper where they'd hosted Grover Scott. Solon must have run his scheme by Mama first because she raised no objections. Nellie was blindsided.

"I'm going to get a position," she said.

Solon scratched his chin, the sound of his nails across his whiskers as rough as a rasp. "Uh-huh."

Agnes popped up from her chair. "She studied. And passed the exam. Right, Nell?"

"Right," she said. Jessa could see the care Nellie was taking to appear calm and rational. Nellie put on a little smile. "I plan to help Mama with expenses as soon as I'm able."

"You can help now," Solon said in equally measured tones. "You know Grover. He's got manners, a good disposition, and he's kin to me. I wouldn't urge you forward if I thought for a minute he'd treat you unkindly."

Jessa had noticed Grover's manners at supper. He'd complimented each dish, made sure to inquire after Papa, and helped carry the plates to the basin even though Mama had said to sit.

He'd also asked Nellie if it pleased her to show him the barrows, but she'd declined. He had accepted her refusal gracefully. "Another time," he'd said.

"I don't wish to marry," said Nellie.

"Me neither," said Agnes, standing next to her sister in solidarity.

Maggie stepped forward, and even before she spoke, Jessa sensed a platitude. "A proof of faith is obedience."

Nellie's nostrils flared just slightly. "Easy for you to say. You were soft on Solon from the moment he stepped on our porch."

"Good Lord willin', it could happen for you," said Maggie.

Nellie made a sound that fell between Ha! and Never!

Jessa thought of Grover's large Adam's apple and jug ears. He towered over Nellie but probably didn't outweigh her by much. Nellie would never swoon over him. Jessa couldn't imagine that anyone would. His hands were his best feature. Jessa found herself watching them at dinner; they were large and well proportioned. He used them to talk. Tie them behind his back and he probably couldn't tell a story. The movement reminded her of Will's fingers on the piano keys, but she shut down that line of thinking as if it were a lid on a box full of rattlesnakes.

"Mother!" said Nellie. She made sort of a stomp, and her burnt-sugar curls seemed to rise from her head. This was the nearest to defiance Jessa had ever seen in her sister. "Please tell me you're not fixed on this."

"We all think well of Mr. Scott," Mama said in a voice that struck Jessa as resigned.

The cords in Nellie's neck tightened as her voice rose higher. "What does that mean?"

"I'm not fixed on it," said Mama, her full attention now on Nellie, "but neither should you be fixed against it." Mama picked up the slop pail and left out the back door. Nellie looked like she'd been slapped.

"Why can't Jessa marry Mr. Scott?" said Agnes. "Rose ain't got no pa."

"Because he wouldn't have her." Nellie's voice had turned shrill. "They only lead the innocent to slaughter."

Solon shook his head. "You are ready for the stage, Nellie Campbell. 'The innocent to the slaughter.' You think awfully high of yourself for one without means, and in an uncertain position. Grover's got a good character and a little money saved. So he's plain-headed, what of it? Ask your sister what comes of falling in love with a Belvedere."

Nellie looked like she had more to say but had lost the position to say it. Her fists were balled at her sides. Solon was missing the point, thought Jessa. Grover wasn't the problem. Nellie had worked diligently at school and studied hard to pass the teacher's exam, yet they had declared all her efforts for naught. Jessa felt the weight of her sister's misery on her own shoulders, her own fault. *If only, if only . . .*

Solon mistook Nellie's silence for acquiescence. "I trust you will think on it." He turned to his wife. "Maggie, dear, let's seek to home." Solon went out the door.

"Don't be mad." Maggie cupped Nellie's cheek. "It's in God's hands." Maggie said it as an encouragement, oblivious to Nellie's feelings. If Maggie had been a different sort, she'd have made a wide circle around her younger sister.

"Go home," Nellie spat.

Maggie screwed up her face. "The eye that mocketh his father, and despiseth to obey his mother—"

"The raven shall pluck it out! I know the verse." Nellie grabbed a fistful of Maggie's hair and got nose-to-nose with her. "Let it! An old crow can take both my eyes! Or will that limit my marriage prospects?"

"Ow! Stop it!" cried Maggie, but not loudly enough to summon Solon.

"Let her go," said Agnes, pulling on Nellie's sleeve. "She ain't done nuthin'."

Jessa grabbed hold of her wildcat sister. "Leave her be, Nell."

Nellie released Maggie. More than a few strands of Maggie's hair entwined in her fingers. Maggie smoothed her hair, adjusted her shirtwaist.

"What is happening to this family?" she said, her voice as soft as moss.

Nellie said, "We're being traded. Us, your sisters. Don't you care?"

"I care that you're safe and loved and healthy. Of course I care," said Maggie.

A wet streak ran down Agnes's face where a single tear had fallen, washing away the ever present dust. "Can I go home with you, Maggie?"

"Another time, sugar." Maggie left, only the sound of her stiff skirts in her wake. The door was left open. Jessa looked outside to the last of the day's sky, sinking streaks of pink and purple on the horizon, the trees reduced to black outlines. Everything felt over. Agnes leaned against her. Jessa could smell her sweaty head.

"Is Papa ever coming home?"

"Yes," said Jessa. Agnes didn't press for more; she'd been told a hundred times that nobody knew when.

OCTOBER 1895

The weeks dragged on. Grover Scott put in twenty or so hours on the place every week. He helped get the cotton in. He repaired the thresher and cleaned and sharpened the plowshare. On Sundays Grover joined them at the table. Nellie put out the tablecloth but no flowers. He asked her on walks. Sometimes she went, sometimes not, polite but never with joy.

One Sunday Grover seemed to purposefully direct his questions away from Nellie since she didn't usually give him much of a response. This must have vexed her because then Nellie asked Grover a direct question—the first Jessa had witnessed. "What's the largest city you've ever been to, Mr. Scott?"

"Louisville, Kentucky," he answered immediately.

"Tell me about it," she said, the slightest spark in her eyes.

"Well, I remember it being noisy."

Nellie practically rolled her eyes, as if to say, you were lucky enough to visit a big city and that's all you took away? When Grover realized he'd answered wrong, he started telling her about a racetrack called Churchill Downs, but he immediately lost her attention when he began describing the horses. "And they heat the barns at the Downs. Can you believe it? Potbellied stoves on either end, maybe ten stalls in between."

Anyone could see they were a terrible match, but Grover plodded ahead like an obliging ox. He came most alive when talking about horses and farming, his father's land in Kentucky, and his deep affection for the Brazos. Nothing Nellie cared a whit about. Jessa had been most impressed with a story he'd told the week before about paddling down the Brazos in a canoe, porting it over the shallows. "I did it in pieces," he'd said. "Made it as far as Cliff Creek but had to trade the canoe for a ride back up here." Solon tried to get at the why of the thing, but there didn't seem to be a reason beyond the challenge and pleasure of it. "You don't know a river 'til you're on it," he said. Jessa thought that sentiment applied to a lot of things, love and motherhood among them. When Grover told of the river's tips and turns, he used his hands. His fingers dipped for the falls, wrists following through, up then down. He didn't seem to know he was doing it. Jessa found it odd, but mesmerizing.

It got real quiet at the table following Grover's detailed description of the barns at Churchill Downs. He twisted his fork in his hand. Nellie failed to stifle a yawn.

"Boy," said Jessa, "they must have a lot of stable hands to manage all that."

He looked up, seemingly grateful. "They do. Have you ever been to the horse races, Miss Campbell?"

"Not on a track like that," she said. "It sounds like quite a show."

"Oh, it is," he said, smiling again, "it is."

Between two sawhorses they laid an old door from an abandoned home-steaders' cabin a few miles away. Papa had used the door once as a divider in the chicken pen, but it cleaned up well. In its present state, it served as a desk for Jessa and Mrs. Posey, who sat side by side. Rose lay on a blanket in the shade underneath. They combed through every newspaper that had come through the post office at Rayner. They were looking for all the adverts soliciting teachers. Mrs. Posey would write the letter of inquiry with Nellie's list of qualifications, as she had the better hand. She also penned letters of reference from Mr. Peabody Hasenpfeffer, in care of the post office. Mr. Hasenpfeffer thought highly of Nellie and had trained her in the Lancastrian system of education (which they'd learned about from reading the adverts), no matter that he didn't actually exist. The mining and border towns of the New Mexico and Arizona territories seemed desperately in need of teachers, so the women didn't think they'd mind the ruse.

"From the frying pan to the fire." Jessa held up an advert for a copper mining company's private school.

Mrs. Posey scanned it. "They board with the families. Surely, she'd be watched out for."

Jessa gave her a look. "Surely?"

"Hopefully," Mrs. Posey amended. "They're strict with the schoolteachers. Moral clauses and all that."

"What if the rowdy ones eat her alive? The boys up at our school gave some teachers a real what for. Miss Peyton didn't last the year."

"Peyton was a mouse. Nellie's no mouse."

Agnes crept into the barn. "This don't look like Bible study." Her knees looked like mud pies. She'd been outside, beneath the cedar trees, building tiny forts and streams and roads in the dirt, using every bit of shell, nut, empty tin, kindling stick, spare button, and piece of broken pottery she could find.

"We did that already," said Jessa.

"Where's your Bible?"

"Put away." They didn't want anyone to get wind of what they were scheming, so they'd claimed "Bible study" to discourage intruders.

Agnes surveyed the scraps of paper. "Whatcha doin' then?"

"*Shhh.*" Jessa pointed to the sleeping baby.

Mrs. Posey said quietly, "On this, the Lord's Day, we're resting and reading the news of the world."

"All the world?" Agnes whispered.

Jessa tried to imagine the whole world's news, every story of every person in every paper. Enough print to fill the barn, she guessed.

"Like what?"

Jessa quickly looked down at the nearest headline. "About the Battle of Kee-lung. Japan seems to have invaded Tai-wane."

"What's Tai-wane?" said Agnes.

Mrs. Posey slid a newspaper over the list they'd made of places to apply in Nellie's name. "A place far away from here," she said. "Probably near Japan."

"Probably," Agnes agreed.

"We're just quietly reading through all papers, every word, so we don't miss anything. Pull up and join us?"

"Naw," said Agnes, desiring a greater diversion than women reading. "But come see my ranch when you're done. The cows are walnuts, and for the waterin' hole, I got a dish."

"Better not be a good one," said Jessa.

"It's not."

The women watched Agnes leave the dim barn and step into the yard, her messy brown hair shining in the sunlight. They continued to work in silence. In the *Austin Tribune*, Jessa saw an advert that caught her eye: Teachers wanted in California. She sat with it a minute before telling Mrs. Posey. California was so far. She reread the advert. California would be much better for Nellie than a copper mine in the desert. California was already a state, not a rough and wild territory. It had an ocean that ran its length and fruit trees along all its streets. Culture as well as commerce. At least according to the ad. "Here," said Jessa, holding out the paper, "a place called Loss Angle-ees."

DECEMBER 1895

On Christmas Eve, seven weeks after the letters had been sent, and without word from California, Grover tapped his glass with his spoon. The family was assembled around the table. "There's news," he said.

He had taken Nellie and Agnes up to church at the schoolhouse two days earlier. With Grover as an escort, Nellie had been cautiously received back into the fold. At least that's what Jessa had gathered. "The singing was nice. I have missed that," was all Nellie had reported. Jessa missed singing too, missed being at a piano, the music moving up through the floor and into the soles of her feet.

The candlelight flickered, the turkey glistened, and Grover stood. Last year the season had been something Jessa endured. This year, her sister seemed on a similar course. Across the table Nellie watched Grover, her face a blank slate.

Grover stood, bumping the table slightly, milk sloshing in the pitcher. "I would like to say . . ." He stopped midsentence. "I mean I am saying . . . announcing . . ." He held out his palms and spread his fingers apart on the word "announcing."

"It's agreed." Nellie spoke from where she sat, without ceremony. "We'll marry."

Silence fell, not because the news was unexpected but because she'd so clearly robbed Grover of his moment, and it pained them all, save Nellie.

"Well, there it is," Grover said, hands limp at his sides. He looked over at his sixteen-year-old bride-to-be. She was dragging her fork through her mashed potatoes.

34

By the time the men brought Mama home, the chickens had gone to roost and the sun had dropped below the horizon. It'd been Mama's first trip to Haskell since the sentencing six months earlier and Nellie's first time since Papa had been jailed. They'd been put up with the Habermehl family, for whom Papa worked. The aim of the trip was to finalize the details related to Grover officially joining the family. Jessa knew from Papa's letters that he was fond of "the boy," as he called him, though Grover was twenty-two, a full six years older than Nellie.

Jessa had considered writing to Papa to let him know of Nellie's misery and her own schemes to remedy it. She was tired of secrets. Some people seemed to feed on them, like Will with his hand up her skirt at the piano, or Mrs. Martin with the photo of her long-lost beau, or even Papa with his silence. Jessa wanted her life in the light, bleached and aired like sheets on a clothesline. But if she proceeded with the plans she was drafting for Nellie in the open, they might be stopped. The family might hector Nellie into staying, invoking God and duty and fear of traveling into parts unknown. Nellie would be nervous. She'd be a fool not to be a little afraid—a fool like Jessa, walking in the dark toward a lamp-lit saloon.

Jessa met Solon, Mama, and Nellie at the buggy. Grover, on horseback, dismounted.

"Got some biscuits left," she said. "Anyone hungry?"

"Naw," said Solon. "Wanna get home to Maggie."

"I best be getting back as well. The Browns'll think I've flown the coop," Grover said. The Browns lived only a mile beyond Solon; he wouldn't have too much navigating to do in the dark.

Grover helped Mama get down from the buggy, a steep step for one so tiny. Just then it came to Jessa, an image of Papa with both his hands around Mama's slim waist, lowering her from their wagon like a doll. It must have been a memory from early childhood, maybe the very day they came to the Shinnery, when Jessa was but two or three. Now Mama's steps were stiff when she reached the ground. Jessa went to her aid.

"I'm not crippled, just stiff from the ride," she said, causing Jessa to back away.

Grover held his hand out for Nellie as well. She took it—it would've been rude not to—but released it immediately when her foot touched the ground. "Thank you. Good night," she said, immediately going into the house.

When the men departed, Jessa reheated the afternoon's coffee for her mother. The December days were shortening, so the sky was already dark. Agnes and Rose were asleep.

Instead of taking a seat at the table as Jessa expected, Mama went straight to the bedroom where the girls slept. When Jessa went in she saw her mother at the cradle, adjusting the baby's blanket. Mama's lips held a smile. You didn't survive a war, six children, and the death of one—not to mention a husband's incarceration—by being soft, thought Jessa. Whatever tenderness was left in Mama seemed to have been kindled by Rose.

"Good Lord!" said Mama, startled by Jessa's presence. "Don't be a sneaker."

The irony wasn't lost on Jessa.

At the kitchen table, after Mama volunteered nothing about the visit with Papa, Jessa spoke. "What's to happen then?" Mama was chewing her biscuit, tomato preserves at the corner of her mouth. It reminded her of Rose, the way milk would sometimes pool at the corner and spill down her chin like a tear. She considered how there was more than one stage of life where you needed wiping and feeding. Someday Mama would need care like that, and Jessa would be the daughter to do it.

"Four weeks," said Mama. "The marriage will take place the second Sunday in February. Here of course. Mr. Scott will secure the preacher. It'll just be family. The less fuss the better, don't you think?"

"Are you asking me what I think?"

Mama sighed. "Grover Scott is a nice, hardworking young man. Nellie's agreed."

"So did I when I went to Rayner."

"The regrets your father has . . ." Mama's words drifted off.

"The regrets *he* has? What about you, Mama?" Jessa made her voice quiet to disguise the ferocity of her speech.

"I was never in favor of you going to town."

"You weren't?" Jessa suddenly felt wide awake.

"No." Mama took another biscuit.

"Did you try and stop it?"

"I said my piece."

"And Papa didn't listen?" Jessa watched her mother take a big bite of the biscuit. She wanted to tear it from her hands, impatient for an answer.

"Oh, I suppose he listened. He just wasn't persuaded."

Jessa wanted to know the whole story. "So when he went for the melon seeds . . . ?"

"The melon seeds. Gracious, that was a long while ago."

"When he went . . . ?"

"The Martins up and closed our credit," Mama said. "Mr. Martin was the one who suggested working it off, came up with the idea of a mother's helper."

Jessa pressed, "But you said no?"

"I didn't think much of the plan." Mama took a long sip of coffee. "Don't hold it against him."

Jessa looked at her mother in the half-light, her cheekbones sunken, shadows hooding her eyes. She looked exhausted. "I don't hold anything against him" is what Mama needed to hear. But Jessa couldn't say it true. "Tell me, Mama, do you think much of this plan with Nellie and Grover? Honestly. Just you and me."

Mama's dark eyes locked with Jessa's. "That girl should be a teacher. She's got plenty of marrying years."

Jessa shot out of her seat and threw her arms around her tiny mother, surprising them both. "Oh, Mama," she whispered in her ear. "Thank you."

The next day Mrs. Posey came with a letter.

35

The sun was just coming up, the road still in shadow. A low band of pink and orange in the distance. Quiet. Even Rose, in her sling, had stopped fussing. Teething had been a trial for all concerned. Better to bring the baby along than to have her wake the house and alert everyone to Jessa's absence. Jessa was grateful for her daughter's body, tucked underneath her breast and held tightly by a shawl. In a few years Rose would be walking this road beside her. Jessa would teach her the names of things. In winter they'd search out the brown thrashers in the shin oak and the prairie falcons on the hunt, flying fast and low to the ground. Like Papa had taught her, she'd teach her daughter to weed and to ride, to plant and to pluck, to nurture and to kill. But Jessa couldn't make her daughter love the hard life on these rolling plains. Rose would or she wouldn't. Jessa would release her either way.

The Browns, where Grover Scott stayed, lived roughly two miles away. Jessa's stomach was jumpy, thinking about delivering her news. But since Grover had only ever presented as a reasonable person, Jessa reckoned he'd understand the logic of the thing. If only she could say it right.

Five days earlier Mrs. Posey had delivered the letter confirming Nellie's teaching position, a position Jessa and Mrs. Posey had accepted on Nellie's behalf. They'd debated about telling Nellie then, but Jessa feared her sister would go to Papa first for his blessing. She'd always been an obedient daughter, as evidenced by her agreeing to marry Grover in the first place. Breaking off an engagement was cause for more scandal.

Jessa's task was to make the men understand. She owed this to Nellie. And if Nellie declined to teach in California—always a possibility—Jessa could sleep well knowing she'd done her best.

Nellie was set to depart on the last day of January—if she chose to go—eight days before her scheduled wedding. Mrs. Posey had arranged her passage to Fort Worth. From there Nellie would board the train to Wichita. She'd next connect with a train bound for Albuquerque, then her final leg of the journey to Los Angeles. Mr. Blake, a Methodist minister and the school superintendent, along with his wife and eldest daughter, would meet Nellie at the station. The school board had arranged the tickets.

According to Mr. Blake, there were two teachers from Oklahoma booked on the same leg to Los Angeles. The superintendent wrote that, all told, twenty-five new teachers had been hired for the spring term. Jessa hoped Nellie would feel more comfortable with a group of like-minded young women. As the wedding day neared, Nellie had turned more glum. For the old Nellie, any occasion to dress up and style her hair would have pleased her. This Nellie was unmoved. Jessa would tell her tomorrow. She also owed the news to Grover. She did not wish to shame him. He was a good man. Planting the winter wheat and pruning the peach orchard with him felt easy, comfortable. On the other hand she didn't know if she could trust him entirely. There was a chance he'd expose her plan out of loyalty to the menfolk of the family.

The sky was lightening when the Browns' dogs met Jessa at the short lane up to the house. Their barking ceased once they got a good sniff. She'd been to their place with Papa many times over the years. A flock of mountain bluebirds flew over, singing their dawn song. Then the winter visitors flew back around to settle in a stand of junipers, where they foraged for berries. Jessa took the appearance of the sky-blue birds as a good omen. When she got to the dugout, where Grover stayed, she pitched a pebble at the single low window at her feet. The black dog they called Get-Um woofed when the pebble pinged the glass. "*Shhhhh*," she said, giving his slick back a pat. She'd prefer not having to greet the whole household when she'd come on singular business.

Grover poked his head out the door. A look of panic crossed his face when he saw her. "Someone hurt?"

"No," she said.

"The baby sick?" he said, gesturing toward the sling.

"No, no." She rocked back and forth a little to keep Rose from noticing her mother had stopped walking.

"What is it?" He stepped out of the dugout, already dressed for the day. Jessa could smell coffee.

"May I speak plainly?" she asked.

"Go ahead," he said, "but I think I know what you're gonna say. Your sister's quit on me." He folded his arms against his chest and looked up at the turning sky.

"Nope. She doesn't even know I'm here." He looked baffled.

"Then what in Sam Hill?"

"She wants to be a teacher. She'll never be happy here with you."

"But I thought she got turned down on account of, you know . . . the troubles." His fingers seemed to grasp for something on "troubles," as if the right word to describe the events of the past year could be found in the air.

"In Kansas, yes, but now she's got a position waiting in California. If she wants it. And if you release her—"

Skepticism flooded his face. "Then why isn't she here?"

"She doesn't know yet. I haven't told her."

Grover took a step back, hands up as if to ward off bad news. "I don't want to get mixed up in any deception."

The dog woofed again. A coyote could be heard in the distance. Then the low *bock* of a hen disturbed the silence.

"Please," said Jessa. "She's a dutiful daughter. She will marry if she's obligated."

"I'm not forcing anyone, Miss Campbell." He had taken to calling her Jessa when they were working.

"No, I know. I didn't mean to imply . . ." Jessa was mucking it up. "I need to know: If Nellie wishes to leave, would you pursue the matter?"

"No, course not. But I have to say, I don't know where that leaves me with your place, with the agreement I have with your father." He crossed his arms again then looked down at his boot, heel digging into the dirt. "I should probably speak with him . . . I don't want to get on the wrong side of your pa."

Though Jessa could sympathize with Grover's position—he'd put in months of labor, along with some money—she had to make sure Nellie was free of her obligation. "Is Nellie released or not, Mr. Scott?"

"She's released." He made a shooing motion with his hands.

"Thank you," she said. Rose stirred. Jessa patted her rump, willing her to continue sleeping. Then Jessa's mouth went as dry as cotton; her lips felt stuck to her gums. She thought how nice it'd be to have a little nip of whisky to help her through the next part, and she bit the inside of her cheek to produce a little moisture. "There's something else . . ."

"What?" His tone said he expected more bad news.

"Grover Scott," she said, as she'd rehearsed. "I am no one's prize. My name and my reputation have been tarnished, and I come with the burden of another man's child. But like yourself, I am a hard worker, and my constitution is strong. While it's true we don't know each other well, I've come to admire you." Here, she faltered, saying what came to mind, not what she'd practiced. "I . . . I like the way you talk about the river, the way you move your hands when you do, and how you went down it for no practical reason, and well, you're so kind with Mama and—"

"Wait," he said. "Is this a . . . proposal?"

"It is."

"I see. One Miss Campbell's riding lead, and the other's riding drag, picking up strays."

"No, I—"

Before Jessa could say another word, Grover plunged into the dugout. Conversation over. She didn't think the words she'd chosen were the problem; the words didn't matter. She was the problem. Why did she think he'd even consider it? She was damaged goods, a soiled dove, a calico queen. So many ways to say the same ugly thing. Her shoes felt wet-heavy as she turned back down the road with her baby. Nellie was going anyway, wife for Grover or no. When she passed the junipers, she heard the bluebirds calling, this time the *tink, tink* of alarm.

•••

Jessa slipped the sling over her head and laid the still sleeping baby in the cradle, shawl and all. Then rocked it a couple of times for good measure. Nellie came in behind her.

"Where've you been?"

Jessa patted the bed beside her. Agnes was asleep in the trundle across the room, so they didn't have to worry about disturbing her. "Can you be brave?" Jessa asked.

"What do you mean?"

Jessa held out her hand. Nellie tentatively took hold of it. How long had it been since they'd been girls holding hands on their way to school or standing knee deep in the Brazos, using one another for support? What Jessa was about to say, she realized, what she had put in motion, would mean saying goodbye to this sister she loved so deeply. Grover had released Nellie, but for the first time, Jessa realized she was releasing her too. "If you want it, you've a teaching position in California."

"A what?"

"A job. A teaching job. In Los Angle-ees."

Nellie's face turned three shades of wonder, eyes and mouth open as wide as they could go. "But . . . but . . . how? How can I?" Her voice as fragile as a drop of dew.

Jessa squeezed her hand then pulled the envelope out from under the mattress. She handed it to Nellie. "Letter from the superintendent."

Nellie took out the letter and read it hungrily. "I don't understand."

"You said no one would hire you, and you stopped sending out. I understand why. But I thought, well, why not try some more? I didn't tell you because I didn't know if it would work. And then, when it did work, when they wanted you, I was worried you'd say no. I wanted to make it as easy as I could for you to say yes. That's why I'm only telling you now."

"You've told Papa?"

"I will. If it's your wish to go."

"And Mr. Scott?"

She wouldn't tell Nellie the whole story; it wouldn't serve. Jessa didn't want any more pity from her sister or anyone. She had been right to think Grover reasonable; what she hadn't rightly understood was the preposterous notion of marrying her. "I have," she said. "You're released, Nell. If you want to be."

A sob rose from Nellie. She wrapped her arms around Jessa like a drowning woman clinging to dry land. "Sister, oh, sister, when do I leave?"

•••

The next morning Jessa pulled out her riding clothes. Rose had just been fed and was sleeping next to her aunt Nellie.

Horseback would be almost twice as fast as going in the buggy, but she still had a lot of ground to cover to Haskell and back. She'd let the horse rest up and then head back as soon as possible, even if she had to steer by the moon. The baby would need to feed, and she'd need the sweet relief that came with it. As it were, her breasts would be rock hard by noon and leaking after that. Nellie would have to give Rose milk from the Krauss's goat until Jessa returned.

Now that Grover was willing to let Nellie go, she had to tell Papa. Pulling on her shoes she thought back to the night before at the Browns'. She felt foolish, a little ashamed even. She'd set herself up to be shot down, and shot down she was. She was done with men. If Rose needed another name, a legitimate name, the child would have to wait until she grew up and got married herself; nobody wanted her mama.

As Jessa was heading to the barn, Mama stopped her with an owl call. Something Mama hadn't done in years. Jessa stopped and turned. Mama was in the doorway. Their eyes locked. The moment stretched on. Mother and daughter. Mama nodded. All the blessing Jessa needed.

36

By the time Jessa arrived in Haskell, the sun was high but the air still cold. Most of the trees around the square were winter bare. Even so, the town buzzed. Jessa could hear the *clang* of the blacksmith's hammer, the *clunk, clunk, clunk* of a barrel rolling down the boardwalk, and the *jing, jing* of the harness on a wagon team, its load stacked higher than the driver's head. It'd been so long since she'd been to any town the mad bustle of it all surprised her. In the center stood the courthouse, so familiar to her now. The place where the second-worst thing had happened: the exposure, before God and everyone, of the first-worst thing, and yet she'd walked out on her own two feet. A miracle really, she thought, the way shame could shrink in the sunlight, her past—at least to herself—becoming a dried-up thing, like a flattened frog in the road. Turning paperlike. Eventually, to dust.

She steered Dan to the livery, where he'd be fed, watered, and rested. Then she made her way to the mercantile, no one paying her any mind. It felt good to blend in, just another dusty homesteader come off the farm. The Habermehls' shop was smaller than the Martins', but with a bigger front window. She stood outside and looked through it. Papa was filling a barrel from a sack; she couldn't tell what was in the sack, beans maybe. He looked thin, his pants bunched around his waist. It'd been over seven months since she'd seen him.

Papa spotted her through the glass. Frozen for a moment he seemed to question whether his eyes were playing tricks on him. Then he knew.

Dropping the sack, he hurried outside; his big hug almost lifted her off her feet. She'd pictured the whole encounter with him as more businesslike: "Here's how it's gonna be . . ." But she got caught up in the warmth of his arms, the scratch of his whiskers, the faint smell of butter in his mustache. God, how she'd missed him.

"Jessamine," he said. He squeezed his eyes, tucked his chin to his chest, and swallowed hard. It wouldn't do to cry out on the street. "Lord, but it's good to see you, gal."

Jessa took a half-step back. "Let's see if you still think so when you hear what I've come to say."

"Is it about your mama?"

"No," she said, sensing his panic. "Everyone's fine."

His forehead furrowed. "The baby?"

"Rose is well," she assured him.

Just then Mr. Habermehl, the barrel-chested proprietor, came outside. Papa introduced them. Jessa offered her hand, but Mr. Habermehl said he'd just been oiling the coffee roaster and didn't want to get oil on her. She hoped that was true, hoped he didn't fear that her rumored licentiousness could be caught like a cold.

"Aames says your pa is two whoops and a holler from a pardon," said Mr. Habermehl. "I've a good feeling Governor Culbertson will see fit to do the right thing and send him home."

"I pray for it, every minute of every day," said Papa. "To go farther away from your mother . . ." He cleared his throat but didn't complete his thought.

"And what if the governor doesn't?" Jessa said.

"I'll go to Rusk. I'll have to. But on the way, I'll collect more signatures in support of a pardon. Let the governor answer to the people."

"Amen." Mr. Habermehl clapped Papa on the back. "You're welcome to retire to the stockroom, have a minute to yourselves."

"C'mon," said Papa. "We got a kettle for tea."

As soon as he shut the stockroom door, Jessa laid out what she'd done, arranging for Nellie to accept a position in California. She said it all in a great hurry.

"I don't want another daughter to go, Jess. Not alone. And she's young. Younger than you were when you . . ." He didn't finish.

His anxiety gave her a smidgen of doubt, but she wouldn't let it show. "She's determined, Papa."

"I don't expect so." He pulled a few sticks from the kindling box next to a small potbellied stove and fed the thing. Then he lifted an old, dented teakettle and put it on. "From what I see, it's you who's determined. Nellie woulda married ole Grover."

Her plan was a good one, and she wouldn't let her father undo it. "And been miserable her whole life."

"Her 'whole life'? That's a seventeen-year-old talking."

"I'm eighteen! My birthday was April." Jessa felt anger rise and settle in her jaw. He hadn't understood any of it. Why did she think it'd be different now?

"That's right," he said. "I missed it. You don't write, so I don't know things about you."

Jessa thought of the letters the family exchanged, talk of apple cakes, cold mornings, and the relative health of cows. They didn't say anything about what any of them were feeling, how lonely or scared they were, or what the next step would look like if Papa's pardon appeal failed and he went to the state penitentiary at Rusk. The letters were filled with pretty words better suited to other families. Families where the father wasn't jailed for killing his daughter's once-sweetheart, and the daughter wasn't raising her out-of-wedlock child, trying to keep things running without him.

"What does your mama say?"

"She trusted me to come."

He cocked his head. "Got it all in hand."

"Someone has to."

"I did. Arranged everything."

Back to that, she thought, the men; she was a daughter, not a son. He had no idea what she'd done on the place, how she was running things, how she was willing to marry Grover herself—even though it turned out he wouldn't have her. And of Nellie he seemed to pay no mind. "She's gotta accept the position while the gate's open. You know about Kansas."

"But Mr. Scott?"

"Mr. Scott? What about your daughter?"

"I'm thinking of my daughter. Thinking about her safety. Her welfare. Thinking of all of you."

"I am too." Her sister's well-being meant everything. She knew in her new-mother's bones that what Nellie needed to thrive was to leave them. She was as sure of it as she was of her own need to stay. For the past two years, at least, she had waited for Papa to acknowledge her place on the Shinnery. Her home was not, as it had been for her sisters, something to leave. It was a calling, at least as she understood the word. And if he would not grant her what she believed was her due, she would seize it.

"Nellie's being met in Los Angel-ees by a minister. There's two other new teachers that'll be on the train in Wichita. She'll board in Fort Worth."

He rubbed his face with his hands. "You know what my greatest fear is?"

His voice had gotten quiet, and she had to strain to hear. Of course she knew. "That she'll turn out like me."

Papa looked perplexed. "No!" He furrowed his brow. "Jesus, girl, no. What happened to you—I don't hold you . . ." He seemed stymied. "I don't blame you, Jess. You hear me?" He took hold of her arms, his hands smoother than she'd ever felt them. "My fear's that if anything goes south with Nellie, you'll carry that too. The guilt, the responsibility. It's too much."

"Too much?" She looked at her father's face, the lines, the paleness that came from being off the Shinnery and inside these walls. He looked almost as pained as that day in the barn when she'd told him everything. She had told him everything, but he still withheld the full story from her. This was the gulf between them; they stood on opposite sides of an uncrossable river.

"What do you know about what I carry?" she said. "I don't even know what happened! What happened, Papa? What happened?" She felt the old wrenching in her heart, the pain she could never move beyond because she still didn't know what had taken place. Had Will possibly been willing? Could she have had a life without Rose marked as a bastard? Without being exposed in a courtroom as a prostitute? Had Papa's anger been greater than his mercy? It couldn't have been self-defense, she knew that. The witnesses had testified that Will had carried no weapon, that Papa had shot an unarmed man. They had never discussed it; they weren't allowed to before the trial, and afterward, he refused. "You went to bring him back. 'He'll marry you,' you said. And then you shot him down? What happened?"

He grabbed her by the shoulder. "Jessamine, hush," he said. Then his face got gentle, his voice like something soft to fall upon. "He . . . he disavowed you."

"How?"

He released her shoulder. "We had words."

"What, Papa? Please, what did he say?"

"He refused you." Papa shook his head. "He was a son of a bitch, isn't that enough?"

Son of a bitch. That kind of language was beyond the pale for Papa. He looked spent. Jessa could see how the telling might cost him, but still she pressed on. "No, it's not enough. From talking to shooting, I don't understand." The water in the kettle made a hiss, a gurgle. She could sense Papa might be ready to tell her, but she had to be still, like Red stalking a rat.

"These old eyes were looking for him and he knew it, so he stayed hid like a yellow-belly," he began. "I waited until I saw him come out of the saloon. Tried to talk to him then. He wouldn't face me like a man, but he said enough to make clear there'd be no wedding." Papa looked her in the eyes, almost pleading. "He had no shame, not an ounce of it for what he forced you to do, the . . . the . . ."

He couldn't say the word "prostitution."

"He'd of done it to another girl, and another. I only shot him in the side because he turned. He wouldn't face me, not even in death."

So Papa did try to talk to him and Will refused. How though? She wanted to know what Will said, wanted to picture how the whole thing unfolded. The trees, the breeze, the birdsong. "The words, Papa? What were the words?"

"Haven't you been beat enough?"

"Tell me and I will put it to bed. I promise. I will never bring it up again if you just tell me what he said."

Her father's eyes went teary. "He said you were the filthiest whore in Rayner, and you gave him and half the town the French pox. As for the child, he suggested we drown it."

The words stung, a dozen arrows piercing her at once. *Filthiest whore. Drown it.* The ugliness of the words brought to mind the ugliness of the deeds, of the men, of the room. She could smell the place, lodged in her nostrils, as inescapable as her shadow. Her father stepped toward her; arms extended. She shook her head. Tears were for snakebites and widowhood. She would not cry anymore. She took a deep, shuddering breath. She understood now what was essential. She had been a mark from the beginning. Will's love, an illusion. And Rose, her beautiful child, was better off with him dead.

The kettle whined. Papa nodded. Time to go home. Her baby needed feeding.

Shiner Gazette, APRIL 9, 1896

SHOULD HAVE A MEDAL

A very unusual occurrence was witnessed at Abilene Wednesday. Mr. J.R. Campbell, of Raynor [*sic*], who is under conviction for manslaughter bought a ticket and, armed with the proper commitments, got on the train for Rusk, where he will report to the penitentiary officials . . . A petition with over 2,000 signatures has preceded him and is now on file in the governor's office.

37

Jessa had made the mistake of feeding Red half a biscuit from her pocket. Now he was underfoot as she harnessed the mules to the buggy. "Scat." She lifted her arms, trying to scare him, but he didn't move a lick, just wagged his tail. She reached down and hugged him, his jowls open, a hot blast of dog breath in her face. Not a wholly unpleasant experience.

Nellie was inside with Mama, Agnes, and Rose. Nellie had packed the night before. Mama's satchel was going on another adventure. Agnes had insisted Nellie take *Peter Parley's Tales* to read to her pupils. Agnes's way of saying: don't forget about me. Agnes also tried to get Nellie to take a switch she'd fashioned from a peach branch. "You can take care of the bad 'uns with this." Mama was taking Nellie's leaving in stride, as if nothing about life surprised her anymore. Nellie seemed calm, as determined to leave as Jessa was to stay.

With a few minutes to spare, Jessa walked along the fence rail, looking for something to pick. Nothing was blooming. A clump of sage, a sprig of juniper, and some woody lavender Mama had planted a long time ago would have to do. She wrapped the stems in a clean handkerchief—less a few breadcrumbs—and tied it off with a bit of creeper vine. It looked homely compared to the nosegay Nellie had sent her off with those many months ago, when she'd first left for Rayner.

Solon and Maggie had said their farewells the night before. Solon wasn't happy his cousin Grover had been stood up, but he didn't take it out on Nellie. His was a subdued send-off. They'd see Mrs. Posey in town. This morning was only the little party of Campbell women. Mama was holding Rose, who stretched out her arms to Jessa. Jessa took her, glad to have something to hold. Mama must have felt the same thing, because when she passed off the baby, she immediately started wringing her apron.

"I wanna go," said Agnes.

"Mama needs your help," said Nellie.

"Mama could take care of a hundred babies."

"With all the other stuff then."

Nellie put her belongings in the buckboard. As Jessa watched, the butterflies in her stomach turned to rocks. Although she had stopped asking God for things, a silent chant ran in her head: *Keep her safe, Lord, keep her safe.* Jessa's face must have reflected her worry because Nellie answered it.

"Mr. Blake and his wife will be at the station, and besides, Mrs. Posey's given me the names and addresses of a hundred postmasters between here and California. If there's any problem, I'll find one of them." With that, Nellie embraced her mother and Agnes and finally Rose, still in Jessa's arms. Nellie leaned in, kissed the baby on her cheek, her forehead, her other cheek, her arm. "Don't you grow too much, baby girl, or I won't recognize you."

Jessa thought about Mrs. Posey, how she didn't see her daughter for eight years and hadn't seen her since. She hoped that would not be the case for her sister and Rose. Surely, Nellie would come back sooner than eight years.

Nellie took a last deep breath of her niece, as if she could take the scent with her. Then she smoothed the baby's almost nonexistent hair. "Take care of your mama, Rosebud."

Jessa had to look away as Nellie embraced Mama. Too painful to witness. Jessa wondered if Nellie was thinking what she was, that Mama wasn't young and that this may be the last time Nellie ever laid eyes on their mother. Jessa bit her lip hard. After she handed the baby back to Mama, she and Nellie climbed into the buggy. Just as she was ready to give the reins a flick, Jessa saw a figure on horseback down the road coming toward them.

"Who's that?" said Nellie. The hounds took off like lightning to inspect the visitor.

"It looks like Grover," said Jessa. What on earth did he want? Would he try to stop Nellie from leaving? Jessa reached behind her and put the Henry on her lap, just in case. She couldn't imagine shooting at Grover, but at least he'd know she meant business.

"What's he want?" said Mama.

"I have no idea." Since the morning Jessa had shown up on his door-step a week earlier, he hadn't been on the place. Her fingers gripped the gun. "Maybe you should go inside."

"You're acting straw-headed. It's just ole Grover." Agnes skipped down the road toward him.

"Agnes!" Jessa barked, but her little sister ignored her.

They all waited. The only sound was Rose smacking her lips on her arm and humming tunelessly.

Soon Agnes was racing the dogs back toward the house. Grover was coming up behind her in his workaday clothes.

"Mornin'," he said, dismounting. "Wanted to give you this, Miss Campbell."

Grover handed up a rectangular box to Nellie, the kind that might hold jewelry. Jessa felt nervous.

"I don't know that I can accept this," said Nellie, her forehead wrinkled.

"Course you can. It's to say no hard feelin's. Unless you have hard feelin's?"

"No, no, course not." Nellie opened the box. It held a beautiful ebony fountain pen.

"A Waterman," he said, by way of explanation, though he seemed the only one to understand the significance of the name.

"I can't, really." Even as Nellie said she couldn't keep it, Jessa could see how much her sister admired the pen.

"It's yours. Godspeed!" His palms came together on the last part, like he was blessing her.

"Why . . . thank you, Mr. Scott. I'm . . . uh . . ."

"Flabbergasted!" said Agnes, throwing her hands in the air.

"Yes! That."

Grover said, "Miss Campbell." Only this time he was looking at Jessa. "Before you go, I'd like a word."

"Back in a minute," she said to Nellie, and she slid the Henry over to her sister and climbed down. She didn't need an audience to any continued humiliation. Jessa headed to the barn and Grover followed, along with Red.

Grover shifted his weight from leg to leg before speaking. "There's something that needs clearin'."

"What?" She tried to steel herself against any unkind words he might say.

"That morning . . . well, you took me by surprise."

"I did," she admitted.

"All I heard was that Nellie didn't want me, and that you were acting as a sacrificial lamb, taking on your family's obligation." He pointed to himself. "A six foot, hundred-and-forty-pound debt. I felt lower than a snake's belly. I did."

She had no idea he'd taken it that way. All she'd heard that night was the anger, the outrage at the idea that she would make a suitable substitute for a wife. She realized how they'd both felt like God's supper scraps, the last thing she'd intended. "I didn't mean to—I'm not good with words, Mr. Scott."

"But that's the thing, Jessa. I can call you that?"

"Of course."

"That day I tried to recall exactly what you'd said. The words. I hadn't really heard them, I was so busted up. So I've been puzzlin' it out." His hands moved as he spoke, counting off the things he was saying, finger by finger. "And I seem to recall that somewhere in there, you said you liked me."

Jessa nodded. She had said that.

"You liked the way I took to the river. The way I tended to your ma.

And something about my hands." He blushed at this last one, his right hand clasping the left into stillness.

"I did," she said. "I said all that." This was not at all what she expected when she saw him coming up the road, and with each word he spoke, she felt lightened. The gift of the pen, she realized, though it appeared to be for Nellie, was actually for her. He was setting things right.

Starting fresh.

He brought his hands to his heart. "Well, that's the thing. I realized over two months ago that you and me were better suited than Nellie and me, much better, but things with your sister had already been decided by then, so I didn't act on what I knew to be true. I should have, and I'm sorry for that."

Jessa could hardly believe what she was hearing. He liked her better? "And what about Rose? And Will Keyes? The trial? All of that?" Jessa wasn't hiding anymore, better to know now where she stood than later.

"I don't have much interest in gossip."

"But it's not all gossip. You have to understand that."

"I see who you are."

Jessa looked deeply into his eyes, maybe for the first time, and wondered if he could truly mean what he'd said. Time would tell, she reckoned. Jessa smiled at Grover but made no promises, no declarations. "I have a sister to deliver, so if you don't mind, I'd better get a move on. Oh, and if you're here to work today, I've got thirty beeves down on Tonk Creek that need checking."

"Sure thing," he said, trying to conceal a grin.

Red sprang up and followed Jessa out of the barn, Grover a step behind. Jessa climbed back in the wagon and secured the Henry.

"Everything all right?" said Nellie.

"As right as rain," said Jessa.

"Bye, Mr. Scott. Thank you!" said Nellie, lifting the gift box.

Agnes hung on the side of the buckboard. "You said not to cry, Nell, but I tell you right now, I'm fixin' to."

"Wait 'til I'm gone," said Nellie, "or we'll all be a bawlin'. Now get down."

Agnes let go of the buggy. Nellie blew a kiss to Mama. Mama sent one back and rocked the baby, who didn't need rocking. Tears spilled down her weathered face.

Nellie touched Jessa's hand. "C'mon, go," she said, her chin to her chest, trying to contain her weeping.

Jessa gave the reins a little slap, and Beck and John moved out, the dogs following for a pace. She turned around to see Grover standing with Mama, Rose in her arms. Agnes's face was buried deep into Mama's side. Jessa urged the mules on again, trying to outrun everyone's tears. As a distraction she reached under the seat and handed Nellie the nosegay. It was scraggly by any measure, devoid of pretty blossoms. But it smelled of home, of sage and juniper.

"It's beautiful," Nellie said, taking it.

"No, it's not," said Jessa.

Nellie gave it a good looking over. "You're right, it's not. It's kind of ugly."

The girls laughed and laughed, like it was the funniest thing ever, this mangy, flowerless bouquet. It felt good to laugh. Jessa felt scrubbed clean by it. She looked over at her sister. Nellie's head was back, teeth showing, light brown hair glistening in the morning sun. Jessa felt like they were all-new creatures, not their father's daughters but grown women unto themselves. Women driving west. One moving beyond the front porch of the frontier, the other laying claim.

Epilogue

As printed in the *Abilene Reporter* on May 1, 1896.

To the entire press of Texas:

With a heart full of gratitude, I tender you my sincere thanks for your noble efforts on my behalf during my recent trouble. It is to the press that I owe the sympathy that has been so universally shown me by the public. I desire also to thank all those who aided me in my great affliction bereavement, and especially do I thank the board of pardon advisers and His Excellency, Gov. Culberson.

Having been released from a felon's cell and restored to those who stand in great need of my services and protection and in whose behalf I have suffered incarceration, it is needless to say that language cannot convey my feelings of appreciation.

I also desire to thank the great army of men, most of whom are to me unknown, who have come to me from the time I left the prison walls and are still coming and call me by name and rejoice in my release and bid me Godspeed. May a kind providence shield me and all mankind from any more such troubles as to which I have just passed.

Very truly,
J.R. Campbell

Acknowledgments

To Clark Whitehorn, my most important "yes," and the rest of the team at University of Nebraska Press. The book couldn't have landed at a better place. Grateful to editor Stephanie Marshall Ward for her keen eye and book-lover's heart.

To those who aided me in gathering the facts and learning about the region: Col. Glendon C. Johnson (1929–2010), genealogist and family historian. I met Glen due to the tireless work of my aunt, Kathryn Barnes Leary, author of *Barnes Roots & Hale Heritage*. The patient staff member at the Haskell County Courthouse who searched musty record books so I could see and touch my great-great-grandfather's signature. The Texas State Historical Association, which runs the largest digital state encyclopedia, dedicated to preserving Texas history. Another key website: The Portal to Texas History, created and run by the University of North Texas Libraries. I used this vast online gateway to find the newspaper articles excerpted in the book. Any factual errors are entirely my own.

To my people at the University of California Riverside: colleagues, students, and staff from the Department of Theatre, Film & Digital Production. I'm continually galvanized by this group of artists and scholars. From the Creative Writing Department, my grad school fiction faculty: Susan Straight, Andrew Winer, Michael Jaime-Becerra, and Cristina Garcia. Their teaching still guides me.

Mentors: Ann Weisgarber, whose generous advice spurred me on and whose work is a major inspiration. Gayle Brandeis, the first writer I met who made everything seem possible. Susan Straight, my swap-meet sister, mother-warrior, line-dancing, kick-ass-writer friend—a source of help and support every step of the way.

Partners in crime and midwives to this book: Thatcher Carter and Julie Higgins. So much here from our exercises. Big, fierce love to our little writing group.

My family: children, Dylan Harder and Veronica Navarro, Gabriel Harder and Shelby McCormick, and Liam Harder, you are everything. Christian Harder, my husband and friend, the biggest of all supporters. In writing and life. Love beyond measure.

CPSIA information can be obtained
at www.ICGtesting.com
Printed in the USA
LVHW012319190822
726385LV00003B/165

9 781496 231383